PRAISE FOR LISA BORK'S *FOR BETTER, FOR MURDER,*
THE FIRST BOOK IN THE
BROKEN VOWS MYSTERY SERIES

A finalist for the 2009 Agatha Award for Best First Novel

"[A] lovely book."

—*CrimeSpree*

"… a fun joy ride."

—*Mystery Scene*

"Entertaining with subtle humor, [a] self-deprecating and complex heroine, and [an] engaging story."

—*CozyLibrary.com*

"… a charming cozy set in the Finger Lakes region of New York and the Christmas season adds extra warmth to the setting. A fun, fast-paced mystery with both a great setting and a great cast of characters and plenty of twists and turns to keep readers engaged and coming back for more."

—*TheMysteryReader.com*

For Richer

For Danger

For Richer

{ a Broken Vows mystery }

For Danger

LISA BORK

MIDNIGHT INK
WOODBURY, MINNESOTA

First Edition
First Printing, 2010

Book design and format by Donna Burch
Cover design by Kevin R. Brown
Cover illustration © Marc Tobin
Editing by Connie Hill

Midnight Ink, an imprint of Llewellyn Worldwide Ltd.

Library of Congress Cataloging-in-Publication Data

Bork, Lisa, 1964–
  For richer, for danger : a broken vows mystery / Lisa Bork. — 1st ed.
    p.   cm.
  ISBN 978-0-7387-1952-8
  I. Title.
  PS3602.O755F675   2010
  813'.6—dc22   2010010461

Midnight Ink
A Division of Llewellyn Worldwide Ltd.
2143 Wooddale Drive
Woodbury, MN 55125-2989
www.midnightinkbooks.com

Printed in the United States of America

DEDICATION

For my husband, Tom

ONE

DESIRE. IT CAUSES HEARTBEATS to accelerate, pupils to dilate, and men to part with their money. Lucky for me, the desire for power and luxurious beauty, coupled with speed, has brought many men to my door. If they experience engine failure, I can help them with that, too. It was just a little trickier now that I had a baby.

From the showroom window of my sports car boutique and repair shop, I watched the Fourth of July parade pass, trying to tell myself it was the reason no one had come in today. Otherwise, surely the 2006 Rosso Corsa F430 Ferrari Spider gleaming under the showroom pin lights would cause someone to salivate.

Even through the showroom glass, I could tell the Wachobe High School marching band was in good form. A ten-foot float of their mascot, the Wachobe Bumble Bee, trailed them down Main Street as a man-sized, costumed version boogied with high-spirited spectators along the curbs. The wind had kicked up with all the heat, no doubt heralding the thunderstorm predicted for later this afternoon. The color guard struggled to keep their flags under control, and the cheerleaders flashed more panty than cheer.

A six-foot-three, 220-pound man hustled past the window, blocking the sun and my view for a moment, a pink bundle in his arms. I headed toward the showroom entrance to greet him, surprised to see Ray and Noelle this early in the day.

"Darlin', I got called in. Car accident. You'll have to take Noelle." My husband, Ray Parker, a county deputy sheriff, took a minute to kiss our baby's cheeks over and over again, generating a storm of appreciative giggles. Then he lifted her flowered shirt and pressed his lips to her tummy, blowing a loud and long raspberry. She latched onto his dark hair and tugged.

"Hey, no. Ouch."

Ray pulled Noelle's hand away from his hair and held out all twenty pounds of her to me. As I took her in my arms, Ray got a proud yet wistful look on his face. He didn't like losing his precious daddy days with our almost-seven-month-old foster child, but he would have countless days with Noelle as soon as we finalized her adoption.

"We'll have to reschedule our picnic. I'll be home as soon as I can."

I swallowed my disappointment. This wasn't the first time Ray's job had come between us and a day in the park, and it wouldn't be the last. "It's a plan."

Ray smoothed the wrinkles from his perfectly creased gray uniform. He looked good in his uniform, all masculine and muscled. Heck, he looked good in anything—and nothing, too. The few white strands in his dark hair and the crinkles around his eyes only added to his allure, especially coupled with his heartbreaking grin. I only hoped when people looked at me they thought thirty-seven looked as good.

He pecked my lips and headed out into the crowd, which clapped for the marching band's rendition of "Cabaret." My gaze followed him as he walked away, feeling a familiar tingle at the sight of his sexy butt and remembering with a grin how irresistible it had been in the shower this morning.

Then I greeted Noelle with a few hugs and kisses of my own. She pressed sweaty palms to my cheeks and giggled. The scent of Gerber rice cereal and formula on her lips and Johnson's No More Tears in her wispy blondish-brown curls were like baby perfume.

Her wide blue eyes studied my nose, then my pearl necklace. She made a grab for it, yanking it off and scattering the pearls across the waxed floor.

Noelle watched them roll. Her fascination killed any irritation I felt. She had that effect on me.

I rubbed my nose against hers. "Help Mommy pick up the pearls."

I bounced her around the showroom, stooping to insert pearls into my pant's pocket. It would be just my luck to have a customer stray in from the parade and slip on them. Even though my insurance was paid up, I didn't want to take any chances.

Something smacked against my showroom window. I heard a cracking sound. I straightened and swung around, cupping the back of Noelle's head with my palm and pushing her into my chest. She stiffened and let out a wail.

Seconds later, my showroom picture window lay in pieces on the floor, mixed with the pearls. Six high school boys in low-hanging Bermuda shorts and exposed boxers struggled to extract the Wachobe Bumble Bee from the window frame.

Noelle's wailing ceased and her eyes grew wide. She gasped.

I thought of an exclamation but managed to keep it to myself. At least no one was hurt.

One of the boys waved. "Sorry, ma'am." The Bumble Bee swayed down the street, and the crowd began to break up. A few passersby shook their heads at the sight of my ruined window. I gave them a rueful smile as I wondered how much this mess would cost me. Lately almost everything seemed to cost me.

An athletic-looking man with blond hair and silver-rimmed glasses strolled through the showroom door. He stopped to gaze in surprise at his sandal-clad feet, which had kicked up loose pearls and glass.

He looked up at me. "Are you open?"

I gave him my best saleswoman smile. "We are. We just had a little accident with the window. How can I help you?"

He stepped closer, almost on tiptoe. I held my breath he didn't slip or get cut.

"I spotted the Ferrari before the parade began. I've been looking for one for months. They're getting to be quite rare. Any chance I could get a test drive?" The man thrust out his hand. "Dave Barclay."

I shifted Noelle to my left hip and shook his hand. "Jolene As ... ah, Parker, owner of Asdale Auto Imports. I'll be happy to assist you. Unfortunately, the police have the parade route blocked for another hour. Can you stop back later today ... or tomorrow morning? That might work out better." I needed time to get both the showroom and my thoughts together.

"Tomorrow morning around ten would be great. I'll bring my wife."

I watched him walk out the door. Had he heard the story about the Ferrari? Normally, I wouldn't allow a test drive for a customer off the street, given the value of the vehicle, but I'd make an exception for this man and this car.

Dave Barclay was the man—a self-made millionaire who hawked Mennonite-crafted wooden furniture and quilts in New York City, furniture and quilts made in the hills around here, Wachobe, New York, the western portal to the Finger Lakes region. Locally, the quilts sold for around six hundred dollars, the furniture less. In New York City, they netted sixteen hundred to three thousand a quilt, with a proportional markup on the furniture. I wished I'd had the foresight to export them instead of importing foreign cars. Maybe I'd own a two-million-dollar cottage on the lake, instead of an arts-and-crafts bungalow in the middle of town and a struggling sports car boutique. Dave Barclay had the money to buy the Ferrari, no doubt about it.

"Do I even want to know what happened here?"

Cory Kempe, my garage mechanic and confidant, stood in the entranceway, toeing the pearls and glass. He wore a cat costume with a huge mane of black fur, sharp claws, and runny makeup that no longer hid his glistening porcelain skin. His poodle-tight auburn curls looked damp with sweat.

I shook my head. "Then you'd be as depressed as me."

He slinked across the showroom, wagging his tail at Noelle. "Would petting the kitty make you feel better?"

Cory's nearby Broadway-quality theater troupe was doing *Cats* this month and a few of the locals with a role in the production had marched in the parade as advertising. He was one of the smaller cats, standing five-foot-one, three inches shorter than me. The makeup artists loved to enhance his girly eyelashes.

"I wish. Who'd you call the last time the window got broken?"

Cory reached for Noelle, who went to him happily. "Marty Simmons Glass. He's in the yellow pages."

I headed toward my office. "Watch the glass doesn't ruin your costume."

"It's hotter than he … an oven in this thing. It could use some air holes."

While Cory set Noelle on the conference table to play peek-a-boo, I dialed the glass company and arranged for an immediate visit. The owner warned me he would have to charge double time for the holiday visit. I had to agree since I didn't think the town fathers would take too well to having the window simply boarded over.

My sports car boutique sat right in the middle of our upscale tourist town, at the head of its seven-mile-long lake which was ringed by million-dollar homes, euphemistically called "cottages." Wachobe's major tourist attractions included lakeside cottage rentals for thousands of dollars a week, delightful restaurants, a dozen wineries, and a trendy shopping district. But the cedar shingles and white trim on my shop contrasted sharply with the 1790s picturesque brick and clapboard storefronts that ran along the rest of Main Street, and my modern cars didn't blend well with the charming Victorian image the town fathers wanted to project. Already they had hinted my shop might be better located on a back street. Certainly boarded windows would not say "Welcome Tourists" in the tried and true Wachobe way.

After hanging up the phone, I took a minute to smooth my bob as well as the creases from my linen pantsuit, which had hung a little loose the last few weeks. The humidity had made my brown hair more wavy than usual, and I didn't need to look in the mirror to know that my blue eyes had dark circles under them. Would I ever get this business permanently in the black?

I walked into the showroom to stand next to Cory. "The glass company will be here in twenty. Don't you need to catch up to the rest of the cast?"

Cory tickled Noelle under her chin, eliciting giggles. "Nah, the parade's over. They're having a picnic in the park. I can join in anytime." He proceeded to blow kisses into Noelle's tummy and was rewarded with more giggles.

I leaned my back against the Ferrari while I explained to Cory about Ray's need to cancel our family's holiday picnic, my ruined pearls, and the nonexistent showroom window. "But bad luck comes in threes, right? So my streak is over."

Cory pried his hair out of Noelle's fingertips. She protested with a wail. He gave her his tail to play with instead. "I thought death comes in threes. The newscasters always say that when someone famous dies, and within a month or so they're usually proved correct."

I put my index finger to my lips. "Shhh. Don't say anything about death." I pointed to the Ferrari. "Dave Barclay is coming in tomorrow for a test drive. I don't think he's heard about the car." A dead man—a murdered one, to be precise—had been left in this Ferrari six months ago, right here in this showroom. But Dave and his wife were summer residents of the town. Maybe the news hadn't traveled.

"Excellent. My lips are sealed."

I doubted the rest of our town would be so cooperative.

Noelle tired of Cory's tail and reached for me. I scooped her up.

One glance at my watch told me it was naptime. We waved goodbye to Cory, who gave us a final, glorious tail wag before disappearing down Main Street. In my office, I settled Noelle on her back in the portable vinyl playpen. She opened her mouth for her pacifier, inhaled it, and closed her eyes. Six or seven loud sucks later, she slept. Such a good baby.

I closed the door behind me as two men in maroon and green Marty Simmons Glass polo shirts appeared in the showroom. The short stout one with no neck was clearly in charge, and he looked me up and down so thoroughly as we shook hands that I felt the need to check to make sure my fly wasn't open. When his bloodshot eyes remained on my breasts a little too long, I resisted the urge to snap my fingers and point to my face.

"Are you Marty Simmons?"

"No, I'm his brother-in-law." He turned his back to me and pointed to the window. "Replacement glass for this is gonna run you. I'm not sure we even have anything this big in stock."

His cohort, a pimply lad of maybe eighteen, nodded vigorously in support of his claim.

I swallowed my impatience and tried to charm them with a smile. "You've replaced it for us in the past. Perhaps you could measure it and check your inventory. I need it fixed today. If you can't do it, I'll have to call someone else."

That got them moving. Apparently they didn't know their company was the only glass company within fifty miles of Wachobe. In minutes, they confirmed the availability and price of the replacement. I tried to recall my deductible and couldn't. Tomorrow I could sort it all out when the rest of the town, including my insurance agency, reopened for business.

By three o'clock, the showroom had a new window. The installers had almost lost it a couple times in the swirling winds, but apparently my streak of bad luck had ended. I wanted to go home but observed the first rule of parenthood—never wake a sleeping baby.

A familiar face appeared in the window and waved an ice cream cone. My attorney, Greg Doran, strolled into the showroom and offered me a lick of his black cherry treat. I declined.

"I didn't expect you to be open today. I planned to give you a call tomorrow." Greg slurped the melting ice cream off his hand and took a few huge bites to get things under control.

"Good news?"

"No." He finished his cone and looked around. "Do you have a restroom?"

I pointed. "In the corner."

"Be right back. I need to wash my hands."

While I waited for him to return, I pondered the possibilities. Greg was handling our adoption, a rather unconventional one to say the least. My sister Erica had talked two of her "friends" into signing custody of their baby over to Ray and me—unbeknownst to us until the baby was dropped in our laps and the birth parents had left town on the lam. Just one of many awkward positions Erica had placed Ray and me in over the years, but now that we had Noelle and our life was so much richer, it was impossible to remain angry.

Greg reappeared and looked around. "Can we sit down?"

"Sure." I led him to the round table next to the reception desk. "What's going on?"

He crossed his hairy legs. I realized it was the first time I'd seen him in anything other than a suit and tie. His flip-flops revealed freakishly long second toes, and his khaki shorts and white polo both had purplish ice cream stains. Greg was the best lawyer in town, maybe even in the Finger Lakes region, but, at the moment, he didn't look so competent. Perhaps that was appropriate for delivering bad news.

"I've run into a wall with the adoption. We may need to hire a private investigator. Or maybe Ray can take some time off."

My heart accelerated, pressing on my chest. Tears blurred my vision, and I looked skyward to contain them. "Why? I thought you'd filed all the necessary papers. I thought we were weeks away from finalizing."

"I did, and we were. But a red flag popped up."

"What red flag?"

Greg picked at the stain on his shirt. "You know I contacted all the birth parents' family members to make sure they didn't want to claim Noelle."

"Yes?"

"Theodore Tibble's family wanted nothing to do with her, or with Theo."

"Right." I remembered doing the happy dance when Ray and I learned that.

"We never found Abigail's parents. Her application at the convenience store and her apartment lease named Theo as her emergency contact. The previous employers she listed had never

10

heard of her. So I wrote her family off since she had signed all the necessary papers to make Noelle yours before she left town."

That was a nice turn of phrase. Greg could have said "before she split" or "before she ran from the law" or even "before she escaped." Must be the lawyer in him that made him so vague. "Okay. So now you've found them?"

"No."

"What then, Greg? Can you just tell me?" Now I understood why the messenger got shot so often—for trying the recipient's patience!

Greg leaned his forearms on the table and folded his hands. "It turns out Abigail's name and social security number don't check out. Abigail Bryce was born in Canandaigua, New York, eighteen years ago."

"So? Lots of eighteen-year-olds have babies these days." Too many, in my opinion, but this one happened to please me.

Greg looked down at his hands. "Yes, but this Abigail Bryce never made it to eighteen. She died in June of last year, five months before her eighteenth birthday. Hit and run. No witnesses. Police thought it might have been a drunk driver, given it occurred around the corner from a bar at two-fifteen in the morning. They never apprehended the driver."

My chest felt tight. I forced myself to breathe. "But that's over a year ago."

"Exactly."

I tried to fill in the blanks. "Noelle's mother stole Abigail Bryce's identity?"

Greg shrugged. "So it appears."

"Then who is Noelle's mother?"

"Damned if I know."

TWO

RAY ARRIVED HOME A little after nine that night. Noelle had gone to sleep an hour earlier, and I sat in our living room staring at the flickering television screen. Who knew what show was on? Who cared? My baby wasn't going to be my baby, at least not yet. I still couldn't absorb the news and now I could no longer avoid sharing it with Ray. But when I said it out loud, I would have to accept it as the truth, something I simply didn't want to do.

"Darlin', aren't we going to sit on the front porch and watch the fireworks? I think we might see a few through the trees."

He didn't wait for my answer. Instead, he breezed into the kitchen and returned minutes later with a turkey sandwich and a Corona in his hands. "Did you want to go out on the porch or not?"

"Sure." Why burst his bubble? Ray didn't need to feel the pain I was feeling any longer than absolutely necessary. I'd let him enjoy his sandwich before I told him the bad news. If I told him now, he'd never eat, and he needed to eat. We were both going to need all the energy we could get to make it through this nightmare. The bag of caramel and chocolate-covered popcorn I'd consumed had energized me for all of an hour before I lapsed back into despair.

I grabbed the baby monitor and followed him outside, sitting next to him in my matching white wicker rocker. My feet skimmed the floor. Ray sat with his legs extended and crossed at the ankle. The thundershower had arrived on schedule at five o'clock and the outside air felt refreshingly cool. But the cushion on my rocker felt uncomfortably damp.

I tried to have our standard end of day conversation. "How bad was the car accident?"

Ray swallowed a bite of his sandwich. "Four boys smashed a Buick into a tree. They'd been drinking. Car must have been going at least sixty in a forty-mile zone. Beer bottles scattered all over the road. The driver's in critical condition. The passenger was dead on impact. Two kids in the backseat walked away."

I made a mental tick mark. One death in our town that could have been prevented. "How old were the boys?"

"Seventeen or eighteen. They all would have been seniors in high school this coming year. Football players."

"Ah. Do we know the families?"

Ray wolfed down the last of his sandwich and wiped his lips on the back of his hand. "I don't think so. Kids' names weren't familiar to me."

I would send a card anyway. Wachobe was a small town, and their families would appreciate it. "How sad."

"Yeah." Ray snorted the word. He had run out of patience a long time ago for teenagers who make bad choices, especially since he was the one who had to help scrape their remains off the roads and deliver the news to their parents. "So, are you going to tell me what's bothering you?"

The man knew me too well. "I need to talk to you about Noelle."

"Jolene, I'm sorry I couldn't watch her today. The Department is short with Gumby's wedding this weekend and Darrel out on disability after his bypass. I'll have to work more overtime while Gumby's on his honeymoon. You know the population in this county more than doubles in the summertime."

I did know and I hated the fact Ray had used my given name. Sometimes it meant he was feeling the urge, but it also indicated when he was ticked at me. Unfortunately, he'd also answered my unspoken question. He would not be able to take time off to hunt for Noelle's birthmother. I skipped ahead with my questions. "Do you know any good private investigators?"

Ray turned to look at me, surprise and confusion doing a rumba on his face. "Come again?"

I told Ray about my conversation with Greg Doran. When I finished, Ray drank his Corona in one long gulp and stared out at the street where other families were gathering to glimpse the fireworks.

After five minutes of silence, I couldn't take it anymore. "Ray, we need a plan to find her."

He eyed the bottle just to make sure the beer was done. I figured he could use another, but I wanted answers before I would fetch him a second.

"I know one guy. He's good, really good. But he charges four hundred dollars a day plus expenses. Have you sold any cars lately?"

"No, but I have an appointment tomorrow." To try to sell the car from hell.

Ray set the empty bottle on the porch floor. "Even if I can get a courtesy discount, we can't afford this guy for long. This kind of investigation could go on for months, even years. All we know about this girl is who she isn't. Finding out who she is will take hours of knocking on doors, and even then, it'll come down to dumb luck. We don't even have a good picture of her."

"I guess that's why Greg was hoping you could take some time off."

"Yeah, well, that's not gonna happen right now."

Even in the dim porch light, I feared Ray would see the tears filling my eyes again. Ever since Noelle had arrived, I'd become all emotional, a new experience for me. If I'd given birth, I could blame it on postpartum depression. Since I hadn't, I blamed it on all-consuming love.

I turned my head to watch a spider crawl up our yellow siding. I wondered how many children the spider had. Then I hoped they hadn't all taken up residency at my house.

Ray took my hand and squeezed it. "Listen, the worst that can happen is Noelle remains our foster child. She'd still be with us. That's the most important thing, isn't it?"

I yanked my hand away. "I don't want to jump every time there's a knock on the door, thinking someone is here to claim her and take her away from us. I want to know she's ours."

"Darlin', even if we are able to adopt her, it's always going to be a possibility her mother or father will come knocking on the door. People grow and change. They may sign away their rights, then decide they still want to meet her ten or fifteen years from now. We're going to have to be prepared for that."

"Fine. But I'd at least like to strive for permanency. Children need stability in their lives. They need ... parents." My voice broke.

Ray reached over to pull me onto his lap and hold me against his chest. He knew I was thinking of my mother, who killed herself when I was twelve and left me to raise my seven-year-old sister, who was now bipolar, often suicidal, and just plain quirky. My father, an eccentric man at best, had spent most of his time hiding under someone's chassis in his automotive garage. When he died four years ago, I turned the garage into a sports car boutique, both in tribute to his passion and in acknowledgement of his influence on my life. We'd spent a lot of time talking about cars, him and me.

Ray hugged me closer as the fireworks began overhead. He whispered close to my ear, "We'll do our best to find Noelle's mother and finalize the adoption. Don't worry."

As the crackle of fireworks filled the air and the acrid scent of gunpowder wafted into the neighborhood, I snuggled against Ray and convinced myself everything would happen for the best if I just had faith. Noelle belonged with us. She'd fallen into our laps and we would not let her go. Period.

Wachobe must have doubled the budget for the fireworks this year, maybe because the number of tourists in our town continued to increase each year, along with our property values and the associated taxes. The fireworks went on for twenty-five minutes at a steady pace. I cranked the volume on the baby monitor to see if the noise had awakened Noelle. Once in awhile, I heard sucking, but that was it. She wouldn't awaken until seven-thirty or so in the morning.

When the last sizzling sparkle faded, I fingered the rough whiskers on Ray's chin. "So where do we start?"

He kissed me on the nose. "We start with what we know. While I'm on patrol tomorrow, I'll stop at the convenience store where she was employed and talk to her old boss Bobby and anyone else she worked with. Maybe they'll know something about her. Then I'll stop by the apartment where she lived and snoop around there. Maybe the new tenant gets a stray piece of mail for her now and then. Maybe she left a forwarding address."

"I think Greg already checked that angle. He came up dry."

"That's all right. We're looking for one tidbit of information that could unlock the case. We check everything twice, ourselves."

I got off his lap and returned to my rocker, my confidence returning. Ray stretched out his legs and shook off my lingering weight.

I continued to plan. "What about this dead girl in Canandaigua? Do we check her out?"

"Absolutely. But I can't get over there tomorrow. I don't know when I'll be able to get there. It would be best to go on a weekday to stop in the high school office, places like that."

Canandaigua was a half hour east, a true Finger Lake at fifteen and a half miles long—more than twice the size of Wachobe's lake. The city shared our town's historic Victorian architecture and spectacular scenery, but exceeded our tourist capacity considerably with renowned wineries, a convention center, chain stores and motels, and even a water park. We were in competition for tourists, although our small town won hands down, in my opinion, for its charm and finer quality shops, of course. And Wachobe's real estate was more valuable, perhaps because it wasn't as citified. Still, it had occurred to me more than once that my niche sports car boutique might do a more thriving business in a city of Canandaigua's size. And I had a soft spot for the place. As a child, my parents had taken me often to the amusement park by the lake, Roseland, where the carousel was my favorite ride. I have a crystal clear and precious memory of my mother waving to me as I spun around again and again. I could still hear the music.

Ray gave me a funny look.

I realized I was smiling. I'd drifted onto memory lane. The amusement park closed in 1985. I needed to stay on task.

"I could go to Canandaigua on Friday."

Ray frowned. "You don't know where to start investigating. You don't know the right questions to ask."

"So you tell me. If I have a question, I'll call you."

"Has it occurred to you this girl stole someone else's identity for a reason? People who do that generally don't want to be found. She may even have been in trouble."

"So?"

"I'm not sure it's a good idea. You may be in danger sniffing around. For all we know, she may have been the one who mowed down Abigail Bryce in the street."

A mental image of that flashed through my head. I winced. But I didn't want to hear any drawbacks to my plan. Just put the pedal to the metal. "Ray, it's Canandaigua. Not exactly the homicide capital of the world. I'm sure the girl's death was a tragic accident."

He conceded with a tip of his head. "What about the shop?"

"Cory can watch the shop."

"What about Noelle?"

That was a little trickier. Cory could watch her at the shop. He would have to keep her in the crib most of the time, though, or ignore his repair and maintenance customers for an entire day to play patty cake and build block towers with her. He'd happily do so, but I hated to impose on our employer-employee relationship by expecting him to care for my child.

Noelle could ride with me to Canandaigua, but her maximum tolerance for her car seat might be exceeded. Things would turn ugly then. And it didn't seem fair to her.

Another idea occurred to me. I dismissed it just as quickly then let it slide back into my thoughts. I dared to voice it. "What about Erica?"

I could see the whites of Ray's eyes as they bugged out of his head. "Now *you've* lost your mind."

My sister Erica had been released from the state psychiatric center months ago. This time when her doctor met with me, he implied they didn't ever plan to welcome her back. Quite a shock since she'd been in and out of the center for the last three years, attempting suicide each time as her golden key to re-entry. Apparently, the doctor had figured out Erica didn't like it on the outside and preferred to live there. From what he said, I guessed the state frowned on that. They didn't consider the psych center a spa and resort.

I braced myself for an argument. Ray had no faith in Erica at all. Amazingly, I still had some. It was part of my job as her surrogate mother. "She takes Noelle to the park by herself."

"That's an hour, not a whole day. And the other mothers keep an eye on her."

I had no doubt. They were probably trying to keep her away from their children. Not that Erica looked or acted peculiar, but the town grapevine made sure everyone believed she was.

"She has a job now. She seems to be doing quite well. I've noticed a significant change in her."

"Has she stopped picking up strangers in bars and sleeping with them?"

"I can't say." It didn't help my case that she worked four nights a week as a waitress in a local bar and restaurant.

"Is she still cutting out pictures of butterflies and hanging them on the wall?"

Of course Ray would remember Erica coveted the butterflies' short life spans. "I haven't seen any." I hadn't been in her apartment recently either, but I kept that to myself.

"What has your mother had to say lately?"

Now that was just cruel. Ray knew Erica claimed to talk to our mother. I didn't know precisely how that worked, but Erica claimed Mom had suggested she obtain Noelle for us. Couldn't fault that idea, whatever the source. "Lots of people go to the gravesite of their loved one to talk to them. That's not so awful, is it?"

"Your sister never visits the grave."

A minor technicality. At least Ray didn't know Erica thought Mom's ghost had moved into our new home with us. That's because I'd sold the family home she haunted previously, of course. My mother had asphyxiated herself to death in its garage with car exhaust. Sometimes I wondered if her method of choice had been a message for my dad or just a perverse use of her knowledge of automobiles, learned at his side. I knew her actions had left Erica, my father, and me feeling abandoned, helpless, and hopeless. It remains debatable as to whether or not we ever truly recovered. On my darkest days, I'd have to say not.

"Let's cut to the chase, darlin'. Do you trust Erica?"

His question stopped me cold. I gave it a few minutes thought and went with my instincts. "Yes. She's never been harmful to anyone but herself. And she loves Noelle."

"I know she does. She loves you, too. But that never stopped her."

This time it might. Erica had said she loved me best. I took that as her promise she planned to stay around, unlike our mother, who thought of herself first and left us.

Ray slapped at a mosquito. "Why can't you ask Isabelle if her nanny would watch Noelle and Cassidy?"

Isabelle was my best friend from college. She ran an advertising agency, and her husband owned a jewelry store in a city an hour east of Wachobe. They were busy people, too. "Cassidy is three now. She has to be driven to nursery school, library story hour, dancing lessons and a whole bunch of other activities." My best friend subscribed to the theory a child was best kept moving until worn out. I subscribed to the opposite theory. "It would be very taxing on Noelle, and she'd be exposed to a lot of new germs. Besides, I'd spend all day driving there and back. I'd never get to ask any questions."

"All right, all right. Maybe your sister and Cory could split a day. I'd be okay with that." Ray slapped another mosquito. "Let's go inside."

It irritated me a bit that I had to supply all the babysitters. Ray knew people, but somehow this responsibility always fell to me. I decided to let it pass. So many more things passed without comment or argument now that he and I had reconciled.

I picked up Ray's empty beer bottle and headed for the door. "Then it's settled. I'll call Erica tomorrow. We need to know everything she knows about Abigail Bryce and Theo Tibble anyway."

Ray breathed in my ear, "Be sure to ask her if she knows where they're hiding out."

"She said she didn't know, Ray." Erica swore she knew very little about their alleged participation in the convenience store robberies. Her sociopath boyfriend at the time, Sam Green, had been a suspect and a psych center escapee as well. Theo was his cousin. Needless to say, the demise of Erica's relationship with Sam had delighted me.

"And you believed her?"

"Ray!" I whipped open the screen door and turned around to retort. "Be nice to Erica. We're going to need her to talk to Sam and his brother to see what they can tell us about Theo and Abigail. They'll be far more likely to talk to her than you."

"Aw, you think they hold their arrests against me?" Ray nuzzled my neck.

I had to laugh.

I was halfway into the living room when squealing brakes and rhythmic thumping of woofers made me stop to look at the street. Ray's gaze traveled in the same direction.

A shiny black classic Chevy Nova with a jacked up rear end and chrome wheels screeched to a halt under the streetlight in front of our bungalow. The passenger door flew open. Erica popped out, all tousled blond hair and in Daisy Duke shorts with a tank top, looking like a teenager instead of a woman in her early-thirties. Braless, if my eyes didn't deceive me. Shoeless, too. Not a good sign. When she was on her game, Erica dressed much more conservatively and fastidiously. Although it was hot today…

Erica leaned into the car. "I am never speaking to you again, you bastard. Don't come anywhere near me. Ever. Do you hear me?"

I checked the street. It had cleared after the fireworks display, but I noticed a few porch lights flick on. Who didn't hear her?

"Erica!" I tried to get her attention, but the woofers drowned me out.

Ray folded his arms and made his I-told-you-so face.

I ignored him, watching the scene on the street play out instead.

Erica screamed, "Give me my purse."

Her purse sailed out the open car door. Its contents spilled onto the sidewalk.

"YOU BASTARD." She slammed the door and fell to her knees to gather up her belongings. The Nova burned rubber, fishtailing around the corner at the end of our street.

Ray pulled out his cell phone and started dialing. I knew the driver had better slow down before the nearest on-duty sheriff's deputy caught up with him.

Erica stumbled up the steps onto the porch and threw herself into my arms, sobbing. "I hate him. I hate him."

I tugged her inside the house and settled her on the sofa. "Okay. Who?"

She accepted a tissue from me, mopping her face. "Sam. You remember Sam, don't you?"

I met Ray's wary gaze as he clicked his cell phone closed. "Sure, we remember him."

"He's an asshole. I'm never, ever speaking to him again."

A muscle in Ray's cheek twitched. "Darlin', we might need a Plan B."

THREE

THE NEXT MORNING WHEN Ray dropped onto a stool at the raised breakfast bar separating our kitchen and dining room, he didn't say anything about the fact that Erica was still asleep on our couch. He didn't say good morning to me either. He simply dug into his plate of pancakes. I poured him a cup of coffee and leaned against the stove to watch Noelle carefully place each piece of her torn-up pancake in her mouth and chew with great concentration. I loved to watch her eat. She took it so seriously.

Ray finished his breakfast within two minutes. He kissed both of Noelle's sticky cheeks and pecked mine. "I'll call you later."

"No kiss on the lips?"

"Is your sister sleeping on our couch again tonight?"

"No." Now I just needed to tell her that.

He leaned in and brushed my lips with his. "Thank you."

I loaded his plate and silverware into the dishwasher and wiped down the granite countertop. Noelle banged her hands on the highchair tray, sending a few pieces of pancake flying through the air onto the floor. I knelt to pick them up.

A cheerful voice called out behind me, "Who's making all the racket?"

Startled, I jerked upright and slammed my head on the underside of Noelle's tray, launching the rest of her pancakes. She wailed. I bit back a swearword a second before it left my tongue.

Erica perched on a barstool with a broad smile on her face. It did little to offset her swollen red eyes with their black mascara rings. She hadn't bothered to clean up before crashing on the couch last night.

I returned her smile with a grimace. "You're feeling better, I take it."

Erica grabbed a pancake off the serving platter and ripped it into tiny pieces for Noelle. Then she tickled Noelle's chin and kissed her hair. "Every time I see this little sweetie, I feel better. Keep drumming, Noelle." Erica tapped a few beats to get Noelle started again.

The back of my head throbbed. I wished Noelle would stop, but I let it pass. "Have some pancakes, then we need to talk."

"No pancakes, just coffee." Erica grabbed a mug, filled it, and added two heaping teaspoons of sugar. "I don't want to talk about Sam anymore."

What a surprise. She'd spent two hours last night filling me in on every detail of their past relationship as well as all his current faults. For a certified sociopath, he didn't have that many. I figured she'd missed something in her analysis, blinded by her own shortcomings, perhaps. I was, however, very clear that he stole fifty bucks out of her purse last night, and she never, ever wanted to speak to him again.

Too bad. She'd suck his toes if necessary to get the information I needed. I had waited until this morning to tell her, though, hoping the night would bring her more perspective.

"Sorry, but you're going to have to. Abigail Bryce is not Abigail Bryce. She stole the identity of a dead girl. We need to know who she is to finalize the adoption. You're going to have to talk to Sam to see if we can find Theo and Noelle's birthmother."

Erica set her coffee mug down with a thump. "No shit?"

I covered Noelle's ears. "Watch your mouth."

"Sorry." Erica looked down at her rumpled and skimpy clothing. "Okay, not to worry. Do you have anything I can wear?"

"Help yourself." I was a size eight. She wore a size four. I silently wished her luck.

She disappeared into my bedroom. I heard muffled words. I followed her in. "What?"

She emerged from my closet. "You wear granny underpants."

"I wear hipsters. They're comfortable and don't make panty lines."

"That's what you think. Take me home. I need a thong."

"What for?" I headed back into the kitchen with Erica in tow and wiped Noelle down before lifting her to my hip and grabbing my car keys.

"Sam's not going to want me anywhere near him. I need a mini-skirt."

I led the way to the garage and strapped Noelle into her car seat in the back of my silver 2004 Lexus ES 330 sedan. A new-to-me import, it was a concession to my family status. The Porsche 944 my father had restored and given to me for graduation had presented too much of a hassle for car seats. But I missed my Porsche. Erica drove it now, and I cringed every time she ground the gears. "I still don't get it, Erica." I wasn't sure I wanted to either.

She flopped into the passenger seat. "When Sam pis…angered me last night, I gave him a squeeze."

"What do you mean, a squeeze?"

"I squeezed his ba…man parts."

No wonder he threw her purse out of the car. I was surprised he didn't turn her into road kill. "So what's the thong for?"

"I'll have to do a little Monica Lewinsky on him. Flash him and…promise to play with his cigar."

"Erica!"

"Do you want the information or not?"

——

I dropped Erica off at my…her apartment and drove to the shop in time to flip the sign to "Open" at eight-fifty-eight a.m. Cory strolled in on the last tick before nine.

"Did you see the fireworks last night?"

"More than I cared to." I filled him in on Erica's road show and the need to learn Noelle's birthmother's true identity.

"So you need me to watch this little cutie tomorrow? That's cool, but unfortunately I'm only available until two. I have an afternoon rehearsal." Cory picked Noelle up out of her playpen and tossed her in the air, much to her delight. I crossed my fingers her pancakes wouldn't reappear.

"Maybe you could take the morning shift." I didn't know what time Erica rolled out of bed after a work night. Or who she might be rolling out of bed with, for that matter.

"I'll try to finish up the maintenance on Brennan Rowe's Jaguar today and get a head start on the McDonalds' Mercedes. We should be able to deliver on all our promises." Cory set Noelle down and headed out to his kingdom, the three-bay garage that ran across the back of the sports car boutique.

I played peek-a-boo and pony with Noelle, hoping to tire her out for a nap before Dave Barclay and his wife arrived at ten o'clock. As she bounced on my knee, I reviewed the selling features of the Ferrari in my head and tried not to picture the dead body falling out of it seven months ago and the furor that followed. The car still gave me the creeps. It also gave me acid reflux every time I made a payment on the outstanding loan. Pretty soon I might be desperate enough to sell it for scrap metal value.

At nine forty-five, Noelle finished her bottle. I laid her down for her morning nap. Perhaps I'd been too entertaining because she popped right back up and held her arms out to me. I laid her down again and offered her pacifier. She took it and started sucking, closing her eyes. I tiptoed into the showroom and eased my office door shut.

I sat at the table by the reception desk for a few minutes then sprang to my feet, not wanting to look like I had nothing to do but wait for them to arrive. I grabbed the phone and tried to think of someone to call who I could hang up on fast. Isabelle didn't answer her cell. Ray either. I started to dial Erica and changed my mind. I didn't want to know what she was currently doing.

Dave Barclay and a pinch-faced woman strode through the door. Where Dave was fair, his wife was dark. Dark hair, dark clothes, dark expression. Where Dave looked athletic, she looked gaunt. Maybe she was ill? Dave introduced her as Kim.

When I shook their hands in turn, her chilly touch felt skeletal. I stifled a shiver. Her voice didn't make me feel any warmer. "You're Jolene Asdale?" She curled her upper lip and said my family name as though it were synonymous with dirt. I could smell her perfume, an overpowering spicy scent.

"Jolene Parker, actually. That's my married name."

Kim Barclay sniffed.

Dave didn't seem to notice anything amiss. "Kim and I couldn't wait for this morning to arrive. We skipped breakfast to be sure we'd arrive on time." He rubbed the palms of his hands together. "It's a beautiful car."

Much better looking than his wife. I wanted to tell him not to let her skip too many meals or she'd disappear. On the other hand, her snarl deepened as she gazed at the car, and I realized her disappearance might not be such a bad thing after all.

"Let me tell you a little bit about it. It's a 2006 F430 Ferrari Spider. I purchased it from a collector in Arizona. It has only 1,502 miles on it and—"

"I thought we were here for a test drive. I didn't realize we were going to be subjected to a sales pitch." Kim Barclay took two steps toward the door. "Maybe I'll peruse the merchandise at Talbots until you're ready to drive, David."

He looked between her and me. "Would it be any trouble for us to take the car out on the road now, Jolene?"

"No trouble at all. Let me get the key." I tried not to let it show the woman had gotten to me, but my hands shook with anger as I entered my office and pulled out the desk drawer for the key. Unfortunately, enough to make me bang the drawer.

Noelle awakened with a wail. I set the key on the desk and tried to soothe her by rubbing her back. She wasn't having any of it.

Cruella De Vil appeared in my office doorway. "Is that a baby?"

I swallowed my first response and managed a politer one. "Yes."

"Is it *yours*?"

I picked Noelle up, stroking and soothing. "Yes."

"I heard she belonged to a couple of thieves."

Dave appeared in the doorway behind his wife as I choked on my outrage. "We've caught you at a bad time. Perhaps we could reschedule for later in the week."

I'd heard those words before. They meant "no sale."

I struggled for composure. "Of course. Here's my card. Please give me a call and let me know what day is good for you."

I heard Kim Barclay say, "Any day that crying creature isn't here" just before the showroom door closed behind them.

———

Cory bought me a tuna sub for lunch to try to erase my new streak of bad luck. He also purchased a chocolate cupcake decorated like a turtle for Noelle from the new bakery on Main Street. The bakery only sold cupcakes—delicious, sugary ones. Cory and I invested almost daily in their success, but Noelle didn't get to participate often.

"Mark and I are going to the Keuka Lake Arts Festival in Hammondsport this weekend. Then we might hit all the wineries around the lake. What about you and Ray?"

Keuka Lake lay forty-five minutes southeast of Canandaigua. It didn't qualify as a true Finger Lake because of its Y shape, but it did lie in the heart of the region. Ray and I had considered exchanging our marital vows at Garrett Chapel, a one-room historic stone sanctuary set on the tip of the bluff between the forks of the lake. Then we eloped to Disney World instead.

"Ray has to work and Gumby's getting married this weekend."

Cory choked on his sub. "Isn't Gumby the guy who hit on you a week after you and Ray separated?"

"That's him. He's quite a prize. The bride's a lucky, lucky woman." I crumpled the wrapper from my sub and tossed it in the trash can. "So you and Mark have been dating since December. That's got to be a new record for you. Do you think you'll ever become Cory Wynn instead of Cory Kempe?" The minute the words left my mouth, I feared they were politically incorrect. New York didn't permit same sex marriages.

Cory didn't take offense. Maybe after three years of working together almost daily and lunching just as often, we had reached the point where none would ever be taken.

Instead he continued, "I'm thinking about asking him if he'd like to live together. The drive between his apartment and mine is getting to be a little too much. I was thinking we could buy a house together. Build some equity—in a home and our relationship."

"Have you talked to him about it yet?" I tried picking the cupcake crumbs from Noelle's hair with little success. They smeared into chocolate highlights, blending with the yellow baby cereal streaks. I decided to give her a baby wipe bath instead.

"Maybe this weekend. We're staying overnight at a bed and breakfast in Hammondsport. I figured that would be a good time."

"Call me when you get home. I can't wait until Tuesday to hear what happened." We closed the sports car boutique on Sundays and Mondays. If the phone didn't start ringing more often, I'd have to close it more days—like Monday through Sunday. Moving the shop to Canandaigua started to look appealing.

The phone rang as if on cue. It wasn't a customer.

"I saw Sam. Good news." Erica sounded as if she'd just finished running a marathon.

"He knows where to find Theo and Noelle's birthmother?"

"No."

Nausea waved over me. "He doesn't?"

"No. He's not even sure they're still together."

That was a lovely thought. They'd be easier to find if they were, since we could get pictures of Theo. If Noelle's birthmother had gone her separate way, we might never find her.

Erica continued, "Sam said to try all the casinos in the state first or maybe the one just over the bridge in Niagara Falls. Theo has a thing for gambling."

Now I was trekking two hours to Canada. Maybe we would need to hire a nanny.

"Is that all he said?"

"No! I told you I have good news."

"So tell me."

"Sam and I are getting married!"

FOUR

GOOD NEWS WAS MEANT to be shared. I phoned Ray. He answered from his patrol car, somewhere east of the lake. I suggested he pull over.

He liked the idea of checking the casinos. "They hid out at Turning Stone last year. I'm sure they've gone farther away by now, but it wouldn't hurt to check. I got a video from the convenience store that shows Abigail. I'm going to have a print made. It'll be black and white, but better than nothing. I also got Theo's high school yearbook picture and a more candid shot from his parents. I'll fax both pictures to the head of security at Turning Stone and have him look over the current guests. Did Erica say anything else?"

I closed one eye, scrunched my shoulders, and held my breath. "Erica and Sam are getting married."

Silence.

"Ray, are you still there?"

I heard breathing. At least he hadn't died of a heart attack.

"Ray?"

"You are not leaving Noelle with that lunatic. That's final. If Cory can't watch her all day, then you can't go to Canandaigua tomorrow."

Big mistake. Never tell me what I can and can't do. Oddly enough, I liked to decide for myself. "I'll talk to Erica and make sure she isn't planning to spend time with Sam tomorrow."

"That's not good enough. She's unfit."

"Her doctor says she's fit." Fit for society anyway.

"I'd like to hear that from him."

"Maybe I'll call him." He might be able to ease my doubts—and run interference on Erica's pending marital disaster.

"You do that, Jolene. Let me know what he says. I have to go now." The dial tone came through loud and clear this time.

I flipped through my Rolodex and found the number for Erica's psychiatrist, who continued to monitor her medication and progress through monthly appointments. His secretary paged him. He picked up the line within a minute. "Dr. Albert."

After I identified myself, I gave him the rundown on Erica's recent activities. He listened without interruption. I wrapped with "I'm very concerned."

"Jolene, I'm not sure how I can help you. Rushing into a marriage is not a certifiable offense."

"But her judgment is impaired. She's fallen right back into her promiscuous patterns and now it's escalated."

"Promiscuity is not a mental illness. Marrying the wrong guy isn't either. I'm on my third wife myself. You can't hold your sister to a higher standard than the rest of the world. You can only offer her advice when she asks for it."

I choked back a sigh. "Is my child safe with her?"

Dr. Albert chuckled. "My wife and I let the thirteen-year-old down the street babysit our son. I think Erica has at least as much going for her, but there's no guarantee."

I had my answer. Ray wouldn't like it. But I felt silly now for even calling Dr. Albert, although he assured me I'd been no trouble at all.

Erica would watch Noelle tomorrow afternoon as planned. It would be for less than three hours. But I'd threaten Erica and make her swear not to let Sam near Noelle. The man had stabbed his own mother's hand with a fork last year when she tried to serve him pork chops. I didn't want to take any chances.

I called our attorney and asked him for the address of the real Abigail Bryce, formerly of Canandaigua. Tomorrow I would start my investigation with a visit to her mother and stepfather. Perhaps they would recognize Noelle's birthmother from my description or the photograph. If not, I'd try the high school and any friends of Abigail her parents were willing to name. I would look until I couldn't think of anywhere else to look.

My gaze wandered to Noelle, who sat on her portable crib playing with some blocks. My chest felt full. I swallowed a lump in my throat. Who knew I would grow to love her this much? I couldn't imagine life without her now. Six months ago, she'd filled the void in my marriage, a void that separated Ray and me for three years and almost brought us to divorce. For years he'd asked me to bear his child and I had refused, fearing our child would be born with a mental illness like my mother and Erica. I didn't want the burden of guilt or the responsibility for another wayward soul. Thankfully, Noelle was a happy, healthy baby so far. Now if only she could become ours.

After spending the rest of the day alternating between entertaining Noelle and catching up on my accounting and bookwork, I turned off the lights in my office and headed toward the garage, cuddling Noelle. I planned to ask Cory to turn out the lights and lock up. Oh, we'd leave the spotlights on over the Ferrari all night. Maybe someone would drive by and fall in love with the Italian stallion. Maybe my new improved website or the listing on eBay would draw some interest. Or, even better, maybe someone would steal it.

I should be so lucky.

The phone rang. I debated ignoring it, but ever hopeful, I decided to answer.

"Jolene, this is Dave Barclay."

"Yes, Dave! I'm so sorry about this morning. Are you calling to reschedule?"

Noelle tried to pull the phone from my hands. I hitched her a little lower on my hip and leaned away, praying she wouldn't scream.

"I have to ask you a question. I hope you won't think I'm crazy."

"Of course not."

"Kim heard that you found a dead body in the Ferrari. Is that true?"

Rats. "Yes, I'm afraid so. But it's been thoroughly detailed. The body didn't cause any damage to the interior." As soon as the words left my mouth, I thought I must be crazy for saying them.

"No, of course. It's just … this car might not be the right one for us. Bad karma, you know."

I knew. "I understand. Well, if there's anything else I can help you with—"

"Actually, there is. It's a sort of an unusual request, but hopefully within your line of work."

"Okay. Let's hear it."

Noelle started to whimper and squirm. I set her down on the floor and watched to make sure I'd found all the loose pearls and shards of glass when I swept yesterday.

"Kim's grandfather is dying of cancer. He's got a few weeks left. It's been very stressful on Kim. She's been at his bedside every day." Dave's voice trailed off as if it pained him to have his wife under such pressure.

That might explain her pinched face and gaunt body. Had her death watch sucked the life from her, too? Had it milked all her human kindness? Those were questions one didn't ask a potential paying customer. I settled for "I'm so sorry."

"Thank you. He used to be in the car business, too. And he raced cars in the late sixties and early seventies. Factory show cars. You know, the models the manufacturers put on racetracks as advertising?"

"Yes." My dad used to take me to the track in Watkins Glen, only a couple hours away from Wachobe at the base of Seneca Lake. The Glen offered a number of different racing venues. After new car models made the rounds of the auto shows and the automotive press had a chance to take their pictures, the manufacturers often put the vehicles on racetracks to garner even more of the public's attention.

"He raced one car in particular. A 1970 Datsun 240Z. We believe the car is still racing in vintage series, or at least, it has in the past. Kim's grandfather is sure he's seen it at the Glen in recent years. Anyway, here's our request. If we give you the serial number, can you locate the car for us and purchase it? We'd be happy to pay you a fee for your time."

I didn't really feel like doing Kim any favors, but my business needed the money. With all my inventory money tied up in the Ferrari, my best alternative offer to any customer was to locate the car of their choice, negotiate the deal, and deliver it to their door. Sometimes I had to search a while to find the right vehicle, but I loved the thrill of the hunt. "I can make a few phone calls. What are you willing to pay for the Z?"

"Gramps thinks the Datsun is worth around fifty thousand or so. We'd go three times that."

Three times its value? Wow! "Is your wife's grandfather interested in driving the car again?"

"No. He wants to be buried in it."

———

After Noelle settled into bed for the night, I left Ray parked in front of the television and fired up the computer.

I'd been around cars for all my life. No one had ever suggested them to me as a burial vessel before today. Dave Barclay said it had triggered a lot of debate within his family, but they'd all come around to agreement. Who was I to judge?

The Internet never ceased to amaze me. God bless Al Gore for inventing it. I typed in the year, make, and model of the vehicle, hit the search key, and, presto, up popped an article from a car club that listed all the known owners of the first shipment of Datsun 240Zs to the United States. A quick search of the Internet Yellow Pages produced three listings for the man I needed to contact. They looked like his home, office, and cottage in the Finger Lakes. Would a hundred and fifty thousand dollars be enough to entice him to sell?

He answered his home phone number on the third ring. I identified myself and explained the purpose of my call, leaving out the part about the burial. Maybe the man wouldn't appreciate having his car under six to eight feet of soil for eternity.

"You know, it's funny. The car's been sitting in my garage for years since my last race. I had an offer or two on it after we won the Paine Webber Endurance Championship at the Glen, but no one's asked me about the car in years. Now I've had two calls about it within the last month."

"Really? That *is* interesting." I tried to think of a tactful way to ask about the other caller. Had Dave Barclay already contacted this man?

"The other woman offered me forty-five thousand. I couldn't sell it to her."

A woman? Kim Barclay maybe? "I see." I typed a quick map search into the Internet. This man's residence was only an hour or so from Canandaigua. "Would you be home tomorrow afternoon? I'd love to see the car."

"It's my day off. I'll be in the garage, working on my current project. You're welcome to stop by, but I have to tell you upfront I'm not really interested in selling the Z."

I'd see what I could do to change his mind about that. It's always harder to turn someone down in person than over the phone. We agreed to meet at three the next day.

Ray was flicking through the channels when I entered the living room and sat next to him. He didn't look at me. The flicking stopped when *Dirty Harry* appeared on the screen.

"Will you give me the pictures of Abigail and Theo for tomorrow?"

His gaze remained glued to the television. "I'll have to get them out of the car. Can it wait until morning?"

"I suppose." But I wanted to get a look at the pictures now. My memory of Noelle's birthmother had faded. She'd had a silver nose-ring, brush cut, and spiky eyelashes when I first saw her, as well as a vibrant tattoo of an eagle on the back of her neck. Of course, she'd been noticeably pregnant, too. In six months, she could have grown longer hair, removed the nose-ring, and cut down on her makeup. Given the automatic weight change, she would be next to impossible to recognize. We didn't even know for sure what color her hair was or whether it was curly or straight, and try as I might, I couldn't recall her eye color.

I nudged Ray. "I wanted to examine Abigail's picture. See if she has any distinguishing features, like big earlobes or moles or something she can't hide. Did you notice any?"

A commercial came on with dancing bears. Ray stood. "Nope, but I'll get the pictures. You can look for yourself."

The grainy, gray photos told me nothing. Abigail stood in the middle of an aisle in the convenience store. With the distance from the camera and the conversion from videotape obscuring the clarity of the photo, I didn't think her own mother would recognize her.

Ray's attention was on the television again. I climbed onto his lap, facing him. He leaned to the left to continue watching his show.

I fiddled with the buttons on his shirt. "I'm going to start with Abigail's family tomorrow. Any suggestions on how to approach them?"

He looked at me. "Just tell the truth. The truth will set you free."

Pretty poetic for Ray. A little unnerving for me, considering I didn't plan to tell him Erica would be babysitting for us tomorrow. "I planned to stop at the high school, too. If neither one of those stops produce any leads, where else should I try?"

"Wherever kids hang out. The beach at Kershaw Park, the bowling alley, the graveyard."

"The graveyard?"

Ray nodded. "Very popular with the teenage crowd. Great place to hide from mom and dad and do all the things against the rules."

"Ew. We never hung out there." Ray and I had dated since we were sixteen.

He slid his hands under my shirt. "No, but your father and my mother were always at work. We had the run of two houses."

That was true. We'd had very little supervision, but we were also too responsible to get into trouble. I had my sister to take care of and Ray had his little brother. We were more like parents than kids from an early age. Besides, we both had a parent who resided in the Wachobe cemetery.

I shook off the memories and focused on the plan. "I'm going to take a detour and look at a car for Dave Barclay, too. I'll be home no later than four forty-five."

His gaze shifted to meet mine. "Noelle will be at the shop with Cory?"

"I'm dropping her off first thing in the morning." Then Erica planned to pick up Noelle at one-thirty after her nap and take her to the park before bringing her home. But Ray didn't need to know that. He wouldn't get home until after me.

I thought it best to change the subject. "Have you ever heard of anyone getting buried in a car before?"

Ray squinted at me. "No. The closest I've heard is being buried with a baseball mitt."

I told him about Kim Barclay's grandfather. "Do you think that's legal?"

"It probably takes all kinds of permits and legal maneuverings, but Barclay has the money. I'm just not so sure he's as squeaky clean as he appears to be."

"What do you mean?"

"I've heard rumors he extends financing to a lot of people who are not likely to pay him back." Ray's finger traced the base of my spine.

"So his business is unstable?"

"That's just it. His business appears to be doing incredibly well."

"So is he incurring losses or not?"

Ray's hand began to wander up and down my back, scratching. "I think he's being paid in other ways."

I arched my back so he could get to all the hard to reach spots. In another life, I might have been a cat. "Such as?"

"That's what I'm not sure about. He does his exporting from an office here, but the sales occur in New York City. I don't have enough access to information about his business to figure out if the rumors are true. But he owns an awfully big house and some pretty fancy cars—too fancy to be financed on the sale of Mennonite quilts and woodworking alone."

"Could he be into drugs?"

"Or money laundering. Or something else altogether. Do me a favor and keep your eyes open when you're around him. Maybe you'll stumble onto his secret. But stay alert."

Ray stopped scratching and turned his attention back to *Dirty Harry*, who was about to deliver one of his most famous lines.

I slid off his lap. "You know this town, Ray. Most of the rumors are just that, rumors, spread by people who don't have enough going on in their own lives to occupy their minds."

"It's still smart to keep your eyes open."

I would keep my eyes wide open, but right now Dave Barclay was the closest I'd come to selling a car in months. I needed a sale, not just for the money but for the confidence boost. My business was coming up to its four-year mark and it hadn't shown a profit yet. Cory's work in the garage paid most of my overhead. I worked almost for free. I would believe Dave Barclay was an honest man for now.

Then Clint said it. *You have to ask yourself a question. Do I feel lucky? Well do ya, punk?*

After the last two days, my answer was no.

FIVE

Canandaigua had a six-lane highway leading in and two lanes on each side of Main Street, all of which were packed with traffic on a Friday in the beginning of summer. I tried to pass once and nearly got the passenger side of my car scraped by a boat trailer swaying down the road behind a minivan, its roof loaded with two kayaks and a canoe. This town might offer more business to my sports car boutique, but I didn't know if I could take the crowds. It was a relief to turn onto the side street off Main where the Bryces lived.

Mature trees lined the street, casting welcome shade on sidewalks and sun-parched lawns. The stately homes dated back over a century with front and side porches, tall skinny windows, and real painted wooden shutters instead of the no-paint vinyl ones on most newly built homes. Many of the windows still had the original wavy glass. It looked like a nice place to grow up.

In my naiveté, I thought investigative work was simple. Ring a doorbell, ask a few questions, and uncover the desired answers. I didn't realize it could become a game of cat and mouse from the get-go. Too bad I was allergic to cats and irrationally afraid of mice.

When I parked my Lexus in the Bryces' driveway, I saw the curtain on a second floor window twitch. Ringing the doorbell three times didn't bring anyone to the door. Multiple knocks with the brass lion's head failed to attract any inhabitants either.

I stepped away from the door and gazed up at the window, contemplating whether it would be worthwhile to shout for attention or not. I could yell "Stella, Stella" but someone might call the padded wagon for me. I'd always secretly feared that. Would I be able to talk my way out of a psychiatric ward? When I spent three days there as a child, after discovering my mother's suicide in the garage, my dad rescued me and refused to allow them to take me back. Ray might let them keep me if he found out I had left Noelle with Erica.

On a hunch, I climbed into my car and drove a half-block before turning around and watching the Bryces' house from a down-the-street neighbor's driveway on the opposite side of the road. Sure enough, ten minutes later, a blond in a short blue dress and white sweater left the house and walked down the sidewalk toward me. She didn't seem to notice my car.

I started the car and followed her. She went in the florist shop on Main Street then continued down the road with her purchase of pink carnations in hand. She made another right onto the next street and, after half a block, disappeared into a yard.

Turned out, it was a graveyard. Ray must have had a premonition. I parked my car and started a row-by-row search of the cemetery, taking great care not to walk on anyone. Easier said than done.

I found the blond woman kneeling next to a polished marble stone engraved with Abigail Bryce's name, birth and death dates, and a pair of doves floating heavenward. The woman had removed a shriveled bunch of flowers from a vase at the base of the gravestone and replaced them with her purchase. I stayed out of her line of sight as she prayed. When she stood and started to walk away, I stepped in her path.

"Mrs. Bryce?"

She jumped a foot in the air and yelped. The dried flowers in her hand dropped to the ground at my feet. I stooped to pick them up.

"I'm sorry. I didn't mean to startle you. I hoped to talk to you, just for a minute." I held out the wilted stems as a peace offering.

She accepted them. "Are you here about your daughter?"

Surprised, I skipped a beat. "Yes, in a manner of speaking. I'm here about her mother."

Mrs. Bryce wrinkled her brow. "Aren't you her mother?"

"Not yet. I'm her foster mother."

She continued to appear puzzled. "Are you Cynthia Morton?"

Now it was my turn to be confused. "No. I'm Jolene Asdale." No, Parker. Try to remember to say Parker.

Mrs. Bryce's knees seemed to go out from under her. She reached for the nearest gravestone and leaned against it. Sweat popped out on her brow.

I surveyed the graveyard, but didn't see anyone else. "Were you expecting Mrs. Morton?"

Her eyes bugged out. "No. No. You just caught me off guard. I didn't expect to run into anyone here." She wiped her brow. "It's awfully hot today, isn't it?"

I wished I had something to fan her with. "Are you all right, Mrs. Bryce? Maybe I could buy you lemonade or iced tea somewhere?"

When she failed to respond, I tried again. "I wanted to ask you if you know this girl." I pulled Noelle's birthmother's picture from the pocket of my pantsuit. "I believe my attorney, Greg Doran, phoned you and asked about her. She had your daughter's identification. She claimed to be your daughter. I'm trying to locate her because my husband and I would like to adopt her child. Foster care placed her with us."

I tried not to drown her in details. The poor woman already was half off her feet.

Relief rippled across Mrs. Bryce's face and she straightened. "You're from Wachobe. The deputy sheriff's wife."

"That's right. I'm Ray Parker's wife." I'd never been so delighted to admit it, since it seemed to please Mrs. Bryce. Her whole demeanor had changed from distressed to ... friendly.

"Your attorney called me a couple times." She started to walk toward the street. "I remember now."

I fell into step with her. "We need help finding this girl. We thought maybe she was a friend of your daughter's."

Mrs. Bryce stopped walking. "My daughter didn't have many friends. We were here less than a year before she ... died." She inhaled deeply. "Please, show me the picture again."

I waited in silence while she looked it over. Mrs. Bryce appeared to be around my age, not unattractive but certainly not vibrant. The bun containing her over-treated hair and the bags under her eyes made her appear worn and tired. I thought I caught a whiff of cigarette smoke from her clothing. The white sweater seemed way too much for such a hot summer day, but Mrs. Bryce didn't weigh much. Maybe she needed the insulation.

She handed the picture back to me. "I don't recognize her."

"Did Abigail have any friends I could contact to see if they know this girl?"

"I don't know any names. She never brought any school friends home, but maybe you could ask at the school. I think the office keeps summer hours."

I tried not to feel too disappointed. If it had been a simple task, Greg Doran wouldn't have suggested hiring a private investigator. He'd have tied it all up in a bow instead. "I will. Thank you. Did Abigail have any regular hangouts I might check as well?"

"She wasn't much for hanging out. If she wasn't in school, she was usually home."

We reached my car. "Can I still buy you an iced tea or lemonade? Or maybe give you a ride home?"

"Thank you, no. I have to go on to work. I waitress at the diner during lunch hours."

The blue dress was a uniform. I should have known. "I'd be happy to drive you."

Mrs. Bryce backed away. "Thank you, no. Good luck with your search." She turned and continued on.

I thought of something else and called after her. "Mrs. Bryce, do you think I could talk to your husband? Maybe he would recognize this girl."

She stopped walking but didn't turn to face me. "He's at work."

"Somewhere close by?" A hint of desperation slipped into my voice.

Mrs. Bryce must have heard it. "He works at the water park. He should be there now."

"Thank you, Mrs. Bryce. I'm terribly sorry about your daughter Abigail."

Her hand waved as if to acknowledge my words. She trudged away. By the time I started my car and turned back toward Main Street, she had disappeared.

Back in my car, I took a second to call Cory and check on Noelle.

His day was going better than mine. "Noelle's sleeping now. She had mashed banana with her bottle for a snack."

"Sounds like everything is going well." I could only hope Erica's shift went so smoothly. "Any interesting calls or visitors?"

"Just one tire kicker who got his fingerprints all over the Ferrari. I'm going to polish it again while Noelle is asleep."

Tire kickers. I needed collectors, Magnum P.I. fans, or some wealthy speed demons to take the car off my hands. Maybe next week's group of lakeside cottage renters would include one. All I needed was one. Was that too much to ask? Was everyone buying their cars off the Internet these days? No wonder Isabelle had insisted on improving my website.

It was already eleven o'clock when I hung up. I decided to try the high school next. If the office kept summer hours, I didn't want to miss them. Too bad I had no idea where to find it.

I must have had a lot of testosterone in my body, because I didn't stop to ask anyone for directions. I just drove around the side streets of Canandaigua until I happened upon the high school, a sprawling two-to-three story brick structure with a portico covering the main entrance.

My high school had been much smaller and housed the elementary and middle school as well. Very convenient for me since I was responsible for getting my sister, who was five years younger, back and forth to school every day. I never got to participate in after-school activities, not that I really wanted to. High school, in my opinion, was something to get through in order to move on to real life.

A stout brunette bustled to the counter in the main office when I entered. "Can I help you?"

I pulled the picture from my pocket. "I'm trying to find out if this girl was a student here. Last year perhaps?"

The woman's eyes narrowed. "May I ask why you want to know?"

I told her my sad tale. She wasn't moved by it. "I would need her name to find her record. Sorry."

"What about yearbooks?"

"We have a copy of every yearbook in the library, but the library is closed for cleaning. I'm sorry, we can't help you."

She stared at me until I decided to retreat. I stood in the empty hallway, smelling the weird combination of sweat and mustiness all schools seem to have. My only prudent choice was to leave. But I wasn't feeling all that prudent.

I took off down the hall in search of the library. With any luck, it would be unlocked and the yearbooks readily accessible.

I found it quickly. Its door was wide open. I stepped inside. No one was in sight. I started my search.

After five minutes, I had the last three yearbooks on the table in front of me. I flipped through the pages, studying all the girls. The most recent yearbook didn't yield any clues.

Abigail Bryce's picture was in the prior year. Apparently she had either graduated early or young. In the three books, lots of the girls resembled Noelle's birthmother … and none of them did. A Candace Morton caught my eye, though. Was she related to the Cynthia Morton Mrs. Bryce had mistaken me for? I rose to put them back on the shelves.

A man's voice said "Excuse us."

I turned to find the woman from the office glaring at me. Next to her stood a man in a business suit, a principal-looking man, who didn't look too pleased to see me.

———

By the time I reached the water park at one o'clock, I felt hot, sticky, hungry, and frustrated. The principal had taken me to his office and chewed me out. Thirty-seven was a little old to visit the principal's office for the first time. I left the school red-faced.

My day didn't improve. A cashier charged me nineteen bucks to get into the water park, but she promised me a fourteen-dollar refund if I returned to the gate with my wristband still dry and intact. I was wearing a navy linen pants suit from Talbots and two inch heels for Pete's sake. Did she really think I'd head for the waterslides?

She pointed me in the direction of the food concessions and said Mr. Bryce managed that area. Given it was lunchtime, he was probably busy. I decided to buy myself a burger before attempting to approach him.

I got in line behind a tall man in a Speedo. Ugh! No man should ever fool himself into thinking his gumballs looked good so tightly wrapped. This guy had gray in his hair, too. He should have known better.

"Dad, we need two more orders of fries and another Coke."

He turned to acknowledge the willowy teenager, who approached from our left. She appeared to be with a birthday party occupying a picnic table under a white tent. "Okay, Christina."

The man's voice sounded familiar to me. Could he be a customer? I tried to circle to his left to see his face, but the line moved forward.

After he placed his order for four burgers and two orders of fries and two Cokes, I knew I'd spoken with this man before ... and more than once. I still couldn't place him, but I had to know who he was. Maybe I could sell him a slightly used and abused Ferrari.

I placed my order for a cheeseburger and a Coke and moved over to the line for picking up orders. Again, I tried to get a look at the man's face, but his back was to me.

My order came up before his. I accepted the tray and moved to the condiment area, waiting to come face-to-face with him there. After taking excruciating care with applying ketchup to my cheeseburger—I did resist drawing a smiley face like I do to entertain Noelle, however—the man approached.

"Excuse me. I know you from somewhere but I can't place you. I'm Jolene Parker. I own Asdale Auto Imports in Wachobe."

The man's eyes widened and his tray jerked, bumping into mine. My Coke slopped over onto my wristband. I could kiss my fourteen dollar refund goodbye.

"Dad, can I take the tray?" His daughter slid it from his hands and smiled at me. "My friends are hungry."

I returned her smile. "I'm sorry. I'm keeping your father from you. Is it your birthday?"

"Yes. I'm sixteen."

"Happy Birthday! I'm Jolene Parker, by the way." I held my breath, hoping her sixteen years included the right kind of social training.

"Christina Wynn." She glanced up as a woman under the tent called her name, then offered me an apologetic smile. "My mom is calling. Nice to meet you."

"Enjoy your party." I waited until she was out of hearing distance then focused on Mark Wynn. He was the same man I saw at Christmastime last year when he and Cory began dating, except today a gold band encircled his wedding finger. "I recognized your voice from when you call the shop to speak to Cory."

Unspoken words hung in the air between us. Words like Cory never mentioned you were married.

Mark looked over at the tent.

The woman Christina had identified as her mother, his wife, gave me a curious smile and waved.

Since my hands were full, I nodded and smiled in return. Then I looked at Mark and raised my eyebrows.

His Adam's apple bobbed up and down again. He leaned down. "Cory means the world to me." Then he walked over to join his family.

And left me holding the hot potato.

SIX

WHILE I ATE MY cheeseburger in the scorching sun, dampened the underarms of my suit with sweat, and tried to keep my mind off Cory's doomed love life, I watched the staff behind the concession counters, trying to decide which one was Mr. Bryce. Most of the employees wore polo shirts and looked like teens or college kids. Two men, one maybe in his early forties and the other in his fifties, wore short-sleeved dress shirts. The older man had on a wedding ring. I pegged him as Mr. Bryce.

Wrong again.

"I'm Bryce." The younger, better-looking man sidled over, taking the spot across the counter from me in place of his co-worker.

Bryce's hair was cut an inch on the crown of his head and shaved up the sides. Flecks of gold sparkled in his hazel eyes, along with what I interpreted to be sexual interest. He had that familiar heavy cologne smell—eau de ladies' man. No wonder Mrs. Bryce looked so weary.

I identified myself and explained I had spoken with his wife earlier in the day. Then I pulled out the picture. "This is the girl we're looking for. We think she might have known your stepdaughter. Do you recognize her?"

Bryce took it in his hands and appeared to study it with care. "No. Sorry."

I accepted the photo back. "Do you know of any place Abigail liked to hang out? Maybe someplace she might have met this girl?"

Bryce busied himself with emptying one of the cash drawers. "Abigail didn't go out. She could have gotten in here for free, but she never wanted to come." He sounded almost disgusted.

"Would you know the names of any of her friends that I might ask?"

"No. They've all graduated and left town by now anyway."

"Did Abigail have plans to go to college?"

"You'd have to ask her mother." He glanced at the clock on the wall. "I have to go now."

He left the stand with a vinyl envelope filled with cash and took off in the direction of the entrance to the park. A string of keys dangling from his belt jingled with each step he took. I watched him walk away, frustrated, thinking it's hopeless. In an instant, my mind made a one-eighty. No, persevere.

I pulled the picture out and showed it to all the staff behind the counter, receiving only headshakes in return. Most of the kids were new to the water park this summer. I needed to find longer-term employees who had worked here a year ago when Abigail Bryce was still alive. I asked the kids about hangouts and got the usual responses: shopping plaza, movie theater, and Kershaw

Park beach. If I stood outside the entrances to all those places for an entire day, what would be the odds I would find someone who recognized this girl in the fuzzy picture?

An hour had passed since my arrival. My three o'clock appointment waited.

I stopped at the exit and showed the cashier the picture as well. She didn't recognize it, but she said this was the first summer she had worked at the park. Then I showed her my park band, which was tinged brown. After explaining about the Coke spill, pointing out my hair wasn't wet, and holding out my wrist for her to sniff for chlorine, she refunded my fourteen bucks. At least somebody bought what I was selling today.

I asked her if I could see the manager. She called him on the phone and he appeared, looking flustered. He must have thought I had a complaint. When I showed him the girl's picture, he didn't recognize her. He'd worked there for three years. The water park was a dead end.

My car released a heat wave that shimmered in the air when I opened the door. I considered stripping down to the camisole under my short-sleeved suit jacket and decided to crank up the air instead. While I waited for it to kick in, I dialed Erica's cell.

Erica answered on the third ring. "We're at the park, but Noelle's rubbing her eyes. I'll take her for nappy-bye soon."

"And you're alone with her?"

"No, Jo. We're surrounded by screaming children and their keepers."

I decided to be more direct. "You're not with Sam."

"I'm not with Sam. He had things to do today. I think he's getting me a ring." Erica's voice rose with excitement.

Oh, joy. Sam was only in his early twenties and had never worked a day in his life. I hoped he wouldn't steal a diamond. Nevertheless, nothing immediate to worry about. "Great. I'll see you at four forty-five."

I spent the next hour of my drive trying to figure out why Mr. and Mrs. Bryce made me so uncomfortable. They'd answered all my questions, except the one about college, which really wasn't all that important. Abigail Bryce never made it to college. She couldn't have met Noelle's birthmother there.

Mrs. Bryce had looked worn out, but she'd lost her only child. Every day I feared losing Noelle, but Noelle wasn't going to die. I couldn't imagine how I would take it if she did, but the lone warm tear rolling down my cheek and huge lump in my throat at even the mere thought were pretty good signs.

Why had Mrs. Bryce failed to answer her doorbell? Why was she so afraid I might be Cynthia Morton? Maybe I should have asked her. Ray would have asked her. Could it have something to do with her husband, the ladies' man? Bryce had been polite, but I didn't like him. Polite wasn't always a good thing. Just look at Mark Wynn. He had perfect phone manners every time he called the shop to speak to Cory. Now he smelled like yesterday's garbage. Would he tell Cory the truth about his wife and daughter during their romantic weekend? If he didn't, should I? It was so hard to know if that would be the right thing to do as Cory's friend, or the absolute wrong thing.

————

The 1970 240Z that Dave Barclay hoped to purchase sat in a six-car garage attached to an imposing three-story brick mansion overlooking the churning gray waters of Lake Ontario. The plates on the silver Jaguar in the garage indicated the owner was a member of the judicial society. Maybe he'd recognize a plea deal when he heard one.

He introduced himself as Ed.

"Here she is." He lifted a cover off the Z to reveal a red, white, and blue paint job. Car number 112, at least in its last race.

"How long have you owned the car?"

"Sixteen years."

"When was the last time you raced her?" By habit, I ran my hand along the contours of the hood and circled the vehicle, looking for rust, dents and scratches, hints of Bondo, or other evidence of contact on the track. The car was clean. Not that Dave Barclay had asked or cared. After all, the car was going to be buried. He hadn't even specified that it needed to be in one piece, which was a good thing because often racecars were completely disassembled between races to check every bolt and wire in an effort to improve performance. Cory could have put it back together, if necessary.

"1998 maybe. I changed hobbies."

"Really? What's your new hobby?"

Ed lifted the tarp off something that took up two garage bays. It looked like two wings attached to a bicycle seat.

At first I thought it was a replica of Orville and Wilbur Wright's first flyer at Kitty Hawk, the one pictured on the North Carolina quarter. But I didn't want to guess. "What is it?"

"An ultralight. It's a light-weight airplane."

I'd heard of them. "Where do you buy them?"

"I built this one from a kit. Got it on eBay."

"Really?" A plaque on the garage wall caught my eye. *Flying is the second greatest achievement known to man. Landing is the first.*

"It's great fun. Makes you feel like a bird."

"So you fly it?"

"Every chance I get."

"Where did you learn to fly?"

"I got an instruction manual off eBay."

I choked back a third "really"? Man must have a bird brain. "Don't you need a license?"

"Nope. FAA has no control. It's total freedom. Nothing like it."

"Wow." All the more reason he should be willing to give up the Z. If Kim Barclay' grandfather had more time, we could just wait until the inevitable estate sale after this guy crashed and burned. "Sounds like a great hobby. Are you ever going back to racing?"

"Doubtful."

"So you might be interested in selling the Z?" The sale was in the bag.

"Well—"

A boy of around ten in a grimy T-shirt and black gym shorts trudged up the driveway. "Hey, Dad."

"Hey, Max. This is Mrs. Parker."

The boy held out his hand. "Pleased to meet you, Mrs. Parker."

We shook hands. Nice manners.

Max glanced at the Z. "How come you got the cover off, Dad?"

His father refused to meet Max's gaze. "Mrs. Parker wanted to see the car. How was camp today?"

"Same as always." The kid looked between me and his dad. "Are you selling the car, Dad?" He didn't have to say how he felt about the possibility. His face spoke volumes.

The air was leaking out of my bag. It might as well have been a gust blowing me right out of the garage.

Ed met my gaze. "Max wants to race the car someday. I'm saving it for him."

Max beamed. "Yeah. I'm going to race at Watkins Glen, just like my dad."

Maybe it was my newfound motherhood, but somehow I knew an offer of even one hundred and fifty million dollars for the car wouldn't be enough.

————

The only part of my day that went according to plan was my arrival home at four forty-five. I should have been at least half an hour ahead of Ray, but no, his cruiser sat in the driveway. Panic flowed through my veins. Erica had messed up and he'd been unable to reach me. I jumped out of my car and crashed through the front door.

Ray looked up from his seat on the couch. Noelle lay across his lap, her head in the crook of his arm, drinking a bottle. Ray had his good-cop, bad-cop, whatever-you-need-me-to-be cop look on his face. I never knew exactly what approach to take with that inscrutable look. But I sensed his anger. It resonated through the airwaves and shook my confidence. Even Noelle stopped sucking for a moment to study Ray's face.

I dropped onto the arm of the couch, at the end farthest from Ray. "You're home early."

"You didn't count on that, did you?"

I decided to play innocent. Probably not the best choice with a cop. "Was there a problem?"

"No, Jolene, no problem. Except my unstable sister-in-law was watching my child after I expressly told my wife that was unacceptable to me."

I cringed. "Cory had a rehearsal at two. Erica was the only one available. Dr. Albert said she was capable. I thought she was, too." I glanced around the room. The toys sat neatly in the basket. Noelle looked clean and happy. "She did a good job, didn't she?"

Noelle sucked the bottle dry. Ray lifted her to his shoulder, patting her back. She let out a burp like a sonic boom with a sour odor that drifted all the way to my nose. He carried her over to her playpen, seating her. She began to fiddle with the red and yellow spinning toys attached to it.

Ray crossed his arms over his chest. "For once, Jolene"—he said my name like the crack of a whip—"Erica is not the problem. You are."

"I'm sorry, Ray. I had to do what I thought best."

"That's the problem. Marriage is based on honesty and trust. Never once did it occur to you to be honest and tell me the truth."

I managed not to blurt out that it had, in fact, occurred to me and that I'd dismissed the idea. Why fuel his anger? But Ray was wrong about Erica. She was more capable than he believed.

I tried to distract him by changing the subject.

"I met Mr. and Mrs. Bryce today. There's something funny about them. They don't quite go together." I expected his natural investigative curiosity to take over and relieve the tension in the room. Noelle was fine. No harm had been done by my little omission.

Ray dropped his arms and walked past me to grab a baseball hat off the coat rack. "Maybe they're not the only married couple who don't go together."

After his car backed out of the driveway and laid rubber on the road, I looked at Noelle. "Sh … shoot."

She opened her mouth and let out more gas in agreement.

SEVEN

IN THE MIDDLE OF the night I awakened on the couch with fuzzy teeth and a dry mouth. I'd wanted to wait up for Ray to beg his forgiveness, but all the steamy weather and driving around yesterday caught up with me as soon as I tucked Noelle in for the night and sat down on the couch. I didn't even remember turning off the television or lying down, but I had a pillow under my head and the afghan Ray's Aunt Dorothy knitted us for a wedding present draped over me. Then I heard the snores from our bedroom and realized Ray had returned.

I slipped under the covers beside him. He continued to snore. Given our spat earlier, I thought it too presumptuous to give his shoulder a shove to turn him over like I usually did. Instead, as I listened to him rumble and whistle, I thought about the wedding we had to attend in a few hours where love was supposed to be in the air. I tried to remember the last time only love had been in the air between the two of us and came up dry. Maybe married life wasn't supposed to be that way. Maybe married life meant strife. Maybe that was why the two words rhymed.

Ray slept in the next morning while I attended to Noelle. When he did get up, he said nothing to me. Instead, he chopped fruit and mixed it into a salad for the potluck dinner after the wedding ceremony. I always laughed at how Betty Crocker this big, tough man could be, but today would not be a good time to tease him about it. I ignored him as well.

At one o'clock Ray and I arrived at the park for the marriage of Deputy Sheriff Steven "Gumby" Fellows to Miss Briana Engle, an exotic dancer at the Cat's Meow, a "men's club" conveniently situated in the countryside between the nearest two major cities. Gumby had met Briana when he responded to a drunk and disorderly call at the club one night and found an out-of-state vaccination salesman trying to give Briana a poke. Rumor claimed it was love at first ogle for Gumby.

I had dressed Noelle in a dainty white eyelet dress with pink ribbons and matching ruffled panties. She was the only dressed up person at the wedding except for the bride, since the invitation had specified casual, comfortable attire, suitable for volleyball and swimming. Ray and I had shorts and polo shirts on.

It was a low-budget wedding. The bride, attired in a mid-thigh white halter dress with sequins at the collar—a virginal stage costume perhaps?—and the groom, in his sheriff's department uniform minus gun and holster, exchanged their vows in the gazebo while the attendees encircled the structure. No chairs were provided, so Ray offered to take Noelle off my hands. I didn't hesitate.

The ceremony ended within minutes when Gumby snapped his handcuffs around one of Briana's wrists then one of his. The crowd applauded and cheered.

After a quick champagne toast from glasses distributed by the bride's co-workers dressed in French maid costumes, the bride stripped off her wedding dress to reveal a white string bikini and tattoos of a flying dragon on her tailbone, a heart stabbed with an arrow on her right breast, and a teddy bear on her ankle. No one would ever have trouble identifying her body at the morgue.

Gumby put his deputy sheriff's hat on her head and I got a flashback to a tabloid photo of Pamela Anderson's wedding to Kid Rock. I expected this one to last about as long. When I turned to share this with Ray, he was gone from my side.

I set my empty champagne glass on the nearest picnic table and studied the people waiting in line by the buffet table. No sign of Ray. He wasn't near the volleyball courts or the beach either. Our baby bag no longer sat under the picnic table where we'd left it, though. I headed over to the restrooms to see if he had taken Noelle in for a diaper change.

His voice reached my ears before I saw him. "It's great to see you. You look ... gorgeous." The warmth in his voice made me stop in my tracks.

"Just like Valerie Bertinelli?" The woman's voice oozed sugar and sex, a hard-to-resist combination. I'd heard her voice somewhere before, too. But her words disturbed me the most, because Ray had a thing for Valerie Bertinelli. He'd kept her picture inside his locker all through high school, and my resemblance to her was the first thing that attracted him to me. Of course, with my now-bobbed hair, I didn't look like her so much anymore. Ray still mourned the day I cut my hair.

But who else looked like Valerie?

Then it hit me. Catherine Thomas, the criminal defense attorney Ray had dated while we were separated. She looked like Valerie, right down to the tips of her long brown hair. But what the heck was she doing here?

I stepped around the corner. Catherine held Noelle in her arms. Ray gazed upon them both like they were the Madonna and child. Noelle's fingers stroked Catherine's long hair and Catherine kissed her on the forehead. Ray smiled. The whole picture made me nauseous.

"There you guys are." I strode forward and held out my arms to Noelle. She hesitated then lunged for me. The hesitation stabbed me in the heart.

Catherine handed her over. "Hi, Jolene. It's nice to see you again."

"Catherine, what a surprise." And not a pleasant one, but I kept that to myself. "Are you enjoying a day at the park?"

Ray and Catherine exchanged glances. "Actually, Steven invited me to the wedding. We got to know each other rather well last year."

Catherine didn't say "while Ray and I were dating," but I heard the words loud and clear. While I had mourned our separation and sat on our divorce papers for three whole years, Ray had managed to move on after two years into a year-long relationship with Catherine. "Oh, great. The more the merrier. Have you eaten yet? We could all go through the buffet line together."

Ray gave me the look, the I-see-right-through-you look. I returned it in spades.

Catherine missed our interchange. Her gaze seemed to be searching the crowd in the park. "Sure. Let me find my date and we'll catch up with you."

Relief flowed through me. She had a date. She'd moved on. Ray was still mine. Mine. Mine. Mine.

The way Ray and Catherine looked at me, I feared for a moment I'd said those words aloud. Maybe it was the look on my face. I did have a face that was way too easy to read. Most of the time, I didn't have to say anything in order to let people know exactly where I stood.

Ray grabbed my elbow and tugged. "We'll see you at the buffet table, Cat."

When we were out of hearing distance, I shook him off. "Cat? Her nickname is Cat?"

"That's what I called her."

"How nice. She'd fit right in at the Cat's Meow." I picked up speed and headed toward the portable highchair we'd brought for Noelle. I strapped her into it then took off for the buffet line a few yards away. Ray dogged me every inch of the way. "Of course, she's a little too gorgeous for there, isn't she, Ray?"

He got behind me in line and leaned in to my ear. "You're making a scene."

"No, I'm not." But I did glance about to make sure no one was looking at us.

"Catherine and I are history. You know that."

I placed a few slices of rolled-up ham and provolone cheese on my plate, followed by a big splat of potato salad, two rolls, some red Jell-O with raspberries suspended in it, and some of Ray's fruit salad. It took Ray a little longer to fill his plate. He might as well have taken two plates. By the time he reached the picnic table, I had diced up the cheese and some watermelon for Noelle and shredded the roll into tiny pieces that she stuffed into her mouth until she had chipmunk cheeks.

Gumby's grandparents, who were seated on the other end of the table, admired Noelle and kept us from continuing our discussion. When they rose to throw out their plates five minutes later, Ray picked up where we had left off. "Darlin', you know you're the only girl for me. But Catherine is still my friend. I see her around sometimes. I can't just ignore her."

He'd called Catherine a woman and me, a girl. I decided to let it pass. All of it. Ray slept with me every night again now, and Catherine had a new beau. We could all move on.

Catherine appeared with a plate in hand. "I wanted you to meet my date."

Ray raised his eyebrow at me in warning. "Great. We'd love to."

Catherine sat on my side of the table. I appreciated the gesture. She waved in the direction of the buffet table. "He'll be right over. He's getting a plate. We met last week at a party in Syracuse. When I found out he lived in Wachobe, I begged him to be my date for the wedding. We're just getting to know each other, but he seems like a great guy."

I smiled and nodded. Maybe this guy would be the love of her life. I hoped so for her sake. Missing out on Ray had hurt her, I knew.

Catherine smiled. "Here he is now."

Her date was a remarkably good-looking man. Slender with streaked sandy-colored hair, he had a tanned face and light blue eyes that reminded me of Robert Redford. When he smiled, his pearly white teeth only enhanced the similarity.

"Brennan Rowe, this is Ray and Jolene Parker."

Ray stood to shake Brennan's hand. I waggled my fingers at him. Brennan and Ray sat down side by side.

I turned to smile at Catherine. "We've all met before. Brennan is a customer at the shop." He was a lot of other things, too.

Not the least of which was gay.

———

On the way home in the car, Noelle fell asleep with her neck bent at an awkward angle and drool running down her cheek. After the number of people who had asked to hold her, including the entire exotic dancing staff of Cat's Meow, I tried not think about the germs she'd been exposed to at the wedding. With any luck, all the fresh air and hot sunshine would protect her. I couldn't say as much for Catherine Thomas.

"So, Ray, this is an interesting dilemma. You're Catherine's friend. Did you pull her aside while you were playing volleyball and let her know Brennan was so not into her?"

Ray glanced at me out of the corner of his eye. "No. Rowe will tell her. Or he'll just fade into the sunset and she'll move on to the next guy."

"Do you think he deliberately misled her?"

Ray flipped the turn signal and executed a left off Main onto North Street. "Hard to say. He is in the construction business. I think he likes to cultivate a certain image."

True. In fact, when Cory told me last year that Rowe was gay, I didn't believe him at first. But then I considered Cory to be somewhat of a subject matter expert. "Not very honest of him."

"No, but Catherine said she begged him for the date. He's a nice enough guy. Maybe he didn't see any harm in one date."

"Is there any?"

Ray sighed. "Catherine hasn't had great luck with men. She might not take the truth so well. Hopefully, Rowe will just tell her he doesn't want to see her again."

"And leave her wondering what's wrong with her." Now I felt sorry for Catherine. A couple hours earlier I would have happily wished her off the face of the earth, but the ties of sisterhood had kicked in. I didn't like to see anyone get their heart broken.

"There's nothing wrong with her." His words sounded a little sharp.

I looked over at him, studying his face as he turned right onto our street.

"Oh, that's just what I want to hear. Catherine's perfect." I harbored no illusions that Ray felt the same way about me. My flaws were many. But then even some of the most beautiful diamonds had flaws, didn't they?

"I didn't say that." He made the turn into our driveway and threw the Lexus into park, killing the ignition. "Let's forget about Catherine and Brennan, okay? They can take care of themselves."

I looked in the back seat at Noelle, who slept on, oblivious. "Okay. I guess I was just asking because I don't know what to do about Cory."

I explained to Ray about meeting Mark Wynn and his family at the water park. "I can't believe Cory knows about Mark's family. So if Mark doesn't tell him this weekend, do I tell Cory or not?"

Ray leaned back against the headrest. "I don't know. It's tricky meddling in other people's relationships. Let's think about it for a while. What else did you learn in Canandaigua?"

I filled Ray in on Mr. and Mrs. Bryce. He asked me a few questions I didn't know the answers to, then glanced back at Noelle. "Not much to go on. Maybe you should think about going back tomorrow and showing the girl's picture around in some stores. Or I can go on Monday. I have the day off."

"You go." If Ray went, I'd know the right questions were being asked at all the right places.

The air conditioning dissipated. The car grew warm. Ray rolled down the windows. A slight westerly breeze drifted inside and feathered across my face, drying the sheen of sweat on it. Ray drummed his forefingers on the steering wheel. "I faxed Theo and the girl's pictures to Turning Stone and the two casinos in Niagara Falls. I also faxed them downstate and to the southern tier. I included all the off-track betting outlets and the horse tracks, too. Gambling is gambling. But they could be in Vegas for all we know."

I tried to think of a new approach. "Can you put a warrant out for their arrest?"

"The robbery warrant is still outstanding on Theo. Has been ever since last year when he skipped town on bail. The girl was only implicated in the robberies by her association with him, so there's no warrant on her."

"Why isn't a bail bondsman looking for Theo?"

"His parents paid cash. That's the only reason they want to see him again."

"So we're on our own."

"Pretty much. But we can handle it, don't panic yet." He reached over and ran the back of his hand down my cheek. He leaned over and I closed my eyes, waiting for his gentle kiss. It never came.

Noelle stirred, stretched and let out an impatient shriek when she realized she was trapped in her car seat. When I opened my eyes, Ray rolled his and reached across me to open my car door. He and I scrambled to extricate Noelle from her car seat. We spent the rest of the evening watching her play in the kiddy pool and holding hands while we soaked our feet.

Around seven-thirty, the phone rang. I was busy laying Noelle down for the night. Ray answered. I could hear the low reverberation of his voice, but not the words.

He appeared in the doorway to Noelle's room. "I got a call. I gotta go." He hustled into the room, kissed his fingertips and laid them on Noelle's forehead. Then he kissed me on the cheek, even though I offered my lips. "I don't know how long I'll be. Don't wait up."

I chased after him, stopping in Noelle's doorway. "Okay. Love you."

"Love you, too." Ray's words sailed back to me over his shoulder as he disappeared out the door.

Calls at all hours of the day and night were nothing new. Ray's job as deputy sheriff required unpredictable hours. Accidents and crime didn't occur on a set schedule. And, of course, Gumby had taken off for Cabo San Lucas for his honeymoon and Darrel was still recovering from his bypass surgery.

I just hoped Ray didn't get called in on Monday. We'd have to find another babysitter so I could trek to Canandaigua. And I wasn't ready to broach the subject of Erica again this soon.

I settled in front of the television and began to race through the channels, hoping for a chick flick like *When Harry Met Sally* or *Must Love Dogs*. A movie designed to make me forget my troubles in both life and love, with the promise of a happy ending even when things did go bad. After the third click of the channel changer, it hit me.

When Ray got a call, the first thing he did was put on his uniform.

Tonight he'd skipped out the door in his shorts and polo shirt.

So who called and where the heck did he go?

EIGHT

I DIDN'T GET A chance to ask Ray the next day. Sometime between seven-thirty Saturday night and seven Sunday morning, he had been home, dressed in a uniform, and left me a note about a suspicious fire in a warehouse fifteen miles outside Wachobe. His note indicated he might be tied up all day.

I spent the morning cleaning the house and taking Noelle for a brisk turn around the block in her stroller. I had just flopped onto the couch to nap with her on my chest when the doorbell rang.

I deposited Noelle in her crib without waking her and opened the front door.

"When are you going to give me my own key?" Erica sauntered into the house wearing her Daisy Duke shorts again and a tube top that I'd thought had justifiably gone out of fashion years ago. She dropped onto the spot I'd vacated on the couch.

"When you stop dressing like a hooker." Or when Ray okayed it, which ought to be just about the time hell froze over.

"That's nice, Jo, really nice. You know, Dr. Albert says those kind of comments are damaging to my psyche."

I wished people would stop telling me what I knew. Lately, I didn't know anything until they told me. "So, how have you been feeling?"

Erica picked at a worn spot in her shorts. "Confused. Sam and I had a fight last night."

I tried not to get excited or hopeful, but fighting was good. Fighting might end all their romantic notions as well as their wedding plans. "What about?"

"He wants to get married next week. I want to get married next month, on August 12th. Mom suggested the date. It's her and Dad's wedding anniversary, you know."

This time I did know. I also knew how their marriage had ended. Somehow I didn't think my bipolar, suicidal sister should marry a sociopath on the same date. Call me crazy.

"What's the hurry? I read in *Cosmopolitan* that long engagements are all the rage nowadays." I had read it on the cover while in the checkout lane at the grocery store, along with a tabloid's teaser about a two-headed alien baby. All quite newsworthy.

"Sam lost his job at the nursery. They caught him lying under the dogwood he was supposed to be planting, smoking weed." Erica slumped farther into the couch cushions. "I think he wants me to support us."

A flawed plan, if ever I heard one. As a bipolar, Erica was often angry and demanding, alienating her peers. Always, she was incapable of holding a job, although able to obtain one during her manic periods. The telephone calls to her co-workers at all hours of the day and night usually did her in. Her three-month stint at the local saloon had set her all-time record for consecutive months of employment. No matter what Dr. Albert said about improvements in medications and a new outlook on life, Erica could not be relied on to support herself indefinitely. Nor could she even dream of supporting Sam, who came from a family with expensive tastes including membership at the local country club and several boats docked at the local yacht club. I swallowed my immediate reaction—to laugh—and searched my mind for a more Oprah-like response. "How do you feel about that?"

"Well, someone has to stay home with the kids. Why not Sam?"

I tried not to panic. "Kids?"

"Sure. I want to have a girl like Noelle. Maybe a boy. Sam wants a boy to play football with in the yard."

It sounded picture perfect. Too perfect. "Erica, have you been taking your medicine?"

"Yes, Jolene, I've been taking my medicine. And I've been seeing Dr. Albert like a good girl. I'm not manic. I'm in love." Erica stood and yanked down the crotch of her shorts. "Can you go shopping for a wedding dress with me or not?"

"Now? Noelle's taking a nap."

"Okay. I'll go home and put on underwear so I can try on things. Come pick me up when you guys are ready."

As I agreed reluctantly, I tried not to look at her butt and wonder why she had gone commando today.

———

Two hours later I arrived at Erica's home, my old apartment in an 1870 white Victorian two-family house on Wells Street, where

Erica occupied the first floor and the landlord, the second. The place looked a little different than the last time I saw it.

Garden gnomes covered the entire front yard. Seven of them looked like Snow White's dwarfs marching off to the gem mines with pick axes in hand. The rest had a variety of poses, attire, and expressions. One of the gnomes holding a sword looked like he was eying me.

Erica had collected thousands of wine corks and bottle caps in the past. Now it appeared she'd branched out. Of course, Dr. Albert would probably tell me lots of people collected things and decorated their yards. He'd probably tell me I was holding Erica to a higher standard than the norm again. He could tell me anything he wanted; this time I was the one who knew. Erica was sinking again.

I scooped Noelle out of her car seat and dashed onto the front porch, skirting the gnome with the sword.

I rang Erica's bell repeatedly. No answer. I knocked. Still no answer.

"She's not home." A rough voice from my past wafted over from the yard next door. Mr. Murphy, my old neighbor and nemesis. Was he coming over to complain about where Erica set the trash cans?

"Hi, Mr. Murphy. How nice to see you again."

Mr. Murphy, a sprightly old guy with two tufts of hair sticking out just above his humongous earlobes, loped closer. He didn't seem to have heard me. "She left with some wild boy in a shiny black car. Reminded me of how you used to roar in and out of here."

His comment offended me, but I let it pass. "Okay. I'll call her on her cell phone."

Mr. Murphy tugged on his right earlobe. "That your baby?"

"Yes. Her name is Noelle."

"She looks just like you."

My heart filled with pride, even though she didn't really. We both had blue eyes and brown hair, but the resemblance ended there. "Thank you, Mr. Murphy. Take care."

I waved and rushed back to the Lexus before he could start in on Erica's behavior again. Mr. Murphy loved to spread rumors with the best of them. Sometimes he even got the story right. I knew he contributed to Erica's wild reputation around town. I supposed she didn't make him work all that hard at finding things to talk about.

I dialed Erica's cell number. It went to voicemail. "Erica, Noelle and I are at your house. You're not here. I thought we were going dress shopping. Call me. Bye."

I looked in the backseat at Noelle. She flashed her toothless grin at me. "We're going to have a little talk with Auntie Erica just as soon as we find her, aren't we, sweetie?"

Noelle blew spit bubbles in agreement.

———

The phone was ringing when Noelle and I entered the kitchen at home. I grabbed it. "Erica?"

"No. What's wrong?"

"Nothing, Ray. I was just expecting Erica to call; that's all. What's up?" I set Noelle in her playpen and gave the noisy rolling toys on it a spin. She reached for them.

"Good news. I got a call from security at the racetrack in Canandaigua. They paid out some winnings last Monday to a guy who matches Theo's description. They think he comes to the track every Monday."

"No way."

"They also think they have him on camera with a girl, a girl with light brown hair."

"Hair like Noelle's?"

"From the sounds of it."

I sank onto the couch. "It's hard to believe they've been that close all along."

"Close, but not in our county. Depending on where they're holed up, they might never be noticed in a town the size of Canandaigua."

"But why didn't they leave the state?"

"I don't know."

"I wonder if they're still in touch with someone around here."

Ray's snort created static on the phone line. "Someone like Sam?"

Or worse, someone like Erica. She didn't seem to be as distressed about our losing Noelle as I thought she'd be, especially considering the fact Erica said Mom had suggested she obtain Noelle for me in the first place. Maybe because Erica was working some angle of her own. Not good. Not good at all.

Ray continued, "On Monday I'll head over there and see if I can spot them. Then I can alert the local P.D."

"I don't think that will work, Ray."

"Why not?"

"Theo and Noelle's birthmother know you. You arrested Theo. They're going to spot you, panic, and run."

"They won't spot me."

"Ray, you're six-foot-three. Everybody spots you."

Silence.

"Ray?"

"So what's your suggestion, Jolene?"

"Let me go. We only need the girl. Maybe I can talk to her. Explain how it's all best for Noelle. Get the information we need. Maybe ask her to set up an appointment to meet with Greg Doran."

"And ignore Theo?"

"I don't care about Theo, Ray."

"He robbed at least two stores, Jolene. Possibly another at gunpoint."

"Well, we haven't had any more robberies. Maybe he's seen the error of his ways."

"Yeah, right."

"Then let the Canandaigua police round him up, after we identify Noelle's birthmother. Will a few hours make that much difference?"

"I don't like it, darlin'."

Ray had called me darlin'. I knew I was going to get my way. When he phoned three hours later to say his boss requested he work on Monday, the plan crystallized. All I needed was a babysitter. No way would I ask Erica this time.

I dialed Cory's cell phone number later that evening, hoping his big weekend was over. When he answered, I could hear a shower running in the background.

"Hey Cory, where are you?"

"At my apartment."

"How was your … weekend?" I almost said "big weekend" but I didn't want to make light of it in case Mark had told Cory the truth.

"I'll have to tell you about it later. Mark is in the shower."

That response didn't give me enough to go on. Cory sounded happy, though. "Oh. Well, I think we know where to find Noelle's mother, and I need a babysitter for tomorrow. Are you free?"

"Sure. What time?"

I arranged to have Cory come to our house around 10:30. The racetrack was less than half a mile from the water park in Canandaigua, just off the main thoroughfare of strip malls, car dealerships, and restaurants. I knew almost to the minute how long it would take me to get there. According to its website, the gates opened at 11:30 and post time was 1:10. I wanted to get to the track when it opened so I could watch the wagering windows and check out the enormous gaming room, complete with slot machines and numerous betting opportunities that might attract Theo. The track sounded like a regular amusement park. From the description, I feared I might get lost and never find my way out.

In the last twenty years, I had driven by the track at least a hundred times and never once had I been inside. Now that I read the website, I couldn't wait to check it out. I just hoped all the hoopla wouldn't be too distracting. We couldn't afford to have me miss Theo and Noelle's birthmother.

———

Cory arrived twenty minutes early for babysitting on Monday. Since I had already dressed and Noelle was taking a nap, we sat down over a cup of tea and he told me about his weekend.

"We bought a mailbox in Hammondsport at the craft festival. The lady painted our names on it." Cory's eyes sparkled.

"So Mark agreed to move in with you?"

"He thought it was a great idea. We're going to start looking at houses this weekend."

Flabbergasted. That was how I felt. Just flabbergasted. And pissed. How dare this man trifle with my friend? "So he didn't have any concerns about his current lease or any other … commitments he might have?"

Cory shook his head. "No, it's full speed ahead."

I watched enough Oprah to know she would tell Cory about Mark's family. And she was supposed to be the queen of compassion. Who was I to argue with her advice? "Listen, Cory, I need to talk to you about something. Remember last year when you said you saw Ray in the bar with Catherine Thomas, but you decided not to tell me about it?"

Cory spewed tea all over my breakfast bar then scrambled to sop it up with his napkin. "Sorry, Jo, sorry. I was going to tell you. I can't believe someone told you already. This town cannot keep its mouth shut."

I pressed my napkin over a spot of tea he'd missed. "What are you talking about?"

"Ray and Catherine."

The lump in my throat was not an allergic reaction to my tea. "What about Ray and Catherine?"

Cory froze, his eyes wide. "Isn't that what you were talking about?"

"Cory, tell me about Ray and Catherine!"

He got off his stool and took the dirty napkins to the trash can under the sink, probably to avoid looking me in the eye. "I saw them Friday night at a bar Mark and I stopped in. They were having a drink together. They talked for about an hour before they left."

I blinked back the tears welling in my eyes. "They left together?"

Cory sat next to me and put his hand on my shoulder. "They walked out of the bar together. I didn't see what car or cars they got into."

So Friday night Ray had walked out on me in the middle of an argument about honesty and trust and met Catherine—Cat—for drinks. I tried not to let my imagination run wild with thoughts of what that said about our marriage.

"Jo, I'm sure they just happened to run into each other. I'm sure it's nothing. Ray loves you."

And I loved Ray, but sometimes, okay, often according to divorce statistics, love wasn't enough. I rested my head on my palm and tried to process what Cory had said. What did it mean?

Cory cleared his throat. "I'm thinking that's not what you wanted to talk to me about, since you obviously had no idea. I'm sorry. Should I not have told you?" His long girly eyelashes blinked rapidly.

I thought about him and Mark. Did I need to deliver a blow to Cory that would rock his world the way he just sent tremors through mine? I needed more time to think about it. I sure didn't want Cory to feel as bad as I felt right now. "No, of course not. I'm glad you told me. I guess Ray and I have something we need to talk about. It's fine, don't worry."

Cory's shoulders slumped as though he'd failed me. "So what *did* you want to talk to me about?"

The baby monitor crackled with sounds of Noelle waking from her nap, saving me from responding. I ran out the door and left Cory to get her up.

On the way to the track, images of Catherine with her legs wrapped around Ray's back kept popping into my head. My confidence had taken a hit last year when I realized he dated her for the last months of our separation, unbeknownst to me. Her reappearance now, when our life was in turmoil, only fueled my insecurities.

I re-examined every word of the conversation they had at Gumby's wedding, fixating on Catherine's comment about her resemblance to Valerie Bertinelli. Damn Catherine for having the long hair Ray loved so much. I looked in the rearview mirror and fingered mine, then lunged toward the mirror. Was that a gray hair?

My car hit the rough edge of the road, making a grating noise and snapping my attention back to driving. I swerved and got back in the center of the lane on Route 5 and 20. No need to become an accident statistic as well as a potential divorce one.

Catherine's date for the wedding—Brennan Rowe—sprang to mind. Had she picked him because she knew he was gay and Ray wouldn't be threatened by his presence? Had Ray and Catherine planned to meet at the wedding all along? They'd certainly had a lot of fun playing volleyball together while I sat on the sidelines with Noelle. My head started to pound as doubt filled it.

I took a deep breath. Let it go for now. Let everything go for now and focus on the mission. I needed to find Noelle's birthmother so we could adopt Noelle, beautiful sweet Noelle. The lump filled my throat again. Would Ray and I end up in a bitter custody battle over her some day?

I brushed away the tear that had jumped unbidden from my left eye. I was going postpartum again. I turned the radio on and listened to the words of the song playing, striving to find my focus. I did. Now if I could just hang onto it.

I knew I was in trouble the minute I arrived at the track. A gorgeous red Mustang GT V8 convertible sat in the entranceway with a huge sign announcing a drawing for the car this Friday. I had to enter my name. No self-respecting car aficionado would pass up such an opportunity.

A steady stream of gamblers trailed into the track. It was a motley crew, some dressed for the Kentucky Derby, the majority in casual summer attire. I'd expected them all to look scruffier, like they were here to bet their last dime in order to save their homes from foreclosure. But no, they looked like average visitors to any other tourist attraction.

I headed for the gaming room. Minutes after I took up watch a few feet inside the door, I realized my location wasn't going to work out. The gaze of every single person who entered the room immediately flew to my face as though curious as to why I wasn't playing a machine. I started to circulate, listening to the continuous clanging bells on the machines, feeling their pulsing heat, blinking as the bright lights flashed, wrinkling my nose at the body odors, and almost tasting the smoke in the air from the anxious gamblers who had inhaled one last pack of cigarettes in the parking lot before entering the smoke-free track. My headache intensified. I decided to watch the wagering windows instead. At least they were in the open air.

After an hour of watching for Theo and his girlfriend, I felt drained. My knees ached. My mouth was parched, and the food aromas made my stomach growl. Every broadcast over the loudspeakers sent pains shooting through my forehead. I sidled toward the concession window with my eyes still on the wagering ones. Then I bumped into someone.

I turned to apologize.

"Jolene Parker. What a surprise."

Dave Barclay stood behind me with Kim on his arm. She curled her lip when she recognized me. That must be her standard reflex instead of a smile. I guessed she must have taken a few hours off from her father's bedside vigil.

Both of them were the height of fashion. Dave wore linen pants and a silk shirt with his sandals from the other day, and Kim, a gauzy sundress and a wide-brimmed hat. They looked ready for the Hamptons, not Canandaigua.

I greeted them and tried to make polite conversation, dreading the moment when they asked me about the Datsun 240Z. On Friday night I had decided to wait to call them until I reopened the shop on Tuesday, in no rush to deliver the bad news. I decided not to inquire about Kim's grandfather's health. Why head the conversation in a direction I didn't want it to go? After commenting on the weather, I settled on another neutral topic. "Are you here for the races or the gaming?"

"Both." Dave held up a handful of betting slips. "Our horses are in three of the races."

"Really? You mean you own racehorses?"

"Sure do. Major Ed, Sire Burg, and Speed Demon."

"Speed Demon?"

Dave rolled his eyes. "I let my nephew name him. He's a NASCAR fan."

Kim's lip curled again, in reference to the nephew or NASCAR. Probably both.

Dave lightly touched my arm to regain my attention. "We're glad we ran into you. Any luck with the Datsun?"

Darn it. "I'm afraid not." I explained about my meeting with the owner and his son. Dave seemed understanding, but I feared Kim's lip curl might become permanent.

"But you found a whole list of Z car owners?" Dave looked at Kim and she gave him a shrug. "Who owns car number eighteen?"

I didn't dare to hope this meant they would be interested in purchasing a different Z. "I can't tell you off the top of my head. I'd have to check the list. Can I call you tomorrow?"

Dave gave me his cell and work numbers. I promised to get back to him with the information first thing in the morning. As he and Kim walked away, it occurred to me they hadn't seemed all that disappointed in my results. Maybe I would still be able to sell them a car.

I swung around to check the line at the wagering booth, scanning the ten people waiting. My eyes passed over then returned to a guy staring back at me. He had dark, almost black hair, cut spiky, a sprinkling of acne on his chin and eyes that flickered with recognition as they met mine. Theo Tibble.

He leaned toward a teenage girl standing by his side and said something. The girl had shoulder length light-brown hair that curled in soft waves around her face, hair very much like Noelle's. When she turned to look at me, I saw Noelle's eyes: wide and blue. I started toward them.

Theo grabbed the girl's arm and tugged. They took off running down the aisle toward the parking lot.

I heard the starting bell for the first race. The announcer's voice came over the loudspeaker proclaiming, "And they're off."

How appropriate. I broke into a run, wishing I had thought to wear sneakers instead of sandals that refused to stay on my feet. After scuffing along, I kicked them off and ran barefoot. Not the best idea because my foot struck a sharp edge like a bottle cap. I yelped, but kept on running, falling farther behind Theo and Noelle's birthmother with each painful stride.

The people in the aisles didn't seem to notice me coming. "Excuse me. Excuse me. GET OUT OF MY WAY!"

I bumped roughly into one woman's arm.

"Hey!"

I kept on running, knowing I'd lost precious minutes. Theo and Noelle's birthmother had disappeared. A stone from the roughly paved lot dug into my heel, increasing my agony. After a few more steps, I had to stop to dig it out of my foot, which now bled in two spots.

Theo and the girl were nowhere in sight.

I limped across the parking lot, remarkably full of cars for a Monday. Didn't anybody work anymore?

The cars glistened in the heat of the afternoon sun. I squinted and scanned each row, left and right, as I entered the lot, listening for the sound of an engine turning over. Nothing. The car owners were all inside already, playing the games or eating or cheering on their favorite horse.

I heard a woman scream.

I ran in the direction of the scream, which rose in volume not only with my proximity but the woman's apparent distress. It took me a couple minutes to find the source.

The woman faced the space between two cars. A man stood with his arm around her shoulder. He appeared to be dialing a cell phone.

I moved closer as two more men ran past me and stopped dead next to the couple. More people joined them. When I reached the back of the group, I realized the man on the cell phone was summoning the police.

I stood on my toes and peeked over shoulders. Then I ducked to try to catch a glimpse under elbows. I spotted the cause of the woman's screams.

Between the cars, Theo lay on the ground in a pool of blood that pulsed from his slashed neck. His eyelids fluttered. His eyeballs looked glassy.

Noelle's mother's left wrist was trapped in his right hand. She was trying desperately to disengage it. In her shaking right hand, she held a broken beer bottle, covered with blood.

She freed her hand. Theo's body shook with a spasm. His eyelids stopped fluttering and his gaze became fixed. Noelle's mother raised her stricken eyes in our direction.

The woman stopped screaming. One of the men rushed forward and attempted CPR. The rest of us watched in silence.

I heard a jingling noise. It sounded familiar. I wrenched my eyes from the scene and scanned the parking lot. I expected the jingling noise to move closer—another curious passerby. Instead it moved away.

I looked back at Theo and Noelle's mother. I heard more screaming. This time it was inside my head.

NINE

THE CANANDAIGUA POLICE ARRIVED in three separate cars, one cop per car. The first officer on the scene checked Theo, approached the girl, and asked her to place the broken bottle on the ground. She did. He cuffed the girl and sat her in the back of his patrol car. At no time did she resist or speak.

I hadn't moved from my spot two car lengths away. The man who performed CPR to revive Theo deserved an A for effort, but his final grade was an F for failure. Theodore Tibble was dead. I made another mental tick mark. Two people from my town dead in less than a month. Was a third death looming?

An ambulance careened into the parking lot. The attendants examined Theo. They didn't pull out any life-saving equipment. The word "dead" spread through the crowd. The attendants sat back, waiting for the medical examiner to arrive.

The police continued to work the scene, interviewing the first couple and the two men who happened on the scene immediately after them. The medical examiner arrived. Now a good-sized crowd formed around the area roped off with yellow crime scene tape.

I stood outside the tape, but still close to the action. I forced myself to stop staring at Theo's body. All the blood had made me nauseous. I turned my back and pulled out my cell phone to call Ray. He answered on the second ring just as I noticed a news crew pulling into the lot.

I swallowed the bile in the back of my throat. "I found Theo and the girl."

"Great. Did you talk to them?"

I inhaled deeply and proceeded to fill him in.

When I finished, Ray whistled. I almost dropped the phone from the screech he caused. "Did you actually see her cut Theo?"

"No."

"Was anyone else there?"

"Yes. A couple spotted them first. Then a group formed. I saw them after that."

"Did they see her cut Theo?"

"I'm not sure. The police are interviewing them now."

"Who's the lead investigator?"

I looked over at the three officers hovering around the medical examiner. "I'm not sure. The patrol officers are here now."

"Okay, I'll make some calls in a few hours to find out the status."

"Do you think the police will want to talk to me?"

"Did you see anything other than what you told me?"

I thought about the familiar jingling noise. For all I knew, it could have been collar tags on a stray, frightened animal. "No."

"Then let's wait and see if anyone noticed you chasing Theo and the girl out of the track."

———

Ray arrived home a little after five o'clock. I was in the kitchen feeding Noelle her favorite Gerber squash and peaches. She had plenty of it on her face, but Ray kissed her cheek anyway, then mine. Once again, I wondered why not on my lips. I asked about the girl instead.

"The girl's not saying anything. Not even her name."

"You're kidding."

Ray popped open a Corona and perched on a stool at the breakfast bar. "She refuses to speak. She even refused her phone call. They've been working her for the last three hours and she hasn't even asked to go to the bathroom. She's still got Theo's blood all over her. The guys thought for sure she'd at least ask to wash it off. But she hasn't."

"What did the witnesses say?"

"Not much more than you. No one saw her attack Theo. They said they found her standing over him with the bottle in her hand."

"Does she have a lawyer?"

"She didn't ask for one. When she goes to arraignment tomorrow morning, they'll assign her someone through the public defender's office."

"Will that person have murder trial experience?"

Ray sighed. "That's assumed."

We all know what happens when we assume. "What if she continues to refuse to talk?"

"They'll probably have her mental health evaluated."

"Maybe she's in shock."

"They say she's quite alert, just unwilling to talk."

"I've been thinking about the scene, Ray. I heard something. Do you think I should tell the police?"

He leaned forward. "What was it?"

I closed my eyes and tried to get the sound back. "I don't know. It was a noise, but it faded. It seemed familiar and made me think another person was there."

"Like running footsteps?"

"No, more like jingling."

He took another swig of Corona. "It's not much. It might cast doubt on the case against the girl if you could place someone else at the scene."

"I wish I had seen someone." I pulled out a baby wipe and mopped the remains of Noelle's dinner off her face. She swung her head side to side, trying to avoid my efforts, and banged her palms on the highchair's tray table. Then she fixed those wide blue eyes on my face. The same eyes her birthmother had fixed on me hours earlier.

I knew the right thing to do. "We have to get her a lawyer. We should call Greg Doran. See who he recommends."

Ray choked on his beer. He slammed the bottle onto the countertop. "Are you kidding? We can't afford a lawyer for a murder trial. It could go on for months. Besides, I look bad enough having failed to report Theo's whereabouts. Now you want me to aid an alleged felon? Not to mention that you were chasing Theo minutes before he was killed."

I picked up Noelle and faced him. I looked him right in the eye.

"We need to help Noelle's birthmother. If we don't help her, do you think she's going to help us finalize Noelle's adoption?"

Ray glanced from my face to Noelle's. She reached her arms out to him. He pulled her into his and looked into her eyes. His own softened, emphasizing the creases at their corners. "I'll call Greg tonight. Maybe he can handle the arraignment tomorrow."

That's my man.

I threw my arms around both him and Noelle and held my cheek against his for a long time.

———

Ray refused to attend the arraignment the next morning. He insisted we should let the justice system take its course before we took any more action. In short, he wanted to know all the facts in evidence to finalize our new plan, and he preferred to hear them from a neutral source. He had me so confused by the time he stopped talking that I had to agree. But I suspected there was more to the story.

I packed Noelle and her toys up and took her into the office. At seven months old, she didn't seem to mind this pattern to her life, but I knew once she started to walk and talk, I was going to have to improve the quality of her time beyond home, work, toys, the park, and rides in her stroller. When Ray's office was fully staffed, he got two days off to spend with Noelle. Sometimes one was a Monday, so we could have a family day. Some were Daddy Days while Mommy worked in the shop. Would we ever be able to work a schedule where one of us was home with Noelle all the time or were self-employment and a cop's life not conducive to stability? Worse yet, were the seeds of Noelle's future psychosis already sown? Now that I knew her birthmother might have killed her father, I had to wonder if Noelle would be the child I dreamed of or the one I always feared. The thought had occurred to me more than once before, but after yesterday, it was foremost in my mind, even as I tried to shut it out.

I looked over at her bouncing up and down in the Jolly Jumper positioned in my doorway. From all appearances, Noelle was normal and happy. Of course, I knew only too well how quickly a personality can change. Erica had once appeared normal and happy. Did I have the strength to take on another Erica?

I needed to think about something else. After booting my computer, I found the article from the car club again and checked for the owner of the car with serial number eighteen. "Not Found Yet." So the owner was unknown. I doubted Dave and Kim Barclay would be happy to hear that, but I started to dial his cell anyway.

My cell phone rang. I dropped the office phone back onto the hook and opened my cell.

"Okay, so you are still alive."

"Last time I checked."

"I thought I was your best friend."

"You are, Isabelle." Actually Ray was, but he got listed in the husband category.

She sighed. "Then tell me why I spotted you on the five o'clock, six o'clock, and eleven o'clock news last night, standing beside a police barrier surrounding a very dead body."

Oh dear. "Sorry. We don't get the paper and I missed the news last night."

"You're missing the point now. I'm your best friend. Your confidante and sounding board. The one you come to in a crisis. Isn't a murder a crisis situation to you anymore, or has it become old hat?"

Way to lay on the guilt.

I spent the next twenty minutes filling Isabelle in. By the time I finished, Noelle had bounced herself to sleep with her head resting on the tray of the Jolly Jumper. I thought about moving her into the crib, but remembered the never wake a sleeping baby rule.

"So you and Ray will hire this girl a lawyer? Where are you going to get the money for that?"

"I don't know." The sports car boutique didn't make a profit. I had a business line of credit, but that would only go so far. Last year I sold my family home, but with the rising property values in Wachobe, our new cozy bungalow had eaten the sale price of that much larger but older home. The purchase of my Lexus pretty much ate the rest of our disposable income, not to mention the subsidy of Erica's apartment. "Maybe we'll get a home equity loan."

"Jack and I could loan you some money."

Those pesky tears welled in my eyes again. "Isabelle, you are a true friend. But I want to keep you as a friend. I can't take your money. Ray and I will work it out."

When we hung up, I turned on the thirteen-inch television in my office to see if the local news had additional coverage on the story. They were talking about something else, but I knew they looped stories every twenty minutes or so. I left the television on and picked up the phone to call Dave Barclay.

"Dave, this is Jolene Parker. I wanted to get back to you about the Datsun Z with VIN eighteen. I'm really sorry, but no owner is listed for that car."

"So she still has it."

"Pardon me?"

"Kim's wicked step-grandmother. She and Kim's grandfather had a bitter divorce. She took everything she could from the man, including his balls. She claimed she sold the car years ago, but it makes more sense that she held onto it. Kim's grandfather talked about being buried in that car for years, since he not only drove it but owned it. She's just being vindictive."

Ed, the owner of the Z car I visited, had mentioned a woman who recently made an offer on his car. Was the ex-wife vindictive enough to try to buy that car out from under the grandfather, too? How mean could one person be? "I'm sorry, Dave. I wish I could help you."

"Maybe you still can. Kim's grandfather's ex is named Sylvia Wilder. She lives in Chautauqua, or at least she did. Can you figure out a way to convince her to sell the Z to you?"

"I don't…" I was going to say I don't think so, but it occurred to me I shouldn't walk away from a potential deal, no matter how tenuous. Besides, I didn't like this lady already and I hadn't even met her. Maybe I could help. "I don't see why I couldn't give it a try."

I promised Dave I would look into the wicked ex-grandma and disconnected. Cory appeared in the doorway behind Noelle.

He held up this morning's paper. "I take it you know about Theo Tibble."

"You read the paper."

He sidled around the Jolly Jumper. Noelle stirred but didn't awaken. He sat. "No. I went to the diner this morning for breakfast. Everybody else in town has read the paper."

"If anybody asks, especially reporters, I have no comment about anything."

Cory grinned. "Where have I heard that before?"

Last year when I found a dead man in the Ferrari. I hoped the newspapers didn't see fit to remind everyone of that, poisoning the minds of this summer's flock of tourists against the Ferrari and possibly my shop. But worse, I hoped everyone didn't make the connection to Noelle. I didn't want her to grow up suffering stares from the townspeople who knew about her birth parents. They'd stared at me for years after my mother killed herself and now they looked questioningly at Erica. No child should have to grow up like that.

For one fleeting moment, I thought Noelle might be better off being adopted by a couple who didn't live in Wachobe, where everyone knew her story. Then I pushed the thought out of my mind. She was mine. Ours.

The blond television newscaster caught my attention. "At the top of the hour, a woman was arraigned this morning in Canandaigua in the stabbing death of Theodore Tibble of Wachobe, New York. The woman remains unidentified at this time.

"The stabbing took place outside the racetrack in Canandaigua yesterday afternoon. Police have released a statement that the woman in custody had assumed the stolen identity of a Canandaigua teen killed in a hit-and-run accident last year. Police are asking anyone who might be able to identify this woman"—Noelle's birthmother's mug shot flashed—"to call them at the Crime Fighters hotline number below on your screen.

"After the woman's arraignment in city court, her attorney had this to say—"

A picture of the crowd on the courthouse steps appeared. I looked, expecting to see our family lawyer, Greg Doran, speaking to reporters.

Instead, I saw Ray's ex-girlfriend, Catherine Thomas.

TEN

NOELLE WAS ALREADY IN bed when Ray arrived home. I'd spent two hours trying to figure out the best way to approach the subject of Catherine Thomas with him. I'd planned to be mature and calm. Then I saw the guilty look on his face.

"Why the heck did you hire Catherine, Ray? I would have welcomed anybody else but Cat." I spat out her nickname like a hairball.

"I knew you were going to say that, but Greg Doran said she's one of the best. And she's doing it for free."

The word free bothered me. Nothing in life was free. "What do you mean for free?"

Ray eased into his recliner and leaned back. "Her firm wanted her to do more pro bono work. She's delighted to find something with this much meat to it."

So she took the case to make a name for herself. "But this case isn't even in her hometown."

He shrugged. "Doesn't matter. It could be a pretty high-profile case. You know, young woman refuses to identify herself, refuses to help her lawyer defend her. Great stuff."

I wanted to scream but kept my voice carefully modulated. "Even better when you throw in her abandoned child, now cared for by a foster family, and, oddly enough, the foster mother was at the murder scene and chased the victim and the girl from the racetrack." I dropped onto the couch and took a deep breath. "What are you thinking, Ray? Making this a high-profile case only hurts us. And Noelle. Everyone will talk about it for years. Noelle will be tainted by it forever."

Ray snapped the footrest closed on his recliner and leaned forward to grab my hand. "Noelle won't be tainted by this. She's a baby. She has nothing to do with it. No one will hold it against her."

He pulled me off the couch and onto his lap, hugging me tight. "You worry too much. You were the one who said we had to help this girl. I asked Catherine because she's the best available criminal attorney."

I didn't bother to argue with Ray about Noelle. He would never understand stigma. His fireman father died of a heart attack on the job, in every way a hero. Ray never had to deal with people whispering about him behind their hands—until he hooked up with me, the daughter of a suicide and the sister of a bipolar with suicidal tendencies, not to mention my father, the eccentric. Even then, Ray didn't seem to notice. I guessed Ray was made of Teflon, like a hero's son should be. Maybe that was one of the reasons I found him so attractive.

But Catherine Thomas found him attractive, too. And now she would have plenty of time to spend with him, which didn't bode well for our marriage.

"Were you in a bar with Catherine on Friday night?"

I could tell from the twitch in his arms that I had startled him. Clearly, he didn't think I would find out. He must have been so into his conversation with Catherine that he didn't notice Cory. Very unobservant for a cop.

"Yes. I stopped for a drink and she was there. We chatted. That's all."

"What about Saturday night?"

He sounded genuinely puzzled. "What about Saturday night?"

I pulled back from his chest and gazed into his eyes. "You said you got a call, but you didn't put your uniform on before you left. You came home in the middle of the night and put it on. So where did you go on Saturday?"

Ray's eyes held what appeared to be pity when he looked back at me. "I went to the office to get the faxes about Theo and the girl. That's how I found out about the racetrack, remember? Then there was a fire around midnight that I picked up."

I felt foolish. Jealousy and mistrust are dangerous emotions. They had led me astray before. Still, they were hard to ignore. "You can understand why I don't want your old girlfriend around, can't you?"

He held my gaze and spoke to me with exaggerated patience. "Yes, but she's here to help us, both of us, and Noelle. She's not here to try to win me back. She's here to try to win this case. And she's going to need your help."

"My help?"

Ray nodded. "Pro bono doesn't include an investigator. Catherine's going to have a whole list of questions, and someone is going to have to go around digging up the answers. Catherine has other cases to work on. She doesn't have time to do it herself. It can't be me. I have to work. I was hoping it would be you."

I put aside my immediate reaction, which was that I didn't want to work for Catherine, and struggled to visualize this new plan. Cory could handle the shop, and my attempt to obtain the Datsun Z was most likely doomed from the start. No one else was calling me for cars. "What about Noelle?"

"I can drop off Noelle at Jeff and Marcia's house. Marcia is home all day with the baby anyway. She said it would be no trouble at all."

Jeff was another deputy sheriff, and his wife, Marcia, was a school teacher. I'd met her before. She was bubbly and sweet. Noelle would be safe with her.

I was kind of impressed Ray had made those arrangements. "Sounds like you have it all figured out."

Ray pulled me close and hugged me again. "I do. So what do you say?"

What else could I do but agree.

———

On Wednesday, I hugged and kissed Noelle goodbye, then did the same to Ray. I got him directly on the lips. He smiled and came back for another. I felt better about everything.

While they drove off in the direction of Marcia's house, I headed toward Canandaigua again, armed with pictures of

Noelle. Her birthmother still refused to speak, and Catherine wanted me to spend some time with the girl, talking about the baby to see if she would crack.

Never having been in a jail before, I didn't really know what to expect, but the facility turned out to be like new. The patterned brick exterior was accented with picture windows, and inside, the lobby seemed welcoming enough with bright lights and plants.

Catherine had made an appointment for me to see the girl, so the desk clerk expected me. I signed in and a woman officer patted me down. They allowed me to take the pictures I'd brought into the visitors' room, but nothing else.

I sat on one stainless steel stool in a long row of stools facing windows that reached all the way to the ceiling. The window panels were separated by light blue metal framework into little booths. The walls were gold and the floor, cream-colored vinyl flooring, had been polished until it shone. I'd expected the jail to smell like old sweat and urine and just plain fear, but the place had an aroma more of floor wax and other cleaning products, not altogether unpleasant.

A door opened at the far end of the row, and a female guard led the girl into the room. Orange prison garb hung off her small frame, her face shiny clean, and her hair held back in a ponytail, emphasizing her youth. The girl blinked as though the lights were brighter here than where she had arrived from, then she started to walk down the row of windows, looking for me in each one. She found me at the eighth window, hesitated, then sat on the stool opposite mine.

I smiled at her. She didn't smile back, but I thought I caught a hint of relief in her eyes, the wide blue eyes so much like Noelle's.

Three freckles dotted the bridge of her nose, which no longer held a nose ring, only the tiniest pink spot where it must have been. I grabbed the tan phone off the wall and waited for her to do the same.

"Hi…" Normally, this was where I would insert her name, but I didn't have one for her. "I'm Jolene Asdale Parker … Erica's sister." I figured she would remember Erica since Erica had arranged the adoption.

The girl nodded, and I thought I saw that glint in her eye again at the mention of Erica. She seemed to study my face and like what she found. Or maybe I was imagining things.

"How are you doing? Are they treating you okay?"

She gave a half-nod, half-shrug, and waited with expectant eyes.

I fumbled for a second. I hadn't realized carrying the whole conversation would be so tough. For a chatterbox like Erica, it would be no challenge at all, but I wasn't exactly known for my ability to make small talk. I decided to get right to the point.

"My husband, Ray, and I are the couple who want to adopt Noelle. We've been taking care of her for the last seven months. She's very happy and healthy and sweet, and she loves cats and going for walks in her stroller and swinging in the park and playing in water and jumping in her Jolly Jumper and eating … well, just about everything. I brought pictures."

With the glass between us, the best I could do was hold them up one at a time against it and wait until the girl looked the picture over carefully and nodded that she was ready for the next. I explained each picture in great detail: all about our trip to the zoo where Noelle got to touch a parrot, our picnic lunch at the park where Noelle got her first dip in the lake, and her visit to the Easter bunny at the mall where Noelle cried when we put her on his lap. I got a little choked up, but the girl never took her eyes off the pictures. She didn't smile either, which disappointed me.

The last picture Ray had taken at Gumby's wedding: Noelle in her white eyelet dress with pink ribbons, reaching for a cookie in my hand. It was a close-up with Noelle's hand in the forefront. The girl lifted her hand and pressed it to the window as though she were touching Noelle's fingers. A single tear rolled down her cheek.

Her lips moved, but I didn't hear anything. "I'm sorry, did you say something?"

She dropped her hand and looked directly into my eyes. "She's beautiful."

She spoke! Score one for the defense team. "Yes, she is. She looks just like you." I hated to admit it, but it was true.

The girl blushed. The slightest hint of a smile tinged her lips.

Now it occurred to me that coming here with pictures of Noelle was not such a great idea. What if the girl decided she wanted Noelle back? Where would that leave Ray and me? Of course, first she'd have to admit her name, then prove she wasn't a killer.

I pushed those thoughts out of my head. Catherine had given me a list of questions, designed to trick the girl into giving us a clue as to her identity. I had memorized and practiced them in an attempt to keep the conversation seeming as casual as possible.

"When I took Noelle to our pediatrician's office, he asked me about her family's medical history. You know, allergies, heart disease, cancer, stuff like that. Does your family have any history of those things?"

Her head jerked as though the question startled her. "Not that I know of."

"So your parents are still alive and healthy?"

"No, they're dead." She looked down at the counter.

I tried to hide my excitement, both at the fact she'd answered this question but also at the news Ray and I would not have to compete with grandparents for custody of Noelle. "Oh, I'm sorry. You're very young to have lost both your parents already."

She shrugged, continuing to stare at the counter.

"How did they die, if you don't mind my asking?"

After a moment, she met my gaze. "Car crash."

"I'm sorry. Recently?"

She looked at me without blinking. After a few seconds, I decided to move on to another question.

"So, were you an only child?"

Her expression told me nothing. I waited again for her to answer, then moved on.

"You and Theo signed all the paperwork for Ray and me to adopt Noelle, but our lawyer wanted to make sure your families didn't want to adopt Noelle. Theo's family is fine with the adoption, but we couldn't find your family to ask them." Because you didn't give your real name.

I didn't say the words out loud, but I might as well have. She continued to stare at me without blinking. She knew what I was fishing for.

"It's just that Ray and I can't finalize the adoption unless you tell us your real name. Even Noelle's birth certificate is invalid, since you gave Abigail Bryce's name, social security number, address, and birth date. And you're not Abigail."

She closed her eyes.

"Were you and Abigail friends?"

She opened them again and continued to stare at me.

"Can you tell me your real name?"

She frowned.

"Erica swore you wanted Ray and me to adopt Noelle. If that's the case, we can't, not unless you tell us who you are."

She shook her head.

"Catherine Thomas is a friend of ours"—I choked a little on that white lie but kept going—"She can't defend you if you won't help her. I can't believe you killed Theo. Erica said the two of you were in love. What happened?"

"I'm going back to my cell now. Thank you for bringing the pictures of Noelle and for taking such good care of her." She started to rise and hang up the phone.

I threw my hand up. "Wait."

She remained standing, but returned the phone to her ear.

"If Ray and I can't adopt Noelle, it's possible the Department of Social Services will take her away from us and place her in a different foster home, maybe many different homes. She's going to get lost in the system. There's no telling how she'll be treated. We want to raise her, but they may not let us." To my knowledge, all this was a blatant lie, designed to torment this poor girl, but, then, who knew for sure?

It worked. Panic danced across her face as she grasped the phone with both hands. "No! Noelle has to stay with you!"

I stood up, too. "I can't promise that. Ray and I are not going to be able to finalize the adoption."

"Ray's a sheriff, right?"

"A deputy sheriff."

"Noelle has to stay with you. You have to keep her safe with you."

As her agitation grew, so did my guilt. How unkind to torment her with thoughts about her baby's safety when her own life was in question. Still, Catherine had said it would be for her greater good. Catherine's plan was to make the girl stew in her fears for Noelle until she answered our questions. A cruel plan, but from my new mother's point of view, potentially an effective one. However, Catherine didn't have to sit there and listen to the girl's pleading. In fact, Catherine wasn't a mother, either. She had no idea how this situation affected this girl and me.

Against my better judgment, I kept going. "She'll be safe as long as we have her, but I don't know how long that will be. Foster homes are not permanent placements. Social Services might decide she's better off elsewhere."

The girl put her hand on her chest and seemed to take a deep breath. She leaned toward the window and pointed her finger. "I left her with *you*. She has to stay with *you*. *You and Ray.*" She raised her eyebrows and stared at me.

"Why?"

"Because he won't kill a cop's child."

I couldn't breathe. Cold sweat popped out on my brow and dampened my shirt. I clung to the counter and tried to push the swell of nausea back. "Wh…What? He who? What are you talking about?"

"You heard me. You and Ray have to keep her safe. That's all I'm going to say." She hung up the phone and walked away.

111

The guard took her by the arm and led her into the hallway beyond. After the door closed behind them, I lowered my head between my knees and tried to keep breathing. What the heck was she telling me? Was she just playing games? Or was Noelle really in danger? If so, why? And from whom?

I raised my head and the room swam with gold sparks. I took a few more deep breaths before the colors disappeared. I gathered up my pictures of Noelle and pressed them to my chest as I left the visitors' room.

In the car, I sat with the engine off and the windows rolled up. Even though it was ninety degrees outside and the interior of the car was sweltering, I shivered.

I'd come here to rattle this girl and get her to talk. On some levels, I'd succeeded with the plan. Now we knew her parents died in a car crash, but many couples died in car crashes every day. Catherine had told me to listen for any sign of a regional accent in the girl's voice, but I hadn't heard any. She could be from around here or from anywhere.

What I had heard in her voice was fear. Fear for her baby. My baby. Catherine's plan hadn't anticipated that. Nor had I anticipated leaving this visit more than a little rattled myself.

ELEVEN

"SHE'S PLAYING MIND GAMES, just like you and Catherine. She's smarter than we thought."

Ray poured me a glass of chardonnay and opened a beer for himself. "Maybe we should hire an investigator who doesn't have any emotional investment in the outcome of this case, someone who can see things objectively. You and I are too close to the case, too easily manipulated."

We'd spent the last hour going over my meeting with the girl again and again. I couldn't let go of my concerns and my frustration mounted as I realized Ray didn't share them. "You didn't see her, Ray. She was genuinely upset. You didn't hear the fear in her voice. Someone threatened her ... and Noelle."

Ray eased into his recliner, resting his elbows on his knees as he leaned toward me. "She's definitely afraid of someone or something. Otherwise, she would be talking to us, or at least to Catherine. Maybe this guy did threaten to hurt Noelle if she talked. But it's more likely that he threatened to kill the girl, and she's expanding it to Noelle.

I'm sure this girl cares about Noelle. She gave birth to her. She knows Noelle has a good thing with us. It takes a real wacko to make good on a threat to a baby."

I took a sip of my wine then a couple gulps. "Maybe he is a real wacko. Maybe that's why she's so afraid."

Ray finished his beer and set it on the coffee table. "Maybe."

"What about her parents? Do you think you can identify them, based on the fact they died in a car crash?"

"Maybe."

All these "maybes" were not making me feel any better.

Ray slid to the end of his recliner and leaned toward me. "A lot of couples die in car crashes, even a lot of couples in the right age range. We don't know where the crash occurred. Only local crash information will be easy to access. The rest will take a lot longer. And that's all dependent on whether she was telling you the truth or not."

"So you think she lied about that, too? Why would she do that?"

"Just to muddy the waters enough to throw us off her trail."

"So what are we going to do?"

He reached over and took the glass of wine from my hand, setting it next to his beer bottle. Then he pulled me onto his lap. "We're going to keep Noelle safe. And we're going to keep asking questions because it will be a lot easier to keep her safe if we know where the real threat is coming from."

I burrowed into the warmth of his chest. "Can we keep her safe?"

"Of course."

I pulled back and looked into his eyes. "Are you sure?"

The grooves around his eyes deepened as he smiled. "I'm positive." He brushed his lips over my temple and moved down to nuzzle my neck. "Now I'd like to think about something else for a little while—" He scooped me up in his arms and headed toward our bedroom—"and not burn all our energy worrying."

I hugged his neck, still struggling with all my doubts. "Are you sure?"

"Positive."

———

Catherine called at nine the next morning. Noelle and I were lying on the floor, playing with one of her toys that made crackling, squeaking, and ringing bell sounds. She liked the squeaks best, and I continued to squeeze the toy for her as Catherine talked.

"Ray called me this morning. He's going to check into the car crash angle, see if he can come up with any leads, and he's going to see if he can find out if the girl was ever in the foster care system. I need you to visit Theo Tibble's family today and ask them what, if anything, they knew about this girl he was dating. See if they're going to say anything damaging about her at the trial."

"Are they on the prosecution's witness list?"

"It's too early for lists and discovery. We haven't even had the preliminary hearing. I'm just trying to cover all the bases. They might know something that would lead us to this girl's identity. Ask them if they know where the two met, how long they dated, where they went on dates, who they hung out with, how Theo felt about becoming a father, why they aren't interested in adopting the baby, and any other nosy question you can think of. Call me when you're done."

Catherine certainly had no trouble bossing me around, but I'd let her for now. "Okay. What about the girl?"

"I'm going to see her today. I'll keep the pressure on by telling her the Department of Social Services doesn't think it's appropriate for you to keep Noelle since you were present at the racetrack and are involved in the investigation."

I winced, wondering if Social Services even had a clue all this was going on. I hoped Ray's questions today wouldn't tip them off. It was hard to say what their view would be on the whole situation. Some of these things we were saying actually might come true. I didn't want to find them on my doorstep when I got home tonight.

Catherine snapped me out of my reverie. "What is that noise?"

I realized I'd been squeezing Noelle's toy faster and louder like some sort of stress reducer. "Just one of Noelle's toys."

"I don't know how you stand it. It's very annoying."

I hung up, wondering if Ray had ever discussed his desire to have children with Catherine. She didn't seem very maternal, although she had held Noelle the other day. She seemed much more of a career woman than me, driven to achieve visible status in her profession. That could only work in our favor right now.

After I called Marcia and arranged to drop off Noelle in an hour, I tried to phone Erica for the fifth time since she stood me up for dress shopping. Once again, she didn't answer at home or her cell. Clearly she was avoiding me. She had done so often in the past, usually when she'd done something I wouldn't approve of, like running off and eloping perhaps. I left her a message that if she didn't call me, I would send Ray looking for her. That ought to get her attention.

Then I baked some chocolate chip cookies. Theo Tibble's funeral was scheduled for tomorrow. I would just drop by his family's home with my condolences and my cookies then try to ask my questions.

While the cookies baked, I called Cory. "I'm sorry to stick you with the shop. How are things going?"

"Okay. We've had a lot of foot traffic interested in the Ferrari."

"That's great." Its sale would spell a huge positive shift in my karma.

"Not really. Our visitors are only interested in seeing where the body was found. One of them asked me if we had a ghost."

Perfect. I'd never sell the Ferrari now. Maybe I could sell tickets to a ghost house instead. "Did you tell them only at my house, the one my mother haunts?"

Cory chuckled. "Next time I'll use that."

"Have you come up with any ideas on how to approach Sylvia Wilder about the Datsun Z for Dave and Kim Barclay?"

"I've got one idea. I'm going to have to drive down there and scope out the situation first. I'll ask Mark if he wants to take another road trip this weekend. Chautauqua's always nice this time of year."

Mark. I still hadn't decided whether or not to tell Cory about Mark's wife and child. Ray never gave me his opinion either. I couldn't think about it now. Besides, Cory sounded so happy every time he mentioned Mark.

"Okay. Do you want to tell me your idea?"

"Not yet. Let me see if it will work first."

Ten minutes later, I packed up Noelle and the cookies. Noelle fell asleep on the drive to Marcia's house, a brand-new blue Cape Cod situated on three acres of land off a rural road. I carried Noelle to the door still strapped in her car seat. Marcia took her from me and smiled. "They're so cute when they're asleep, aren't they?"

I smiled in return. "Adorable."

"I'll take good care of her." Marcia started to close the door.

"Marcia?"

"Yes?"

I studied her, trying to decide if she'd be any match for a homicidal maniac. She was five-eight or so, with an average build. She must have dropped her baby weight fast. Her arm holding Noelle's car seat made a nice bicep, but still, she was a woman. Here she sat in this house in the middle of nowhere, with no neighbor in sight. "Do you get many visitors out here?"

"We don't get any. I wouldn't answer the door if we did."

I felt a little better. "It's just that …" What could I say? Noelle's life may be in danger and, therefore, so is yours? She'd hand Noelle right back to me, and my investigating days would be over.

My concern must have shown on my face because Marcia's expression turned quizzical. "Didn't Ray tell you?"

"Tell me what?"

"I was in the Army for eight years before I met Jeff. We met at the rifle range. I'm armed and dangerous, Jolene."

My laugh sounded nervous, even to me. "I thought you were a school teacher."

"I am now, and you better believe the self-defense training comes in handy at the high school level." She set Noelle's car carrier on the floor behind her and turned back to smile at me reassuringly. "Ray told me about the potential threat to Noelle. Don't worry, I can handle it."

————

It bothered me that Ray hadn't confided in me about Marcia's additional babysitting qualifications. Perhaps he thought it would further alarm me. It did. If Ray thought he needed a trained killer to care for Noelle, then he took the threat a lot more seriously than he admitted. Or maybe he just decided to err on the side of caution. Either way, I felt more confident leaving Noelle in Marcia's care, but concerned again about my marriage. Why was he doing so many things without telling me? I set my doubts aside for the time being and focused on the task at hand.

Theo Tibble's parents lived on the edge of Wachobe in a small, dated-looking colonial with peeling white paint and crooked black shutters. Boxes were piled high in the windows and the stair railing wobbled as I climbed the steps. I rang the doorbell and got no response. I rang it again and listened for its tones. Nothing. The doorbell must be broken.

I knocked on the door, once, twice. Nothing. I should have called ahead. I turned to leave and heard the door fly open.

"Yes?" A woman wearing a light-weight flowered house-dress and blackened slip-on sneakers stood in the doorway. Her mousy brown hair was streaked with gray at the temples, but it was neatly pulled back in a French braid. She had a middle-aged paunch and her shoulders slumped forward as though she carried a heavy weight.

"Mrs. Tibble?"

"Yeah."

"I'm Jolene Parker. I'm very sorry about your son's death. My husband, Ray, and I are the foster parents for his child."

She looked over her shoulder then back at me, waiting. She didn't seem all that upset about the loss of her son.

"I was wondering if I could ask you a few questions ... about your family's health history, things like that. My pediatrician always asks when I take Noelle in for her checkups."

She frowned. Her hand moved toward the door.

"I brought you some chocolate chip cookies." I held them out so she would have to slam my hand in the door to get it closed.

Instead she accepted them and stood aside to let me in.

The stench of garlic and broccoli hit me as soon as I stepped through the doorway. On my right lay the living room. It was filled with stacks of yellowed newspapers and cardboard boxes. Empty whiskey cartons. It also held a plaid couch with two holes in its cushions, a mauve recliner with a cream-colored tatted doily on its headrest, and a blue leather recliner with a man slumped in it. His eyes were closed. He wore a soiled white T-shirt, and an empty bottle dangled from his hand. A television blared *The Price Is Right.*

Mrs. Tibble nodded toward him. "My husband, Theo's father."

That explained a lot.

I followed her into the kitchen. The linoleum was cracked and chipped, the counters covered with pot burns, and the stove was circa 1940, just like the icebox. But the room was spotless and smelled of Pine-Sol.

Mrs. Tibble picked up a coffeepot from the stove and pulled a mug from the cupboard. She set it in front of me and filled it.

"Thank you." I don't drink coffee, but I wasn't going to spoil the moment.

She sat down opposite me and filled her own chipped mug. Then she pushed the sugar and creamer toward me.

"No, thanks. I take it black." I picked my mug up and pretended to take a sip.

She opened the tin of cookies and took one. I watched as she ate it with great relish.

She wiped a smear of chocolate from her finger onto a dish towel lying on the table. "My husband's a diabetic—and a drunk. I don't make cookies, but these are good."

"I hoped you would enjoy them." I sat up taller in my chair. "I am sorry about Theo. I didn't know him, but his daughter brings my husband and me great joy. She's a happy, healthy, cuddly little girl."

Mrs. Tibble smiled faintly. "Do you have a picture?"

"I do." I dug the picture of Noelle at the wedding out of my purse and handed it to Mrs. Tibble.

She glanced at it and passed it back. "She's pretty. She don't look nothing like Theo."

"She looks like her birthmother. Exactly like her, to tell the truth." I hated to admit it. Somehow the admission took something away from me.

Mrs. Tibble nodded. She grabbed another cookie and bit it in half.

"Did you know her birthmother?"

Mrs. Tibble finished chewing the cookie before she answered. "Never met her. Theo never brought any of his friends around here."

"Do you know where Theo met her?"

"I don't know nothing about her. First I heard of her was when Social Services called, asking if we were interested in the babe."

"So Theo didn't live with you?"

She shook her head and took another cookie.

I congratulated myself on bringing the cookies. Mrs. Tibble seemed content to answer any question as long as she could talk with her mouth full. "Where did he live?"

She shrugged. "Not here. Not for the last year anyway."

"Do you know the names of any of his friends?"

"Nope."

"Do you know where Theo worked?"

She snorted, showing her chipped front tooth. "He robbed convenience stores, last I heard."

"Do you think your husband might know more?"

"He don't even know what day it is."

Talk about a dysfunctional family. The Tibbles made the Asdales look like positive role models.

"It's my understanding Theo is Sam Green's cousin. Is that correct?"

"Yeah." Her hand hovered over the cookies once more then dropped to her side. Apparently, three was her max.

"How are you related to his family?"

"Sam's father is my husband's half-brother."

"Oh." Awfully big contrast between the Green mansion and the Tibble hovel.

Mrs. Tibble smiled like she could tell what I was thinking. "I got knocked up with Theo when I was eighteen. His brother didn't want my husband to marry me, so he don't talk to my husband no more. My husband hurt his back on his job four years ago. He needs constant care. He drinks to kill the pain. We can't care for a babe. We barely have enough for ourselves."

Mrs. Tibble stood up, waiting.

I stood up as well, knowing I was being dismissed. She led me to the front door.

"Thank you for talking with me, Mrs. Tibble, and again, I'm very sorry for your loss."

I stepped outside on the stoop and turned back to her. "It really would be helpful to know your family's health history for Noelle's records."

She sucked her front teeth. "Tell your pediatrician the only family history to worry about is alcoholism. Alcoholism and stupidity."

Then she closed the door right in my face.

TWELVE

"ALCOHOLISM AND STUPIDITY. AT least she's kept her sense of humor."

"I'm not sure she was kidding, Ray." In fact, I was doing my best not to add it to my growing list of concerns about Noelle's future.

I took a sip of ice tea from the bottle I'd just purchased from a convenience store. Ray had called seconds after I returned to the car with it in hand. I felt like he was checking up on me. He'd already called Marcia to check up on Noelle. When I called her five minutes ago, moments after she'd hung up with him, Marcia got a little irritated. "You didn't tell me Marcia was G.I. Jane."

"She's more lethal weapon. She was a sharpshooter in the Army."

"So you are concerned about Noelle's safety." I held my breath.

"Not really. Marcia's the only stay-at-home mom I know, and Jeff said they could use the extra money. But I'm not denying her training could be beneficial."

I had to agree, even though his words reassured me. As I hung up, I realized this was the first time in my life I wished I had something more than just self-defense training. In that class, the instructor said it was important to look like a predator rather than prey. To anyone with a gun, unarmed me would always look like prey. But I wasn't going to be a rabbit frozen in anyone's sights, that's for sure.

Catherine Thomas' office and cell phone numbers were now programmed into my cell phone, just like Ray's. Talk about ironic. I dialed her number to report as requested.

She sighed when she heard the results of my meeting with Mrs. Tibble. "Not much to go on. You say the half-brother's family has plenty of money? Maybe there's some kind of inheritance Theo and therefore Noelle are entitled to. Why don't you visit the Green family and ask?"

I had spoken to Sam Green's father last year when Erica and Sam went AWOL together from the state psychiatric facility. He hadn't been warm and fuzzy then. I could only imagine how he would be now that Erica might be marrying into the family. "I could ask my sister to find out. She's engaged to Sam Green." That was, if Erica ever called me back.

"You don't say." Catherine sounded half-amused, half-revolted.

"Unfortunately, I do."

"It would be less obvious we're fishing if you do it that way. In that case, why don't you take the mug shots of the girl back to Canandaigua and show them to the Bryces again? Now that she doesn't look like some kind of grunge queen, maybe they will recognize her."

I checked my watch. An hour to Canandaigua, a couple hours there, and an hour back. I'd be able to pick Noelle up by five o'clock. "Okay, I'm on my way."

No one answered the doorbell or my repeated knocks at the Bryce home. The curtains in the upstairs window didn't even twitch this time. My watch and my growling stomach told me it was past lunchtime. I cruised up and down Main Street in Canandaigua, looking for the diner where Mrs. Bryce said she worked lunches.

Only one restaurant with gingham curtains and the promise of home-style potato salad on a poster in the window seemed to fit her description. Inside, the restaurant had red-cushioned booths, black-marbled Formica tabletops, and a worn but shiny beige tile floor. Miniature American flags rested in overturned miniature flowerpots on all of the tables. The smell of fried chicken and some kind of tomato-based soup filled the air, along with the chatter from the still almost full dining room.

An elderly woman led me to an empty table by the kitchen doors. Every time someone went through the doors, the rush of air lifted the hair on the back of my head, and I could hear dishes clattering, food sizzling, and men discussing Sunday's race. I'd eaten in worse places.

The waitress who took my order for a grilled cheese and to-mato sandwich, a Pepsi, and, of course, home-style potato salad, said Mrs. Bryce was off.

"So she's gone home?"

The waitress clicked her gum. "She's in the back, cleaning."

"Would you tell her Jolene As ... Parker is here to see her?"

She stuck her pencil into her hair and tore my order sheet off her pad. "Sure."

Two minutes later the waitress returned to set my Pepsi on the table. "She'll be out in a second."

When Mrs. Bryce appeared, she had my sandwich and potato salad in hand. She placed them before me and waited. I greeted her and asked if she could sit with me for a minute.

"Just a second." She walked away and returned with a cup of coffee, sliding into the booth opposite me.

I pulled the girl's mug shots from my purse. As soon as Mrs. Bryce spotted them, she waved them off. "I saw the pictures on television. The police came and showed them to us as well. I don't know that girl. Neither does my husband."

I tucked the pictures away again. "I'm sorry. I didn't realize the police had already shown you the pictures."

Mrs. Bryce took a sip of her coffee and set it carefully back on the saucer. "The night my daughter was run down, she had her purse with her. It had all her I.D. in it. It wasn't there when the police arrived." She closed her eyes and pain crossed her face. After a moment where she seemed to fight for control, she opened them again. "They think my daughter laid there for an hour before she was found. She was on the edge of the parking lot, behind the bar. It was three a.m. when the police got the call, four a.m. before they woke my husband and me to identify her."

Mrs. Bryce closed her eyes for a moment then continued.

"It's possible when she got hit, she flew in one direction and her purse, in another. The girl may have found the purse and not seen my daughter. Someone else may have found the purse and sold or given the I.D. to this girl. Or in the worst case, the girl was involved in the hit-and-run and stole Abigail's purse. The police don't know. I don't know. All I know is my husband and I don't recognize this girl."

She glanced down at my sandwich. The cheese was starting to congeal. "Aren't you going to eat?"

"Yes. Would you like half?"

She shook her head. "I already ate, thank you."

I took a bite and scalded the roof of my mouth on the still hot tomato. I grabbed my Pepsi as my eyes started to water.

Mrs. Bryce winced. "Hot?"

I nodded and took another swig.

"Sorry." She sipped her coffee, watching me.

I managed to swallow another bite without hurting myself. "Did your daughter have a boyfriend?"

"No. Boys never called our house. She didn't even go to the prom."

"You said you had moved here recently. Where did you live before?"

"Lockport. My husband worked at Six Flags."

"Why did you decide to move here?"

She fiddled with the handle on her coffee cup. "This was a better job. When the water park closes for the season, my husband William works at the ski resort."

"Could this girl be someone your daughter knew in Lockport?"

Mrs. Bryce shook her head. "I don't think so. I knew her friends there. She wasn't one of them."

A red-haired woman of around forty stopped next to our table. She stared at Mrs. Bryce, who looked up at her and blanched.

The woman didn't speak. She just kept looking at Mrs. Bryce, who seemed to shrink into her seat.

My waitress appeared next to her. "Everything all right here?"

I looked between the three women. "Fine." A bald-faced lie, if ever I told one, but I sure didn't know what the problem was.

The waitress turned to the red-haired woman. "Do you need anything else today, Mrs. Morton?"

Without a word, the redhead backed away and walked out of the diner.

The waitress nudged Mrs. Bryce in the shoulder. "Gotta watch out for them fiery redheads, eh?"

Mrs. Bryce managed a weak smile in return. After the waitress left, she stood up as well. "I'm sorry I can't be of more help, Mrs. Parker, but I wish you the best of luck with your adoption."

I thanked her and watched as she left the restaurant, shoulders hunched and looking more than a bit dejected.

I finished my lunch. The potato salad was every bit as delightful as promised. While I chewed, the tension between Mrs. Morton and Mrs. Bryce continued to haunt me. Wasn't Mrs. Morton the woman Mrs. Bryce mistook me for the day I approached her in the cemetery? Apparently they'd met since then. What was the deal between them? Both their daughters had graduated the same year from the high school. I remembered seeing Candace's picture in the yearbook. I couldn't help but be curious.

My waitress reappeared and leaned in to clear the dishes. "Can I get you anything else? We have fresh strawberry pie."

"No, thank you. But I am curious. Mrs. Morton seemed to upset Mrs. Bryce. She ran off before we had a chance to finish our visit. Do you know why?"

The woman clicked her gum. "Mrs. Morton is a hothead. She gets upset at just about everything. I'm not sure what's eating at her this time. Maybe she didn't get her food as fast as she wanted." She pulled my check out of her pocket, dislodging a couple straws at the same time.

She leaned down to scoop them off the floor. "Have a nice day."

I thanked her again and headed toward the cash register. A pay phone with a phone book dangling off a cord sat right next to the entrance. I paid my bill, then took a quick peek in the white pages. Mrs. Morton lived on West Street. I remembered seeing that road on my map. It wasn't more than a block or two away.

Maybe I'd just wander over to her house with a few questions next.

———

The Morton house was an ordinary gray ranch from the 1950s with dark-green shutters and rosebushes lining the front walk. Mrs. Morton did not answer the door in response to my repeated rings of the doorbell. I started back to my car.

An elderly neighbor woman was pulling weeds from her garden. She had watched me ring the bell and now struggled from her knees to her feet as I approached her side of the driveway.

The knees of her jeans were grass stained and the buttons in her shirt gaped open at the belly. Her white hair seemed almost iridescent in the sunlight.

"Can I help you with something, Miss?"

"I was just looking for Mrs. Morton and her daughter, Candace, but no one answered the bell." I stepped closer to her and caught the scent of musty clothes and fresh soil.

The woman worked her lips back and forth. "Cynthia went out. Candace doesn't live here anymore."

"Oh. Is Candace in college now?"

"That's what her mother says." She made it sound like a joke.

"It's not true?"

The woman looked over her shoulder at the houses behind her. I took a quick look around myself. She and I were alone on the street, except for the occasional passing car.

"I got a piece of mail in my mailbox by accident the other day that belonged to Cynthia. I didn't want to bring it back to her door, because she doesn't like me." She worked her lips some more. "Not that she likes anybody." The woman rocked back and forth as though blown by a sudden breeze.

I waited, but her eyes grew vacant. Apparently she had forgotten her train of thought. "You were saying something about a letter for Cynthia?"

She started then nodded. "I put it back inside her mailbox, and I noticed a letter from Candace to her. The return address was the Wardmont House in Buffalo."

"I'm not familiar with the Wardmont House."

She leaned closer to me. "Neither was I, but I looked it up on the Internet. I'm real good at the Internet. I buy and sell all kinds of stuff on eBay. I bought this antique gold ring just the other day." She thrust her hand at me. "Isn't she a beauty?"

I admired the rather unremarkable ring, then tried to get back to Candace's letter. "The Internet is a wonderful thing. I could look it up myself, but since you already did, what is the Wardmont House?"

Her expression grew conspiratorial. "It's a home for unwed mothers. They also have an adoption service for their babies."

I took a minute to process her statement. Another pregnant teenager, just like Noelle's birthmother. Statistically perhaps not so significant, but I had the feeling the two girls might be connected.

I pulled the picture of Noelle's birthmother out of my purse and showed it to the woman. "Do you know this girl?"

The woman took the photo in her hands and studied it carefully. She handed it back. "No."

I tried not to feel disappointed. "Did you know Abigail Bryce, by any chance?"

She shook her head. "Isn't that the girl who got run down in the road last year?"

"Yes. Did you know her family?"

"No. I think they were new in town. I don't know if they even live here anymore."

My cell phone rang. I pulled it out and checked the incoming call number. It was Erica, with her usual bad timing. "I have to take this call, but thank you so much for talking with me."

The woman waved. "It's nice to chat with a new young face. Come by again, dear."

I slid into my car as I hit the send button on my cell. "Erica, where have you been?"

"I'm sorry I haven't called you. I heard about Theo. And I'm sorry about the other day. Sam came by and insisted I go look at some rings with him. Then we decided to look at apartments. We couldn't find any we liked so we looked at houses. We put a bid in on one. It's on Lofton Street. It has four bedrooms and two baths, all hardwood flooring, and the kitchen is real cherry. It's gorgeous."

Perfect. She had been out getting herself into trouble "Erica, who is going to pay for this house if they accept your bid? You don't make enough to pay for the apartment you have now."

"Sam's going to talk to his dad. His dad's got money."

Indeed he did, but he wouldn't have it for long if he started buying things for her and Sam. I took a deep breath and decided to mind my own business on that score.

"Listen, I need you to find a subtle way to ask Sam about his dad and any potential inheritance. Theo Tibble's father is Sam's father's half-brother. They don't speak anymore, but Theo might have been killed for some reason related to inheritance money, either inheritance for him or for his offspring, which would be Noelle. It's very important. Can you handle it?" I tried not to let my own doubts creep into my voice.

"Sure, I'll ask Sam. If he doesn't know, he can ask his father when we go over there for dinner tonight."

"You're having dinner there?"

"Yeah, Sam thought it was time for me to meet his family."

I had a sick feeling. "You've never met them before?"

"No. Sam's going to announce our engagement to them and ask his dad for the money for my ring and for the house."

"You're going to spring all that on them in one night?"

"Sure. Sam's a grownup. He can get married anytime he wants. Why would they care?"

A better woman than I might try to explain to my sister. I elected to let her run the gauntlet without any warnings from me. Who am I to block the course of true love?

Still, I was perverse enough to want to be a fly on the wall when the Greens sat down to dine with their future daugther-in-law tonight.

THIRTEEN

I PICKED UP NOELLE around four thirty. Marcia had her son curled up on her right arm as she handed over Noelle, strapped into her car seat and ready to go, with her left. Her son had just celebrated two months on this earth, so his tiny bald head flopped about and his unfocused eyes blinked drowsily. Noelle, on the other hand, screamed her fury at being strapped into the car seat yet again. She didn't like being confined.

I shouted over her screams, "Did everything go okay today?" I wanted to ask Marcia if she'd seen anyone lurking in the brush outside her home, but I settled for the more subtle question.

Marcia smiled. "No problems until now. We're not really anticipating any."

As I leaned into my car and buckled in Noelle's car seat, I wondered who she was referring to as "We." Ray and her? Jeff and her? All I knew for sure was I had been left out of the loop. I saw a familiar pattern. It pointed to Ray, who never shared anything with me he thought might create any agitation, for him or me.

He tried to keep the peace at home that way. I didn't know if it was a trait common to all law enforcement officers or not, but it wore my patience. I liked to know everything that might have an effect on my life, so I could plan and control it. He liked to control it for me, one of the reasons we had difficulties in the past.

Noelle fell asleep five minutes after I left Marcia's driveway. I welcomed the silence as my conversation with Mrs. Morton's neighbor replayed in my head. Tomorrow I would have to drive to Buffalo and visit Candace at the Wardmont. Perhaps she could identify Noelle's birthmother. Maybe the girl had even been a resident at the Wardmont herself before moving to Wachobe. I mentally crossed my fingers.

When I pulled into the driveway, a Mercedes sat behind Ray's patrol car, a black 2008 CL600 Coupe, one of the grandest new touring cars on the market, retailing around $145,000. I tried not to salivate. Who did I know that could afford one?

Noelle continued to sleep as I pried her car seat out and carried her into the house through the kitchen door. I almost dropped her when I got inside.

Ray stood in our kitchen, in front of our stove, with his arms wrapped around Catherine Thomas. Her head rested against his chest, her face turned away from me, and he appeared to be murmuring in her ear. For a moment, they didn't realize I was there. For the same moment, I wasn't. My stomach clenched and my head swam. I rocked back on my heels, leaning against the wall for support. My eyes told me one story, my heart another, and my brain, well, the synapses had clearly stopped firing. Then Ray spotted me.

He released Catherine and took a step back. "Hey darlin."

Catherine stiffened and her hands rose to her face, her back to me. I got the impression she was wiping tears from her face. When she turned toward me, her eyes looked red and swollen, but she had a brilliant smile on her face. The smile she most likely showed to the jurors when the defense lost a crucial point in a case. "Hi Jolene. We've been waiting for you."

I matched her smile with one of my own, my best saleswoman smile—the one that says customer satisfaction comes first, even if the customer was a dickhead. I flashed it at Ray, too. Know any of those, Ray?

"What's up?" I placed the baby carrier on the kitchen counter and unfastened Noelle's safety straps. She'd started to stir when she heard our voices and any minute now the screams would erupt if I didn't get her out of the seat. I lifted her and sat her on the edge of the counter, kissing her cheeks to hide my expression from Ray and Catherine. I fought for control.

"I wanted to get a progress report from you and map out our next steps." Catherine took a few steps toward me, waiting for me to look up and respond.

I caught the scent of a wet diaper and rejoiced. Changing Noelle would give me enough time to collect myself. "Okay. I just need to change her. I'll be right back."

I darted out of the kitchen and into Noelle's room, where I took my time, fighting my doubts. Was Ray cheating on me? Was Catherine just so much more appealing to him? She was younger, better-looking, taller, firmer, bigger in the bustline, more successful, and, as evidenced by her car, wealthier. And she still had her long brown, Valerie Bertinelli hair.

Then I reminded myself Ray could have had her last year, but he picked me. Me, me, me. And Catherine said they had been waiting for me. Would she really be embracing Ray as a lover when she knew I'd walk through the door any second? I doubted it. And Ray would never be that cruel.

I set my doubts on the shelf again, picked up Noelle, and walked back into the kitchen with more confidence.

After easing Noelle into her highchair, I pulled out the rice cereal mix and heated some water. Ray and Catherine watched my every move, Catherine seated at the breakfast bar, Ray leaning against the stove with his arms crossed over his chest.

I decided to break the silence. "The police had already questioned Mr. and Mrs. Bryce. Mrs. Bryce said she and her husband didn't recognize the picture of . . . the girl." I almost said "of Noelle's mother," but at the moment, I really needed to be Noelle's mother, since I didn't feel confident as Ray's wife.

I stirred the heated water into the cereal. "I met a woman who told me another girl from Canandaigua is in a home for unwed mothers in Buffalo. Her mother seems to have an issue with Mrs. Bryce. It's all too coincidental, so I thought I should drive to Buffalo tomorrow to speak to the girl."

"Excellent." Catherine nodded. "This might be the break we need."

Or it could amount to nothing. I kept that thought to myself as I carried the bowl over to Noelle's highchair and gave her a spoonful. "Erica is having dinner with the Greens this evening. She's going to have Theo ask about inheritance . . . among other things."

All of a sudden I wished I really was a fly on the wall at the Greens tonight, especially since entering my own home had been such a shock. "That's all I have to report." I swiped the spoon around Noelle's lips to scoop up the cereal overflow. She opened her mouth for more.

"All right. I agree you should head to Buffalo tomorrow, but I need you to save Saturday, if you would." Catherine looked at Ray. He nodded as if to encourage her, and she returned her gaze to me. "On Saturday, I was hoping you would take Noelle to visit the girl at the jail, then call me at the office and let me know what she says. She still isn't talking to me except to ask to see the baby. I'm hoping she'll crack once she does."

Noelle wailed when the spoon stopped halfway to her lips. "Sorry, sweetie." I managed to continue feeding her while I considered the significance of the girl's request.

Perhaps sensing my hesitation, Catherine rambled on, "I know you're probably not too excited about the idea—taking a baby to jail and all—but I think it could help move things forward. And you're the only one she's really said anything to so far." Catherine tilted her head as though waiting for my decision.

I didn't want to take Noelle to the jail, not so much because babies don't belong there but because the girl was sure to fall in love with her—and almost as certain to want her back. I couldn't bear to give her back.

Noelle ate her cereal happily, pushing it off her lips with her tongue and smearing her fingers in the drops of it on her high-chair tray. Then she lifted her fingers to her hair and rubbed a little in to condition it, I supposed. She'd need a bath when we were done. She loved baths, splashing in the water and playing with her rubber ducks.

"Darlin', did you hear Catherine?"

I realized Ray and Catherine were staring at me. "No, I'm sorry."

"She asked if you would take Noelle to see her mother on Saturday." Ray's words were gentle, but they still tore at me.

I slid the last spoonful of cereal into Noelle's mouth. "Yes, of course I'll take her."

———

Catherine finally left sometime around eight. Ray had ordered a pizza that arrived while I bathed Noelle, soaking the cereal out of her hair and pores. I laid her down for bed and joined the two of them at the table to eat. Catherine told us about another case she had where a father and son wanted to plead not guilty to robbery, even though their fingerprints were all over the crime scene and the police found the victim's flat-screen TV in their living room. Then she told us a few more cases with equally amusing circumstances. I might have enjoyed her company if I didn't resent her so much.

Ray cleaned up the pizza box and the dishes while I took a shower. The air conditioning in our little bungalow left much to be desired on a ninety-degree day like this one, but the cool shower water relieved some of my discomfort. The rest of it wouldn't go away.

I lay down on the bed. The image of Ray holding Catherine pushed its way into my mind and refused to leave. The only other image that could overtake it was the image of me handing Noelle over to her birthmother—for good. I curled into a fetal position and pulled my pillow over my head. I could cry—or go have it out with Ray.

This time, I couldn't just let my misgivings pass.

I found Ray in front of the television with his feet on the coffee table and his eyes closed. I sat diagonal to him and studied his face. Was it the face of a cheater? I'd dated him since junior year in high school. He'd been my one and only love. I didn't even kiss that many toads before I found him. But I'd never asked him about his experiences. He'd dated Catherine for a year while we were separated. She thought he wanted to marry her. He had bought her a diamond ring, but he never said the magic words she waited to hear. At least I knew about her.

But what about other women? Was I his first? Had he slept with other women while at the police academy? While I was away at college? During our separation before he met Catherine? Had he gotten a taste for variety? Was he a cheating rat-bastard like a lot of other men I knew, including several police officers? It seemed to be a common complaint among the wives of policemen and firemen. His buddy Gumby was now a week into married life. Based on his track record, he'd probably already strayed. Had I missed the signs all the years Ray and I were together?

Ray's right eyelid rolled open. "Are you trying to burn a hole in my forehead?"

"Maybe. Or etch a big red A."

His other eye opened. "What's that supposed to mean?"

"A for adulterer, like *The Scarlet Letter*."

"I read the book in high school. I got that part, thank you." Ray lowered his legs to the floor and leaned forward with his elbows on his knees. "What are you trying to say?"

"You had Catherine in your arms when I got home today. It looked very … intimate. It seemed intimate when you met her at Gumby's wedding. Are the two of you still … intimate?"

Ray looked at me like I had two heads. "Why would you leap to that conclusion? Wouldn't it be more appropriate to ask me why I was holding her or why she was crying? A good investigator doesn't leap to conclusions."

"Don't patronize me, Ray. A good husband doesn't do things that make his wife question him. But when he does, he damn well better answer the question." I locked gazes with him and waited.

A hint of irritation ignited his gaze. "Catherine was crying over Brennan Rowe. I was just comforting her. That's all."

"So he told her he was gay and not interested in dating her."

Ray nodded. "He also said he was looking for a woman to bear his child. He wondered if she might be interested."

"Ew. Like a surrogate mother?"

"I think he meant more like a shared custody arrangement. Both of them as parents, but, of course, not a married couple."

I wondered how he planned to impregnate Catherine, but didn't want to wander too far off topic. "Why would she cry over that?"

"She didn't cry over that. She cried because her clock is ticking and she wants a child." Ray looked at his hands. "She thought at one point she'd be having her children with me."

Why didn't that make me feel any better? Nice to know she coveted him as both a husband and a father.

Ray continued, "She doesn't want to have a child with Rowe, but she's upset at the thought she might not ever have any children at the rate she's going."

I felt bad for her, really I did. But she couldn't disrupt our lives this way. "She understands that the two of you are through, right?"

"Completely."

Ray might omit the truth once in a while, but he never told a bald-faced lie. I'd already given him a pass on the year he spent with Catherine. We'd been separated for a couple years, one signature away from divorce—mine. A surge of happiness flowed through me, drowning any lingering doubt. "I'm sorry. I guess I'm just feeling a little unsettled. You and Noelle are my whole world. I don't want to lose either of you."

I dropped my gaze, fighting tears. I hated feeling so uncertain and out of control.

"Everything will work out for the best. Don't worry." He studied me for a moment, then stood and walked over to my side. "I'm going to bed. Are you coming?"

I swung back toward the keyboard. "In a minute. I want to find the map and figure out how to get to Buffalo tomorrow."

"Okay." He brushed his hand over my hair before he walked away.

I should have chased after him, but I didn't.

FOURTEEN

In the morning, on my two-hour drive to Buffalo, I thought about all the times Ray showed up when I needed him the most. All the times he wrestled with Erica's issues when I no longer had the energy. The three years he waited for me to realize that I still loved him. All the slack he cut me last year when I looked like the prime suspect for murder. Maybe I didn't know everything about him, but I knew everything important, just like he knew everything important about me. I needed to have faith in him.

My cell phone rang at nine a.m. I swerved to the side of the road like a good, law-abiding citizen before I answered it.

Erica's voice blasted over the airwaves as though she were in the backseat. "Last night was a freakin' disaster."

I refrained from saying "No kidding?" and settled for "What happened?"

"Sam's parents wigged out. His father is a son-of-a-bitch. He won't give his only son a nickel. He's 'a self-made man.'" Erica mimicked Sam's father's gravelly voice. "He thinks Sam should be 'a self-made man', too. He's leaving all his money to foundations so they name hospital wings and other stuff after him. He said it's 'his legacy' and a living testament to his hard work. There's no money for anyone else."

"So the dinner was a disaster?"

"Dinner was great. Shrimp cocktails, filet mignon, and baked Alaska for dessert. I ate the whole thing. But my future in-laws hate me."

"So now what?"

"Sam's getting another job."

"Really? Where?"

"He's having a sign painted today. He's going to put it up at the yacht club, offering private sailing lessons. He said he could charge $50 an hour."

That would employ him for the next month and a half if he was lucky, but then what? "That's a start, Erica. Listen, I'm on my way to Buffalo. Can I call you later?"

Erica was too wrapped up in her own affairs to ask me about my trip. Just as well. My hopes of identifying the girl today were very high, and I was afraid to curse my luck by admitting it to Erica. After we disconnected, I checked my mirrors and glided back onto the road.

So Theo and Noelle had no money coming to them. Inheritance was not a motive for Theo's murder.

Wait a minute. Didn't Ray say Theo's parents had paid his bail money after his arrest for robbery? Didn't he say that was the only reason they wanted to see him again? Where did all that bail money come from? Mrs. Tibble said they had no money. The condition of their home and persons certainly bore that out. Did they get the bail money back upon his death? Would they have killed him just for the money?

I'd lost my mind. No parent would kill their child for money. Besides Mr. Tibble was too drunk to leave the house and Mrs. Tibble was too slow to catch Theo. Still, I needed to find out where they got the money for Theo's bail. Maybe I would have time to stop by their home later today. But first I needed to meet Candace. I stepped on the gas.

The Wardmont House sat on an overgrown lot on the west side of Buffalo. Its parking lot held only two cars, both ready for the junkyard, in my professional opinion. The deep grass in front of the house made me wonder if a snake might slither onto the cracked cement sidewalk, and the austere brown stucco building itself said "Run for your life!"

I rang the doorbell anyway. It gonged and echoed for a few vibrations.

A middle-aged black woman with long dreadlocks opened the door. "Yes?"

"Hi, I'm Jolene Parker. I'd like to see Candace Morton, please."

"Is she expecting you?"

"No."

The woman arched an eyebrow and waited.

I turned my smile on full blast. "I'm a friend of her neighbor. She suggested I stop by to see Candace."

"What's the neighbor's name?"

Rats. I supposed any investigator worth her salt would have taken down the woman's name for future reference. Think diversionary tactic. "Did I come at the wrong time? Do you have special visiting hours?"

"No."

"Then would you please ask Candace if she would see me?" I took a step forward and the woman moved out of my way. "Thank you."

She closed the door behind me and gave me a look that said "I don't like you."

I ignored her, glancing about the foyer of the old house. It was beige and brown, just like the exterior. Beige wall paint and brown-stained gumwood trim. Even the commercial grade carpeting was beige. The air in the house felt heavy, almost oppressive, even though the air conditioning had cooled it enough to raise goose bumps on my arm. Or maybe they were a reaction to the mental climate.

Candace Morton was a ray of sunshine. Her wide toothy smile grew and her sparkling eyes danced with excitement when she caught sight of me. She wore black leggings and an orange maternity T-shirt that reached her knees. "Hi, are you Jolene?"

I introduced myself and asked if we could chat.

"Sure. Come on in and sit."

She grabbed my elbow and propelled me into the sitting room off the right side of the foyer. Surprise! The room held brown furniture. Only the red mat around the picture of the house which hung over the fireplace cut the bleakness.

"You're a friend of Mrs. Binder?"

"Is she the elderly lady who lives next door to your mother?"

Candace grinned. "Yeah."

"I chatted with her a couple days ago when I stopped at your mother's house."

"She knew I was here?"

It was my turn to grin. "Yeah."

"My mom wanted to keep it a secret. How did she find out?"

"She got a piece of your mother's mail in her mailbox."

Candace nodded. "They make me write weekly letters to my mother. If I don't write one, they won't let me watch television."

I glanced around the room. It didn't hold a television or a book or a magazine, just brown furniture. "Is this place like a prison?"

Candace's laughter echoed in the room. "No, but they have rules. You have to follow the rules."

Opening my purse, I fished the pictures of Noelle's birth-mother out. "Do you know this girl?"

Candace accepted the pictures and studied them. "No. Who is she?"

Candace listened to my story without interruption, appearing starved for companionship and something novel in her day.

When I finished, she frowned. "I do know the Bryces, but not this girl."

"Were you a friend of Abigail's?"

She shook her head. "Not really. I saw her at school and we were in ski club together, but we didn't hang out with the same kids. She was quiet, real quiet."

"How do you know her parents?"

"Her mom works at the diner. The kids from school ate there a lot. And her dad works at the water park. I worked there last summer, too." Her tone sounded wistful.

I slid the pictures back in my purse. "I guess it's not much fun living here, huh?"

Her eyes glistened. "It's for the baby. I'm giving it up for adoption. Then I can go home and start over."

"What about the father, if you don't mind my asking?"

She picked at a cuticle. "He didn't want anything to do with it. I don't blame him." Her cuticle started to bleed. I handed her a tissue from my purse, and she pressed it over the spot. "I made a mistake, and now I have to pay the price."

She sounded like she was parroting an adult's words. I checked my watch. Eleven thirty. "Are you allowed to leave here? Can I take you out to lunch?"

She leapt to her feet. "Would you?"

Absolutely, I would.

———

Candace asked to go to the pizza parlor. While we ate our mushroom and green pepper pizza and sipped lemonade, she told me all about the other girls in the home, even their names. It occurred to me the information might be confidential, but I wouldn't be telling anyone. I hadn't realized in this day and age that so many families still tried to keep unwanted pregnancies a secret.

After we ate, she asked to buy some magazines at the drug store. She picked *Cosmopolitan* and *Glamour*. I tried to seem enthused, but I would have picked *Car and Driver* myself.

I dropped her off in the driveway. She opened the car door, but didn't get out.

"Is everything okay, Candace?"

"Yeah." She looked out the window toward the Wardmont. "I just think I should tell you about Mr. Bryce."

"What about him?"

She moved her gaze to her lap. "He hits on all the girls who work at the water park. He even hit on me, but when he found out I was under eighteen, he didn't talk to me anymore." She twisted her maternity shirt in her hands. "I think he does more than talk to the older girls."

"I'm not surprised. Thanks for telling me, though."

"You're welcome, and thanks for taking me to lunch. My mother doesn't come to visit me. She's still mad at me because I wouldn't tell her the baby's father's name. For a while she thought Mr. Bryce was the father. I told her he used to talk to me and the other girls a lot."

Ah, that explained the way she glared at his wife—as if it was Mrs. Bryce's fault her husband was a philanderer.

"Mom wanted to speak to him and make him take responsibility, but I convinced her Mr. Bryce wasn't the one. My baby's father is only seventeen. He's got one more year of high school." Candace's gaze met mine. "And sometimes taking responsibility sucks, you know?"

I thought of Erica. Yeah, I knew all about that, too.

———

The drive home to Wachobe started to drag around two o'clock. To avoid falling asleep, I called Cory and put him on speaker phone, filling him in on the latest events.

"Geez, Jo, you've been busy. You have more drama in your life than I do, and I'm in the theater."

"Yeah, but what I really need is a car sale. Any prospects?"

"We got two new maintenance customers: a BMW and a Saab. The Saab came in for an inspection, and I couldn't pass it. It needs about two thousand dollars worth of work."

"Excellent." If I couldn't sell a car, at least Cory could repair one.

"And Mark's going with me to Chautauqua tomorrow. I found Sylvia Wilder's address on the Internet. We'll swing by and pay her a visit, see if we can spot the Datsun."

"Don't you have a performance scheduled?"

"At eight o'clock. We'll make it a quick trip."

Cory sounded so excited to spend time with Mark that I couldn't burst his bubble by telling him about Mark's wife and child.

Cory entertained me with a few tales from the cast of *Cats* until I reached the thruway exit. Then he hung up. At the stoplight, I headed in the direction of the Tibbles' home.

Mrs. Tibble answered my knock within seconds, wearing the same housedress and sneakers as the other day. She gave me a hint of a smile before inviting me inside. Her husband sat in the same recliner, asleep, but without a whiskey bottle in his hand this time.

Today the house smelled of fried liver, rather nauseating. I declined Mrs. Tibble's offer of coffee and waited while she poured herself a cup before getting directly to the point of my call.

"The other day, Mrs. Tibble, you mentioned you and your husband didn't have much money, but the sheriff's department"—I didn't mention Ray deliberately—"said you paid Theo's bail. I know it was high. May I ask where you got the money?"

Mrs. Tibble took a sip of her coffee and smacked her lips. She stared at the cracked ceiling for a few minutes then shrugged. "I don't see any harm in tellin' you. A man paid us a visit and gave it to us. Said it was back wages he owed Theo anyway."

"Do you know his name?"

She shook her head. "He didn't say. We didn't ask."

"What did he look like?"

"In his thirties, maybe early forties. Blond, good-looking, expensive clothes. Drove a Jaguar."

I thanked Mrs. Tibble for the information and went outside to my car, where I sat considering the possibilities. Only one man I knew was blond and drove a Jaguar. Brennan Rowe. But what business would he have had with Theo Tibble?

Last year one of Rowe's collector cars was used as a getaway car in a convenience store robbery, one of the robberies Theo was accused of. Brennan Rowe claimed the car had been not only stolen but returned, detailed. Ray bought his story. But Rowe really was too good-looking a man to be trustworthy, and his behavior with Catherine was inappropriate at best. Everybody around town always had said he put more than concrete in the foundations of the buildings he constructed. Maybe this time the rumors were actually true.

I checked my watch. Three thirty. Ray had to work until seven today, but Marcia didn't mind watching Noelle until five. Maybe I would just mosey on over to Rowe's latest construction site and see if he had funded Theo's great escape.

———

Rowe's bulldozers were clearing a building lot of hundred-year-old trees to make way for a much-contended office building. I found Rowe in his trailer office, talking on the phone. He waved me to a chair after he caught sight of me hovering in his doorway.

His Robert Redford-like grin brightened his already gorgeous face as he hung up the phone. "Jolene Asdale, or should I say Parker? Cory did a great job tuning up the Jag for me the week before last. He's amazing."

"That he is."

I must not have sounded enthused enough, because Brennan's grin dimmed. He leaned his elbows on his desk and peered over his folded hands at me. "So what brings you to my door?"

"Theo Tibble."

"The kid who got stabbed at the racetrack?"

"And the kid who supposedly took your Mini Cooper last year and used it as a getaway car for a convenience store robbery."

"Supposedly? I thought Ray included that in the charges against him."

"He did."

"So what's changed?"

"I just chatted with Mrs. Tibble. She said a good-looking blond man driving a Jaguar gave her the money to bail Theo out of jail on those robbery charges. He told her the money was due to Theo as back wages. You're the only good-looking blond with a Jag that I know."

He leaned back in his chair with a thump. "You don't pull any punches, do you, Jolene?"

I waited.

He sighed. "I should be flattered, I think, that you find me good-looking, but I'm not the only blond guy in town with a Jag. I've seen another guy driving one around, a 2007 Porcelain White XJ. Did you ask Mrs. Tibble the color of the Jag?"

No. Yet another question an experienced investigator would have known to ask. I did know Brennan's was Frost Blue, because Cory serviced it. Service Brennan paid me for in much needed cash. I didn't know about the Porcelain Jag, and I couldn't decide if I was more embarrassed to admit my ignorance … or the fact Asdale Auto Imports didn't service that car.

I smiled. "Forgive me. I'm trying to find out the identity of Noelle's birthmother. She's under arrest for Theo's murder, and every lead I undercover just seems to send me on another wild goose chase."

He held up his hand as if to say "it's okay." "I understand. Catherine Thomas told me a little bit about the case. It's going to be a tough one if the girl refuses to talk."

"Yes. I have to take Noelle to visit her tomorrow. She only wants to talk about the baby."

He must have heard the catch in my voice. "Babies are a popular topic these days. Catherine and I discussed babies."

"Yes."

His eyebrows rose. "She told you?"

"She told Ray."

"Of course. The man of choice."

"I'm sorry?"

"Ray. Catherine said she would prefer to have Ray as a sperm donor instead of me. She said she asked him about it, but he didn't give her an answer yet."

FIFTEEN

BY SOME MIRACLE, I managed to extricate myself from the conversation and Brennan's office without throwing up all over his desk, but I sat outside his trailer for at least five minutes with my head buried in my hands before I felt calm enough to drive. Only one thing was perfectly clear—Ray was holding out on me again. Maybe I was overwrought, but when another woman asked my husband for his sperm, I would think he might mention it to me. Unless, of course, he knew how I would react and didn't want to deal with it. Just keeping the peace, that's Ray.

Before I left the parking lot, I dialed Mrs. Tibble, who confirmed the Jag in question was white. I wondered if Brennan Rowe would ever bring his cars in to be serviced at my garage again. He couldn't possibly appreciate my visit and its implication that he had something to hide. I couldn't afford to lose his business. Maybe I should have thought of that before I charged into his office unprepared. Shame on me.

I drove to Marcia's and picked up a very alert Noelle. The entire drive home, she screamed with rage at being confined to her car seat. Since my nerves were on edge already, I felt positively wired by the time I walked in the kitchen door with her. I managed, without too many lapses of attention, to feed her, play with her, bathe her, and cuddle her while she had her bedtime bottle, but as soon as I laid her down for the night, I dialed Isabelle.

"I can't believe Catherine asked Ray to father her child. Is she nuts?" Isabelle could always be counted on to see things my way.

"Apparently. She's probably wondering why I didn't call and report today's findings to her. I'm afraid if I call her, I might explode." I dropped onto the couch and laid back to stare at the cracks in the stucco ceiling. And the brown stain. Was that a water leak? Great, just one more thing I couldn't afford.

"You need to talk to Ray. Your marriage is going to be in trouble again if you both aren't completely honest with each other."

I squeezed the phone a little tighter in my hand. "Completely honest?"

"Well, don't tell him his breath smells when he's leaning in to kiss you, but you know what I mean. Honest about the big stuff."

I wasn't sure I knew what constituted 'the big stuff' anymore. It seemed like all the little stuff piled pretty quick into a mountain. Ray and I were both in professions where being completely honest with people didn't serve our purposes. He'd never be able to solve a case if he spilled all the details to everyone he encountered in the course of an investigation. I might never sell another used car if I admitted to all the engine-tuning and touch-up paint Cory did on them.

Which reminded me. "I have a problem involving Cory, too. I met Mark, his boyfriend, at the water park—celebrating his teenage daughter's birthday with his wife."

"His wife? Does Cory know he has a wife?"

"I don't think so. Cory is talking about buying a house with Mark."

Isabelle whistled, piercing my eardrum. I held the phone a few inches out from my ear.

"I think you need to tell Cory, Jolene. It'll be a huge mess that will take years to straighten out if they get all tied up financially in a house, then break up over this."

"You're right. I just hate to break Cory's heart. He gets so excited every time he talks about Mark."

"It doesn't mean they're through, necessarily. It just means Mark has to choose."

I sighed. "You don't think his dishonesty will turn Cory off? It would be the end for me."

"I don't know. Cory's used to a world where things are not always as they appear. He may even have had a suspicion that he's kept to himself all along."

Like my suspicions about Ray. When Isabelle and I hung up, I closed my eyes to review all the failures in my interrogation skills the last few weeks, beginning to comprehend why lawyers never asked trial witnesses questions they couldn't answer themselves.

Ray called me at seven-ten. "Have you eaten yet?"

I hadn't even thought about food, except for Noelle's. "No."

"Chinese, subs, or more pizza?"

"Chinese. An egg roll and Moo Shu shrimp please."

When Ray appeared thirty minutes later with takeout bags in hand, I set the table and waited until we'd both had a few bites. Then I tested out my new, improved interrogation skills.

"Candace Morton didn't recognize the girl's picture, but she thinks Bryce cheats on his wife with girls from the water park."

Ray's fork froze halfway to his mouth. "Is he the father of her child?"

"No. It was a boy from school, not Bryce. But Bryce apparently slept with other girls who worked at the water park."

"That's statutory rape." Ray picked a cashew out of his chicken and popped it in his mouth.

"He only goes for the girls over eighteen, but I thought maybe you should pay him a visit in uniform and see what you can ferret out."

Ray nodded as he shoveled rice and chicken into his mouth. "Maybe early next week on my day off. Gumby will be back from his honeymoon then."

"Mrs. Tibble said a good-looking blond man who drives a Jag gave them the money to bail Theo out of jail. I thought it might be Brennan Rowe, but it's not. Do you know who drives a white Jaguar XJ?"

Ray shook his head. "Doesn't Cory service it?"

It killed me to admit that Cory did not.

"I'll run it through the DMV tomorrow." Ray finished his entire pint of cashew chicken and eyed the two remaining Moo Shu shrimp pancakes on my plate.

I held the plate out to him. "Want one?"

"Thank you, darlin'." He made up a pancake and took a bite.

Time to zero in for the kill while his defenses were down. "Brennan Rowe did tell me Catherine asked you to donate sperm to father her child. Apparently you haven't given her an answer yet." I bit into my egg roll as though his reply didn't matter. Inside, my stomach churned. I feared I wouldn't be able to swallow.

Ray stopped chewing. I could see him considering answers and discarding them. I waited.

"She did ask me the other night when she was crying. I didn't give her an answer then because she was already so upset, but, of course, the answer is no."

"Why didn't you tell me?"

"Because then I'd have two upset women on my hands." He winked.

I tried to wither him with a glance. He ignored me. "Ray, I'm concerned that you hide things from me. You cannot simply choose not to tell me because you don't want me to get upset. I have a right to know what's going on."

"Nothing is going on. And if nothing is going on, why tell you?" He swallowed the last of my shrimp and wiped his fingers with a napkin.

"You're missing the point."

"Am I?"

"Yes. For instance, you didn't tell me Marcia is an expert sharpshooter. I think I have a right to know who is taking care of Noelle, and if you think she's in danger."

"First, if I really thought she was in danger, I wouldn't let you drive her around alone and unarmed. Second, I seem to recall you neglected to tell me your sister would be caring for Noelle last week."

Oops. Caught in my own trap. Time to change direction. "Maybe we should hire a professional investigator. I haven't made much progress. We still don't know the girl's name."

Ever the gentleman, Ray allowed me to change the subject and avoid responding to his comments. He reached across the table and covered my hand with his. "I disagree. A lot of these women have opened up to you in a way they might not have with a professional. You're confiding your story, and they're reciprocating. It's good. It's really good. We'll fill in the blanks soon enough."

"I dread taking Noelle to see … the girl tomorrow. What if she wants her back?"

Ray rubbed his thumb against my palm. "First she's going to have to get out of jail and that's not looking likely the way things are going. Her fingerprints are all over the murder weapon."

"I don't know, Ray. I think someone else was there. I didn't see anyone, but I sensed someone. It's been in the back of my mind ever since, but I can't tell you why I think that. I just do."

He leaned forward and squeezed my hand tight, too tight.

"What was the girl looking at when you got to the scene?"

I closed my eyes. "Theo. Definitely Theo. Then at the crowd that gathered."

Ray released my hand and leaned back. "How about footsteps? Did you hear running?"

"I don't think so. The crowd, the girl, and Theo were still, totally still." He stood and gathered the dishes and cartons off the table. "We could try hypnosis, but I don't think you'll be susceptible."

For some reason, I took offense. "Why not?"

Ray gave me one of his lazy and sexy grins. "Here comes the unvarnished truth, darlin'. Because you're too much of a control freak, that's why."

———

Normally when I took Noelle visiting, I dressed her in her best dress and most adorable hair bows. This morning I put her in plain pink shorts and a T-shirt, trying to make her less appealing to her mother. But with her wide blue eyes, wispy curls, and happy smile, she'd never be anything other than adorable. Maybe I could keep her strapped in her car seat the whole visit, screaming at maximum decibel level? That would test the girl's love. It would test mine, too.

Instead, I carried Noelle inside the jail in my arms and gave my name to the officer at the visitor's desk. The young woman leaned through the window to admire Noelle.

"What a beautiful baby. She looks just like you."

Apparently this woman hadn't gotten a peek at all the jail's inmates yet. I thanked her for the compliment anyway.

I sat Noelle on my lap in the visitors' room. Since it was Saturday, other visitors occupied the dozen or so stools in the room. I'd snagged the last one available, the one closest to the doorway from the inmates' cells.

The girl appeared in the doorway, a guard on her left flank. She spotted me immediately. Her eyes brightened when she saw Noelle, who was oblivious to her until the girl sat down across from us and tapped her hand on the glass. Noelle looked up. Then she reached for her. The girl beamed.

I held Noelle tighter as though it might prevent them from bonding. The girl picked up the phone and waited while I resituated Noelle on my lap to do the same.

"She's so beautiful. Pink is her color."

Actually, blue made Noelle's eyes pop, but I kept that secret to myself.

"What does she like?" The girl wiggled her fingers and made faces at Noelle, much to her delight.

Then Noelle twisted on my lap and reached for my lips. I ducked her. "She likes to be talked to. She likes songs."

The girl bounced with excitement. "Can I sing to her?"

"Sure." I held the phone to Noelle's ear. She tried to grab it. Then I heard the girl's voice singing "Somewhere over the Rainbow" in a strong, pure voice. She knew all the words, hitting just the right notes. Noelle even stopped grabbing to listen.

When the girl finished, the other inmates clapped. I couldn't see them, but I could hear them. Even a few visitors clapped.

"You're a singer. Or you should be."

A mask dropped over the girl's face. "I sing a little. Nobody ever paid me."

She was lying. Someone paid her to sing. Another clue to her identity. I tried to hide my triumph.

When she leapt off her stool and slammed the phone onto the hook, I knew I'd failed. I didn't even make it to my feet before her back had disappeared down the interior hallway.

Well, at least I'd managed to distract her attention from the baby.

I took Noelle outside and settled her in the car. She started to cry, so I revved the engine and peeled out of the parking lot.

When she fell asleep halfway home to Wachobe, I called Ray from the side of the road on my cell phone.

"She's a singer. She sang to Noelle. She has a great voice. She has to be a singer. Someone has to know who she is."

"I'll call the detective in charge of the case and have him add that to her profile. Maybe it will ring a bell with someone."

I heard the click of computer keys. "Are you in the office?"

"Yes, I'm doing a report. I got the results from the DMV. No one has a white Jaguar registered in the Wachobe area, but plenty of them are registered in the state. Any idea what model year we're looking for?"

"Brennan said 2007. He knows his cars." Brennan Rowe had amassed quite a collection of cars, in fact. One of them I'd been fortunate enough to sell him. If he was a forgiving soul, I'd have the opportunity again in the future.

"Okay, that narrows it down. Let me look at the list again."

I waited, my Lexus rocking in the wake of the other cars flying past me on the road.

"I don't recognize any of these names, darlin'. I'll bring the list home tonight for you to look at. Maybe Cory can look it over, too."

"Okay. What should I do now?" I couldn't think of any more places to visit or people to question.

"Call Catherine and fill her in. See if she has any more assignments for you."

I dialed Catherine's office number after he disconnected. Her secretary answered. When I identified myself, the woman lowered her voice as though sharing a secret.

"Hi, Mrs. Parker. Catherine is in conference at the moment, although … maybe you should hold on a second. I'll let her know you're on the line."

O-o-o-kay.

"Jolene, it's Catherine. Can you come to the office right away?"

Startled, I glanced at Noelle in the rearview mirror. She slept on, undisturbed by my conversation or the cars whizzing past us. "I have Noelle with me."

"That's fine. Bring her. I'll have my secretary give you directions." She put me back on hold before I could ask any questions.

The secretary's directions were excellent. It took me only an hour and a half to find Catherine's office building, a twenty-story modern building in the heart of the city. Inside, the elevators were encased in green marble walls with polished brass doors and frames. Catherine's office was on the top floor, with etched-glass windows facing the hall and a lobby filled with brocade and cherry furniture. It all said "expensive," just like her car.

While I waited for the secretary to announce me, I noticed the building swayed a bit at this height. I couldn't wait to get out. I preferred to keep my feet on firm ground.

Catherine appeared in the lobby behind her secretary, dressed for court in a black pantsuit and red satin blouse even on a Saturday. I felt dowdy in my capris and T-shirt, even though they were Talbots' best.

"Jolene, I'm glad you made it." She glanced at Noelle, still sleeping in her car seat. "What if you leave Noelle here with my secretary just for a minute? I have someone you need to meet."

I handed Noelle over to the secretary, who cooed over her just enough to make me feel confident of her care. Then I followed

Catherine down the hall to the very last door, which opened into an office with a fabulous view of the city skyline. A brown-haired woman in a pale blue linen suit sat by the window. She turned to face us as we entered the room.

She looked familiar. She looked like—

"Jolene, this is Karen Hamm. She saw the picture of Noelle's mother on television. She came here to identify her."

That's who she looked like. The girl. An ever-so-slightly more mature and better-groomed version of the girl.

Karen stood up and walked toward me with her hand outstretched. "It's nice to meet you, Jolene. I understand from Catherine that you've been caring for my sister's child."

SIXTEEN

Heather Graus. The girl finally had a name. Oddly enough, I felt disappointed that I hadn't been the one to find it out. I would have been very proud of that achievement, even though it meant the beginning of the end.

Catherine gestured to the sitting area in the corner of her office. "Shall we make ourselves comfortable?"

Karen sat on the couch. Catherine and I took the chairs on either side. Karen smoothed her skirt down over her knees, either as a reflex or because of nerves, I couldn't tell. I tried not to squirm in my seat, but her presence made me uncomfortable in all sorts of ways, not the least of which was her potential interest in Noelle.

Catherine glanced between us. "Karen was just telling me about Heather. Why don't you start again from the beginning, if you don't mind?"

Karen tugged at the hem of her skirt again. "Heather is my younger sister. She's nineteen. I'm twenty-four. We both lived with our stepfather until two years ago when I got married. My husband and I got an apartment, and Heather wanted to live with us. I thought she'd be fine for another year with Dad before she left for college. He's not the warmest, most affectionate man, but he's very responsible. He raised us after my mother died of breast cancer seven years ago. We pretty much took care of ourselves anyway."

She pushed a stray lock of hair behind her ear and looked at the floor. "But with me gone, Dad focused more attention on Heather and gave her what she called 'lectures on life'. She got upset with him all the time. He made her come home at ten on weeknights and midnight on weekends, when she wanted to stay out longer. She had to do all the household chores we used to split. She started staying out later and leaving the work undone. He didn't take that too well.

"They fought all the time. She begged me to let her come live with us, but my husband said he thought Dad's rules were fair. Maybe they were. I don't know. The next thing I knew, Heather took off.

"She was seventeen. The police wouldn't do anything to help us. We hired a private investigator. He took us for lots of money, but he didn't find her. We had to give up."

Her face brightened. "But then I thought I saw her picture on the news. And Catherine said she has a tattoo. It's definitely her. The tattoo is one of the last things she and Dad fought over before she left town."

The big eagle with its talons bared on the back of Heather's neck. I could see where that might get her dad a little excited. I wondered if he ever got a peek at her piercings. And, of course, how he'd feel to learn that he and his wife had died in a car crash, according to Heather. Ray was right, the girl was a liar. Had she lied about the danger to Noelle as well? My heart hardened toward her.

Karen shifted on the couch toward me. "Catherine said you and your husband are foster parents for Heather's daughter. I'd love to see her."

My stomach turned over. Catherine and I exchanged glances. I could tell she hadn't told Karen that Noelle was here in the office, leaving me an out if I didn't want to bring Noelle into the room. Which I didn't.

I stood anyway. It was inevitable. "She's just outside. Let me get her."

Karen smiled with obvious joy.

Noelle had awakened and was now sitting in the secretary's lap. The secretary handed her back over to me with a smile. "She's a sweetie."

I blinked back a tear. My heart beat a little faster, its rate increasing with each step I took down the hall with Noelle in my arms.

When I reentered Catherine's office, Karen leapt to her feet and held her arms out. "May I hold her?"

Catherine frowned, clearly sensing impending disaster.

I managed to plaster a smile on my face. "Of course."

Karen gathered Noelle into her arms and kissed her cheeks. Noelle didn't seem at all afraid of her. Did she realize her relationship to this woman?

Karen sat with Noelle on her lap and examined her tiny fingers, and even pulled off a sock to see her pudgy little toes.

Noelle smiled, but when Karen blew raspberries into her tummy, she giggled. It pained me to see her take to Karen so quickly, as though she sensed their connection.

Then she grabbed a handful of Karen's hair and yanked.

"Ouch. Oh, she's got me good." Karen tried to pull Noelle's hand from her hair, succeeding only in hurting her scalp further.

"Let me help you." I untangled the hair from Noelle's fingers. "Here, I'll take her from you now."

Karen reluctantly handed Noelle back over to me. "She's beautiful."

"Yes." I kissed Noelle's cheek to hide my face. And she's mine. You can't have her.

Catherine cleared her throat. "I'm going to call the jail and make an appointment to see Heather this afternoon. Karen wants to see her sister. You're welcome to join us, Jolene. I'm hoping Heather will be willing to answer more questions now. Of course, you may want to drop Noelle off at the babysitter's first."

"Yes." I welcomed the opportunity to leave and regroup.

Catherine ushered me to the door. "I'll call you on your cell phone as soon as I know what time we can see Heather. Is Ray working?"

"Yes. Until five."

"Okay. It might go better if it was just us girls for now, anyway."

The heat of the early afternoon sun did little to warm me as I scurried across the parking lot to my car. After strapping Noelle into her car seat, I climbed in and rested my head on the steering wheel. Why hadn't I seen this coming? Why hadn't I realized the girl could have family, a rather nice sister, at that? I guessed

I'd been secretly hoping she'd be a forgotten, unloved child, only too eager to give up her own. I should call Greg Doran to let him know what was going on. We might need him for some legal custody maneuvering soon.

Noelle let out an impatient shriek from the backseat.

"Okay, okay, I'm going." I fumbled for the ignition key in my purse, managing to spill its contents all over the passenger side floor. Noelle only shrieked louder. I turned the key. The radio blasted and Noelle quieted down.

I had to pull over and call Marcia to make sure she could watch Noelle. She didn't mind. Jeff had to work today along with Ray. The whole department would rejoice when Gumby got back from his honeymoon tomorrow. Ray and I needed more time with Noelle, now more than ever.

Catherine called just as I was backing out of Marcia's driveway after dropping Noelle off. "Can you meet us at the jail in half an hour?"

"I may be a few minutes late." I stepped on the gas pedal. How unfortunate Marcia lived miles from the thruway.

"Listen, now that her sister has identified her, Heather's trial date will be set. I'm really going to press Heather for more information today. Whatever I do, follow my lead. We need her to tell us what happened the day Theo was killed. Otherwise, I'm going to have a heck of a time building her defense."

"Okay." I was more worried about our adoption now. Would the girl want her sister to take custody of Noelle? Had Karen told us the whole truth? Would Heather be happy to see her?

I pressed the gas pedal a little harder. I couldn't afford to be late.

I entered the jail and found Catherine and Karen at the reception desk. Catherine managed to get us inside with minimal questions and inspections, although only she was allowed to carry her briefcase inside. We all left our purses at the desk.

This time we were escorted to a room on the opposite side of the building from the visitors' booths, a room furnished with a table and four folding chairs. None of us sat after the door closed. Karen and I stood facing the door, waiting. Karen wrung her hands. I tried to harden my heart for what might be a rather emotional reunion and conversation. Catherine opened her briefcase and took out some legal pads and a pen, clicking it then scribbling a few notes.

The guard who opened the door blocked Heather's view of the room for a moment. But when Heather stepped around her and spotted Karen, I saw happiness flash across her face. Then her expression froze. So did she, refusing to come any closer even as Catherine beckoned her forward.

"I want to go back to my cell."

But the guard had already closed the door.

Heather looked at Catherine. "I want to go back to my cell. Call the guard, please."

Catherine took charge. "Let's all sit down for a minute, shall we?"

I moved to the closest chair in compliance. Karen took two steps toward Heather, paused, then crossed the room to the chair next to me. The forbidding look on Heather's face must have discouraged Karen from embracing her sister, although Karen's smile never wavered.

Catherine sat next to Karen, looked at Heather, and waited.

Heather sighed and moved over to sit next to me, dropping into the folding chair with a thump. "I have nothing to say."

Catherine adjusted the legal pad in front of her. "That's fine. I'll do all the talking." She pointed to Karen. "Your sister has identified you as Heather Graus, age nineteen, a runaway from outside of Jamestown, New York. Is that correct?" She met Heather's eyes. "A nod will be sufficient acknowledgment for now."

Heather pursed her lips, then nodded.

"You're going on trial for murder. The evidence supports the prosecution. You were found, alone, standing over Theodore Tibble's body with a broken and bloody beer bottle in your hand, a bottle since identified as the murder weapon that sliced open his jugular vein, causing him to bleed to death."

Heather and Karen closed their eyes, Karen grimacing.

"According to the prosecution, your motive was financial. You and Theo bet on the winning horse in the first race that day, a—" Catherine shuffled through several pages of her legal pad "—Prince Majestic. Your winnings totaled—" she checked her notes again "—$50,000. The ticket was logged in as one of your personal possessions the day of your arrest. Apparently you had it in your pocket."

Karen gasped. Even Heather appeared surprised. I knew I was surprised. How come Ray had never mentioned this winning ticket to me? Were his sheriff's buddies one county over holding out on him?

Catherine flipped to a blank sheet in her legal pad. "So now the prosecution has motive, opportunity, and evidence. Let me tell you what we, the defense, have."

She was silent so long I stole a glance at her.

"That's right. Nothing. We have nothing. No defense. Nothing." Catherine leaned back in her chair, folded her arms, and glared at Heather, who lowered her gaze to the table.

Her sister shifted as though uncomfortable, but she kept her mouth shut. Maybe she'd gotten the same instructions from Catherine that I received.

The silence grew heavy. My stomach growled to remind me I hadn't eaten yet today.

It growled again. Catherine's frown deepened.

Karen parted her lips, then closed them.

We must have sat that way for ten minutes. Then Catherine threw her notepad and pen in her briefcase, snapped it shut, and stood. "Heather, I can't even plead not guilty by reason of temporary insanity if you refuse to talk. Psychiatric examinations are required for that defense. You're going to have to plead guilty. You can expect to spend at least the next ten years in prison, maybe even the rest of your life."

Catherine stepped toward the door. "Let's go, ladies. We can't help her if she doesn't want to be helped."

I followed her, but Karen ran around the table, threw her arms around Heather and burst into tears. Seconds later Heather was sobbing, too.

I tried not to cry, but a tear escaped and rolled down my cheek. So much for my hardened heart. Catherine spotted my tears and sighed with disgust.

"I'm sorry. I'm a little postpartum," I whispered.

Her brow furrowed.

The guard knocked on the door. She swung it open and leaned against it. "Your time is up. I have to take the prisoner back to her cell."

Karen released Heather. "Her name is Heather, Heather Graus. She's my sister."

The guard gave her a look that said "Who cares?"

Heather scuffed her way to the door, taking her time, perhaps dreading being alone in her cell again after leaving her sister's arms.

Karen smoothed her suit jacket and spoke to Heather's back. "Don't worry about the baby, Heather. Curt and I will take care of her. I'll call Social Services as soon as I leave here."

"No!" Heather whirled around to face Karen. "Noelle has to stay with Ray and Jolene. She'll be safe with them. She has to stay there. Don't call anyone. Don't do anything. Just go home. Go home and forget about us."

Karen started to sputter, "But, but …"

The guard got hold of Heather's arm and pulled her toward the door. Heather looked back over her shoulder toward her sister.

"I'm going to plead guilty. If you love me, do as I say, Karen. Just go home."

Heather and the guard stepped into the hall. The door clicked closed behind them, leaving the three of us staring at each other in disbelief.

SEVENTEEN

Sunday morning Catherine and Karen joined us for breakfast at our house. Ray did his Betty Crocker routine and whipped up some Belgian waffles with fresh strawberries and cream. Karen wanted to cuddle Noelle more than she wanted to eat, but Noelle wanted to eat, not cuddle. I satisfied them both by letting Karen feed her. Catherine talked strategy between bites of waffle.

She addressed most of her comments to Ray, which irritated me more than a little, not because he wasn't better at detecting than me but because I had done the detecting in this case.

"Heather thinks Noelle is only safe if she lives with you. She implied that someone, a man, would harm Noelle if she didn't live with you, mainly because you're a police officer. Isn't that right?" Catherine fixed her gaze on Ray.

Ray looked to me to answer. He probably sensed I was seething.

I nodded. "She said 'he wouldn't kill a cop's child.'"

Catherine speared a strawberry and popped it in her mouth, speaking around it. "So a man threatened to kill Noelle."

Ray finished pouring the coffee and sat down next to me. "If Heather talks."

"Talks about Theo's murder?" Catherine asked.

I swallowed. "Or something else. I've been thinking about what you said yesterday, Catherine. There's one problem with the prosecution's motive theory."

Catherine's eyes glittered with excitement. "Do tell."

"I heard the starting bell for the first race just as I spotted Theo and Heather. They ran for the parking lot. I chased them. I don't think the winner of the first race was even announced before Theo's neck had been slashed. How could Heather and Theo know they held a winning ticket?"

"Excellent." Catherine bent down to the floor where her briefcase rested, snapped it open, and extracted a legal pad. She noted my statement.

Ray rubbed my neck. "Darlin', have you told Catherine what you told me? About the noise you heard at the murder scene?"

"No, she hasn't." Catherine's frown encompassed both Ray and me.

I set down my fork and shifted in my chair. "I heard jingling." I felt myself shrug. "That's all. It could have been the collar tags on a stray animal, but, for some reason, it seemed close by and familiar. It made me think a person was there."

"Let's try hypnosis." Catherine sat up straighter and smiled as if to persuade me. "I've used it before to trigger a witness's memory."

Ray's amused eyes met mine. "Not this time, Catherine. I'm sure Jolene's not going to be susceptible."

"Why not?"

Cringing, I waited for him to say "because she's a control freak."

He didn't. "Because Jolene likes to stay in control of her mind and body. She has solid self-protection mechanisms in place that no hypnotist will be able to breach."

I sat up a little taller. Ray made me sound whole and healthy this time, not like I flew a freak flag. It was times like these when I remembered most why I loved him.

I ran my hand down his thigh. He grabbed my hand and squeezed it under the table.

"Fine, if you say so." Catherine doodled a star in the corner of her legal pad. "Let's assume for now that Jolene was correct and someone else was present at the crime scene. Let's assume it was the killer, and he threatened Noelle's safety if Heather revealed him to the police. How do we find him?"

Ray stirred some creamer into a second cup of coffee. "I don't think that's the right question to ask. Theo and Heather had to be staying somewhere in the area. Someone had to see them come and go. Someone had to see who they associated with. Ultimately, I think that's who we're looking for—one of their associates who wanted Theo, and maybe Heather, dead."

Catherine wrote the word *associates* on her legal pad. "Okay, how do we find the associates?"

"Jolene and I could knock on doors, post flyers, and that kind of thing, but the fastest way would be to offer a reward for information on television."

Three women turned to look at him in unison. "Really?"

"Really. That's why we have a Crime Fighters program. Money's not just a motive for murder, you know."

Catherine looked from Ray to me. "How much money can we offer?"

"How much do you need?"

We turned toward Karen as she spoke up. She wiped Noelle's mouth with her bib and laid the baby food jar on the table. "I talked to Dad last night. He said to do whatever it takes to bring our baby girl home, and he's got the money to do it. So just name your figure. I'll have him transfer it to whatever account you specify."

"Excellent." Catherine stood. "Let me make a few calls."

Ray started to clear the breakfast dishes, but I continued to stare at Karen's flushed face as she lifted Noelle out of her highchair.

Her presence made me more fearful and insecure. Her interest and budding affection for Noelle was obvious. And I had to wonder when she said "bring our baby girl home"—was she referring to Heather or Noelle?

———

Ray left for work. Catherine headed off to talk with the press. Karen hinted that she'd like to spend more time with Noelle, but I rushed her out the door. At ten-thirty, just as Noelle and I sat on the couch to cuddle in peace, Erica breezed in.

"You never called me back."

She wore tan chinos, a pink Izod polo shirt, and one of those fabric belts with pink palm trees on it. Her blond hair was slicked back into a ponytail. She sported a French manicure on her fingers and toes, and her makeup appeared professionally applied. The whole look was new to her.

Erica held out her finger to Noelle, who grabbed it.

I leaned against her and nudged her shoulder. "Is this your yacht club look?"

"No, it's my 'I'm so over that boy' look."

I noticed her ring finger remained bare. "You're not engaged to Sam anymore?"

"Nope. I've met someone new."

"Who?"

"A more mature man from a fine family with prospects."

I made a face. "Who are you, Jane Austen?"

"Don't laugh. I met him last night at the bar. He's a stud muffin, and Mom thinks he's interested."

Mom's ghost was frequenting bars now? She'd never had an alcohol problem before. "So when did you break it off with Sam?"

Erica flipped her ponytail. "I left a message on his answering machine this morning."

I tried not to laugh. "I guess that beats a Post-it note, but it seems a little cold."

"You said yourself he's a sociopath. I wasn't going to tell him in person. Who knows how he'd take it?" She stood and headed for the kitchen. "I smell waffles, Ray's waffles. Any left?"

I followed her. "In the refrigerator. You can warm them up in the toaster."

Erica prepared her waffle and leaned against the stove to eat it. Her new look bothered me. Every time she'd made herself over in the past, it had only been a matter of weeks before she'd sunk into depression and tried to take her life.

"Are you taking your medicine?"

Erica licked whipped cream from the corner of her mouth. "Why do you keep asking me that? Of course I am. Don't I seem okay to you?"

"What about the gnomes—"

The kitchen door banged open. Cory trotted in, carrying clipboards and walkie-talkies and dressed in khakis, a pink Ralph Lauren polo shirt, and mirrored sunglasses.

Somebody forgot to call me and tell me the uniform of the day.

"Good, you're both here." He waved the clipboards. "We've got to move."

I hugged Noelle tighter. I hadn't planned on going out today. Instead I was looking forward to spending the day with her for a change. "What are you talking about?"

"We've got to go to Chautauqua this morning."

"Why?"

"I found Sylvia Wilder. The Datsun's in her garage under a car cover, but she's leaving on a cruise at the end of next week. If Kim Barclay's grandpa wants to be buried in the car, we need to buy it today—unless you think he's going to last awhile longer."

I had the impression every day might be his last.

Erica poured syrup on her waffle. "I can watch Noelle."

"No, you can't." Cory and I spoke in unison.

She blinked, a little too rapidly as though tears might be imminent.

I didn't want her watching Noelle, because then both of them might be in danger. Noelle was safest staying with Marcia for now. But why was Cory objecting?

He handed Erica and me each a sheath of paper. "Here's the scenario. You'll need to learn your part while we're in the car."

"Scenario? Are you kidding me?" Erica shuffled through a few pages.

Cory turned to me. "Call Isabelle. Tell her you'll need her to be on standby. She has to call us to make this work, okay?" He glanced toward Erica then back at my shorts and T-shirt. "Can you put on khakis and a pink polo shirt, too? Then we'll look like a team."

A team of what? I wasn't sure I wanted to know. "I guess so. First, let me call Marcia to make sure she can watch Noelle."

Erica tapped her script with a fancy fingernail. "Who am I playing?"

"You'll be Mark." Cory sighed. "He didn't want to participate. Said it was wrong to lie to the woman. But if you read it, we're not going to tell any blatant lies. I don't know why he's being so uptight."

Neither did I, considering Mark had lied about himself. I resolved to tell Cory the truth about Mark's family as soon as this day was over. I couldn't tell him now. It might interfere with his creative juices, which were overflowing like a flooded stream.

When I stepped outside on to the driveway and spotted a white Ford F150 hitched to a car trailer with Kempe Productions lettered with a flourish on the side decal, I wanted to stop and read the script. I didn't, choosing to have faith in my friend.

I waited until I had dropped off Noelle, called Isabelle to place her on standby, alerted Ray, and climbed into the truck next to Cory to read the proposed scenario. Erica sat in the back seat and promptly fell asleep as soon as we hit the thruway for Chautauqua.

I finished reading. "Are you sure this will work?"

"I think so. Sylvia Wilder is an amateur actress, a really bad one from what we heard. Spends a lot of time at the Chautauqua Institute, trying to perfect her craft. She wants to be on the big screen. I'm betting she bites." Cory accelerated and passed a senior who was driving the speed limit.

An educational and cultural center, the Chautauqua Institute offered art, education, religious, and recreation programs to the surrounding township and thousands of summer visitors who assembled there each year. Located on the edge of its namesake lake, it was a good three hours drive southwest from Wachobe and the Finger Lakes region. A long way to go to fail.

I expressed my doubts. "What if we bite?"

"I beg your pardon." Cory frowned. "We never bite."

"You know I'm not that fast on my feet. If she doesn't respond the way you expect, I'm not much of an improviser." I spent days learning all the attributes of my sports cars. Being put on the spot made me blush, and red was not my color.

"Don't worry, Erica and I will be there. Just let me lead."

As an actor, Cory lived to perform. He would excel at this plan—most likely why he thought of it. Erica, on the other hand, was theatrical as well, but not one to follow a script. She might improvise by setting her hair on fire.

I looked at her over my shoulder. She was fast asleep and snoring ever so slightly. "You know Erica is unpredictable."

"She's a lot more with it these days. You're not giving her enough credit."

"Cory, she's been dressing like a hooker for weeks, running around with a boy barely out of high school who stabbed his mother in the hand with a fork and who hit Erica in the forehead with a ping pong paddle. Just because she looks fine today doesn't change the fact that she's collecting a whole tribe of scary-looking gnomes in her front yard—gnomes armed with weapons, no less."

"I don't know about the gnomes, but I've been hanging out in the bar with her and she seems fine. People are leaving her nice tips, and not just guys she leans over either. She's very affable lately."

He made her sound almost normal, but I knew different. "She met another guy at the bar last night. That's why she's a new person this morning. She dumped Sam and gave herself a makeover, all in less than twelve hours. Were you at the bar last night?"

"No, but I definitely want to meet this guy. She looks refreshed."

I glanced at Erica again. Except for the spittle in the left corner of her mouth, she did look more vibrant—just not recognizable as my sister, who never wore this preppy, yuppie look. She did, however, run through men at a rate of one or two a week when she was manic. Or maybe Dr. Albert was right. Maybe her promiscuity wasn't related to her illness. I couldn't decide if that was a good thing or not.

These unanswerable questions and the hum of the truck's wheels on the thruway put me to sleep a few minutes later. When I opened my eyes, Cory had parked in front of a glorious 1800s Victorian brick mansion with arched windows, sparkling white painted trim, and double black doors at the main entrance. A smaller brick building like a carriage house sat several yards behind the home, which was encircled by a black wrought iron fence.

Way at the back of the grounds, an old barn leaned ever so slightly to the left, like a modern-day Tower of Pisa in the making.

"Erica, wake up." Cory reached back and shook Erica's knee.

"I'm awake." She swiped at the edge of her mouth, leaned forward on her seat and stuck her head in between ours. "Is it show time?"

I swallowed.

"Yes. We need to find out if the Datsun is in the garage or the barn. Jo, wait until you see Mrs. Wilder, then call Isabelle and get out of the truck." Cory handed Erica a clipboard. "Ready?"

She grinned. "As ever. Lead on."

Cory and Erica hopped out of the car and began to stride up and down the sidewalk. Erica appeared to study the home and make notes on her clipboard. Cory stared at the house as he paced. Moments later, the front door swung open and a fashionably dressed woman, maybe in her fifties, with perfectly coiffed shoulder-length blond hair appeared on the porch.

I dialed Isabelle. "Call me in five minutes."

I slid out of the truck and went to stand beside Cory.

"Here she comes," he said.

Mrs. Wilder glided down the front steps and approached with curiosity in her eyes. "Can I help you?"

Cory waved. "We're sorry to disturb you. We're just admiring this beautiful home. Are you the owner?"

"I am. Sylvia Wilder."

Cory held out his hand. "I'm Cory Kempe, from Kempe Productions. We're scouting locations."

Locations of Datsun Zs, not lovely Victorian homes. Not exactly a lie.

Mrs. Wilder took a few steps closer and shook his hand. She glanced at the trailer, her eyes moving over the lettering. "And you're interested in my home?"

To Cory's left, Erica continued to make notes. Mrs. Wilder tried to catch a glimpse of her clipboard.

Cory started walking along the fence, jotting down a few lines himself, and Mrs. Wilder followed him. "Your home is a bed and breakfast, is that correct?"

"Yes." Her face brightened then fell. "It's booked for the entire summer, though. Are you looking for someplace to shoot soon?"

"You know the movie business. It's always hurry up, then wait for the final production budget. Still, it would be wonderful to see more of this location. Can we take a tour of your lovely home, or would we be disturbing your guests?" Cory turned on the charm with his high voltage smile.

Mrs. Wilder clapped her hands together with evident excitement. "I can show you the common areas, if you like. Please, come inside."

We followed her up the sidewalk and into the foyer. A guest parlor sat to the left of the entry and a spiral walnut staircase led to the second floor. The twelve-foot ceilings, inlaid floors, ornate woodwork, and cast iron appointments made the home magnificent, but I couldn't wait to get to the garage.

I trailed behind as Cory and Erica oohed and aahed with enthusiasm, referring to their personal friends as if they were movie production people who would love to film in this home.

As Mrs. Wilder shared the home's history with us, we followed her through the dining room with its walnut table, sideboard, and servers, and a marble fireplace, then into what she referred to as the reception room, a white room with bright blue trim, furnished with antiques, including a clock that ticked ominously.

Mrs. Wilder paused in her tour. "So, if I may ask, what is the film you're making?"

Cory started making notes on his clipboard to avoid meeting her eyes. "It's a love story."

About a man and his racecar. I crossed my fingers she wouldn't ask too many more questions.

"Who's starring in it?"

My cell phone rang right on cue.

Cory didn't look up from his clipboard. "Are you familiar with Isabella Rossellini's work?"

Mrs. Wilder gasped. "I adore her."

I hit the send button on my phone. "Hi, Isabelle."

Mrs. Wilder's eyes bugged out. "Is that her on the phone now?" she stage whispered to Cory.

"That's Isabelle." He smiled. "May we see the grounds?"

I repeated everything Mrs. Wilder had told us about her home, plus many accolades, to Isabelle, who kept interrupting to ask if I'd lost my mind by going along with this charade. I thought I had, but luckily Mrs. Wilder was losing hers, too. She almost salivated at the thought of a film company using her home as a location.

When I disconnected, Mrs. Wilder practically danced across the grass in the backyard. "I've done some theater myself. Will you be looking for extras for the film? The Chautauqua Institute is just minutes from here. I'm sure you could find a lot of wonderful players here, if you film in the summer. But if you want to use my house, spring would be best. I know a lot of people at the Institute who would be available as extras then."

"That's a great idea, thank you." Cory wrote it on his clipboard, and Mrs. Wilder preened. "What about the barn in the back? Is it safe for occupation?"

Mrs. Wilder's expression changed to one of sadness. "No, it's my old horse barn. All the animals are gone. I haven't maintained it at all. I haven't even been in it since…"

I would have liked for her to finish her sentence, but Erica leapt into the void.

"What's in here?" Erica pointed to the brick garage.

"It's just the garage."

"May we see inside?" Erica's question sounded innocent enough.

"Of course." Mrs. Wilder swung open the old-fashioned doors.

First, I spotted her Mercedes. Bed and breakfasts must do all right. Then I spotted the Datsun Z under a car cover. "What's that?" I pointed to it.

Mrs. Wilder waved dismissively. "That's an old car. It doesn't run anymore."

"Too bad." Cory looked at Erica and me. "Have we seen enough, ladies?"

Erica stepped closer to the Datsun. "If we were able to film here, are you saying this car can't be moved, Mrs. Wilder?"

"Oh no, it can be moved. It just hasn't run in years." She crinkled her brow. "It might start, but I'm not sure."

Cory grabbed the car cover. "May we take a look?"

She nodded.

He whipped the cover off, revealing the red, white, and blue paint job. I took a few steps closer and found the VIN number. Eighteen. I tried to look bored, but excitement coursed through my veins.

Erica studied the car. "What kind of car is this, Mrs. Wilder?"

"A Datsun 240Z."

"What year is it?" Erica ran her hand along the hood line.

"I'm not sure. From the seventies."

Erica exchanged a meaningful glance with Cory. Mrs. Wilder didn't miss it, just as we'd hoped.

Cory pulled out his phone, pretending to dial. "We have another production we're currently working on. Do you remember the movie *Gumball Rally* from the seventies?"

Mrs. Wilder shook her head.

He pretended to listen to his cell, shook his head as though he'd reached an answering machine, and snapped the phone shut. "That car would be perfect for the remake."

"I'm sorry, it's not for sale." Mrs. Wilder tugged the cover from Erica's hands and tried to flip it back on the car.

Cory cleared his throat. "That's unfortunate. The producer is the same for both the projects we're working. He'd probably look more favorably on this location if he knew we got the car from here."

Mrs. Wilder smoothed the car cover over the trunk with trembling hands. "Where is the remake shooting?"

I slid my gaze to Cory. The scenario hadn't covered that question.

Erica piped up. "The original was filmed in New York City and Arizona. It all depends on where they'd close the roads to allow cars to travel at racing speeds."

Maybe she was full of it, but it sounded good. I nodded and smiled as though she spoke the gospel.

"Not to mention the car crashes, of course." She held out her hand to Mrs. Wilder. "Thanks so much for showing us around. You have a lovely home."

Cory nudged me, and I shook Mrs. Wilder's hand next. "A really lovely home. Thank you."

"Mrs. Wilder, it was a pleasure. Thank you for your time and the information." Cory shook her hand last.

Mrs. Wilder dogged us out of the garage. "You mentioned car crashes. Would you be crashing this car if I sold it to you?"

Erica should never have mentioned crashing cars. It wasn't in the script. No one liked to hear that their prized possession was going to be destroyed, just like they wouldn't want it buried six feet under.

Cory shrugged. "As you said, it's not for sale, so it's a moot point. Thank you again, Mrs. Wilder."

We got three yards away from her before she called out to us. I turned in time to catch the malevolent gleam in her eye. "Mr. Kempe, if you can promise me that this car will never see the light of day again after your movie, I'll sell it to you."

———

Erica got in the Datsun and steered as Cory and I pushed the car onto the trailer. Cory handed over a bank check made out for fifty thousand dollars cash with a big smile.

Mrs. Wilder's last words to us were "Just make sure you smash it to smithereens."

EIGHTEEN

We crowed all the way home. Erica's car crashes had been a stroke of genius. The whole scenario had worked more easily than we imagined, but I did regret that poor Sylvia Wilder would never get a chance to star in any other Kempe Productions. That was, until I thought about the malicious look on her face when she insisted we smash the Datsun to smithereens. Clearly, she still felt a lot of venom over her ex-husband and didn't want him to have the car. I felt a little guilty tricking her and dumbfounded as to why she was so bitter. But I was more pleased to grant a dying man's last wish.

I called Dave Barclay to share the good news.

"That's fantastic, Jolene. Kim's grandfather had a rough day yesterday. He may not make it to the end of the week. I'll get a check ready for you and drop it by tomorrow."

Normally the shop was closed on Monday, but we'd make an exception in this case. I couldn't wait to get his check, which would include a handsome finder's fee. "Fine. Cory will bring the Datsun to you as soon as the check clears."

I disconnected after he thanked me profusely.

I turned to Cory. "Do you mind working tomorrow? Dave Barclay is going to bring the check by. Once we deposit his check, then you can deliver the car to him."

Cory nodded. "Sounds like a plan."

We had reached the Wachobe town line where big old Victorian homes sat back from maple tree-lined sidewalks.

"Cory, where did you get this rig anyway?"

"I rented it from Brennan Rowe and had a friend make up the decals. Brennan uses the trailer to transport his racecars to Watkins Glen."

Good news that Brennan was still speaking to us, or at least to Cory, his favorite mechanic. "Did he mention I visited him last week?"

"No, but he did ask me if you'd been under a lot of pressure lately. I didn't know quite how to respond."

Neither did I, but his comment seemed like a clear indication he thought my questions were inappropriate at best. Perhaps as long as I continued to employ Cory, he'd forgive me.

Cory dropped Erica at her apartment. As she mounted the steps, at least a dozen wind chimes lining the porch tinkled in the breeze. Erica had started yet another collection. It might have been my imagination, but the gnomes appeared to be looking at the chimes as though ready to attack.

I should spend more time with her, maybe meet this new flame and try to ward off any future forest fires, but the mystery behind Heather's silence and the sorry state of my business took precedence for the time being.

Cory pulled away from the curb. Now that we were alone, I tried to think of a subtle approach to the Mark Wynn–boy-friend–married man situation. Nothing came to me, so I leapt in head first, hoping Cory's satisfaction over his first successful pseudo writing, acting, and producing role would ease the blow.

"Cory, you know the other day when I went to the water park to talk with Abigail Bryce's stepfather?"

"Yeah, sure."

"Did Mark tell you that I ran into him there?"

For a second, Cory's gaze left the road to move to my face. "No."

"We had a chat at the refreshment stand."

"That's nice."

I waited for Cory to ask me who Mark was with. And I waited. Didn't Cory have any natural curiosity? Then I plowed on. "I met his daughter, too."

Cory continued to watch the traffic, but his fingers tightened on the wheel. "Really."

"She was having her sixteenth birthday party there. And her mother waved to me from under the tent where all her friends were eating lunch."

"Her mother?" Cory's voice was barely a whisper.

"I didn't ask Mark any personal questions, but I got the impression they're still married."

Cory inhaled deeply and blinked rapidly. "You could be wrong."

I felt for him, I really did. But Mark didn't deserve any excuses. "Mark had a wedding ring on. When his daughter walked over to meet me, he got all nervous and twitchy."

Cory's jaw clenched.

I wanted to ease his pain, if only a tiny bit. "But he did say that you meant the world to him."

Cory stopped the truck at the end of my driveway. He left the engine running as he turned to face me. "You've known about this for over a week and you didn't tell me? You let me go to Hammondsport with him ... and look at houses ... and buy a mailbox—" his voice rose to alto "—and you didn't tell me."

Tears burned in the corners of my eyes. "I know how much you love him. I didn't want to break your heart. I know how much it hurts to lose someone you love."

I reached out to touch his arm, but he jerked it away.

"And you also know how much it means to know your friends and lovers are telling you the truth. I can't believe you didn't tell me, Jo. You were my best friend."

One of the traitorous tears escaped from my eyes and rolled down my cheek, leaving a cold trail. "What do you mean, I was? I'm still your friend, Cory."

He shook his head. "No, you're just my boss ... and maybe not that for much longer. Get out."

"What?" Obviously he was angry at Mark and I was going to bear the brunt of it.

He reached past me and opened the door. "Get out."

"Cory—"

"GET OUT!"

I got out. I'd never seen him this angry. Come to think of it, he'd never shown any anger about anything before. Cory was the most placid, affable person I knew, which was most likely why I enjoyed being with him so much. And now he hated me.

He squealed the tires on the truck as he pulled away from the curve. He took the turn at the end of the street way too fast, and the trailer rocked dangerously close to flipping on its side.

"Slow down, slow down." I reached for my cell phone, thinking Ray might be able to intercept him and calm him down. But I didn't dial, fearing Cory would be even angrier at my interference.

Cory had never told me I was his best friend, but now that he'd said it, I knew it was true. His strapping, hunky boyfriends came and went. The theater troupes changed every six weeks or so during the season with each new play. His married brother called often, but lived miles away with his wife and children, in the same town as Cory's parents. Cory traveled to Hilton Head every spring to golf with his college buddies and to the occasional football game in Buffalo to meet up with a friend from high school, but he didn't talk about anyone else on a regular basis. When Ray and I were separated, Cory had invited me to the movies or dinner once a week. I thought he was being kind, but maybe he needed me as much as I needed him. And I'd disappointed him.

For a second, I considered chasing after him, but he needed some time to cool off. He probably wanted to talk to Mark and hear the truth from him. Maybe when he did, he'd call me. I could only hope he didn't call to offer his resignation. My business wouldn't survive without him. And I didn't want to lose his friendship forever, either.

I decided to pick up Noelle. At least she'd be happy to see me.

The glaring sun made my eyes burn and water, or maybe the water was really tears I wanted to shed, grieving that I'd hurt my friend. I fumbled in my purse for my sunglasses and a tissue, blowing my nose loud and long.

When I reached Marcia's rural road, a sheriff's car passed me, doing over eighty miles per hour, siren blaring. I only caught a glimpse of the driver, but he looked like Jeff, Marcia's husband. Something was terribly wrong at Marcia's.

I hit the gas and tried to match his speed.

Ray passed me two minutes later, doing at least ninety.

My hands shook. My heart beat so hard I could hear it over the roar of my engine. The tears clouding my eyes forced me to slow to sixty.

By the time I pulled into her driveway, Gumby had joined Jeff and Ray in the front yard. Jeff pointed to the roofline as he spoke into his cell phone. I couldn't spot anything, including my child.

I jumped out of the car and rushed over to them, my whole body trembling.

Ray met me halfway. "Noelle is fine, Jolene. Marcia and the baby are fine, too."

"What happened?" Then I saw the black holes dotting the house's siding.

"Someone shot at the house about ten minutes ago." Ray indicated the line of bullet holes. "He shot high. Apparently he didn't want to kill anyone, just scare them."

"He?"

"Marcia caught a glimpse of a guy in a black baseball hat and T-shirt before he took off through the woods on an ATV. She thinks she winged him." He laid his hand on my shoulder. "We're going to search the woods. Why don't you head inside?"

Marcia flung the door wide and threw her arms around me, her hug crushing my ribs. "Noelle is fine. Don't worry." She seemed calm, but she sounded as though she spoke to reassure herself as much as me.

She led me to the windowless bathroom in the middle of the house and opened the door. Noelle sat on the floor inside next to Marcia's baby, who gurgled as he lay on the throw rug.

Noelle's eyes lit up when she spotted me. Her hands reached for me.

I picked her up and held her tight to my chest. She grabbed my earring and yanked. The pain didn't bother me a bit.

I perched with her in my arms on the edge of the bathtub. "So what happened?"

Marcia sat on the lid of the toilet seat, cuddling her son. "I heard two shots. I grabbed the kids and shut them in here. Then I grabbed my gun and looked out the front window toward the woods to the left of the house. I spotted the sun reflecting off his rifle before he shot up the house. I knew he'd probably have to reload, so I opened the front door and got off a few rounds. I think I hit him because I heard a grunt after one of my shots. He didn't fire again, and I heard an ATV moving north, away from the house."

"Ray said you saw the guy."

"Just his hat and the sleeve of his shirt when I took my first shot. He hit the dirt after that."

Marcia's son nosed at her breast, and she lifted her shirt, pushing her bra cup aside. I couldn't believe how calm she was after all that had happened. My hands still trembled as I rubbed Noelle's back.

Jeff appeared in the doorway. He stood just under six feet, burly and bowlegged, with arms like tree trunks. "There's no tracks. It's too dry. And no shell casings. But we found a few spatters of blood. You hit him, baby. Nice job!"

Marcia grinned, looking more than a little proud. "Maybe he'll turn up at a hospital or a doctor's office."

We should be so lucky. In the meantime, Noelle wouldn't be staying with Marcia again.

NINETEEN

Ray followed me home from Marcia's. Noelle slept the whole way, seemingly unaffected by her brush with danger this afternoon. When we reached the house, Ray stood with his back to it and his hand on his firearm while I removed Noelle from the car and carried her into the house. Now I knew how the President felt with his Secret Service detail and the threat of violence always hanging over his head. He could have that job. No thanks.

When Ray closed all the blinds, the house felt like a tomb. Very unsettling. I started to prepare dinner, but my mind kept drifting, first to the unknown gunman, then to Cory. I'd half-hoped he'd heard about the sniper and would call. It struck me as a little odd that even Erica didn't call. The town grapevine must be limp due to heat exhaustion.

After putting a frying pan on the stove, I wandered into the living room where Ray sat giving Noelle a bottle. "Ray, did you release any information about the gunman or the shooting to the press?"

"We decided to keep it quiet for now."

"Who's we?"

"The Sheriff's office, Marcia . . . and Catherine, of course. The office will tell anyone who heard the call on the police scanner that it was kids playing with guns."

"Why?"

"Because we want the guy to think it's safe to seek medical treatment. We did alert the hospitals and local doctors to be on the lookout for him and notify us at once of any suspicious wounds."

Ray jerked his chin toward a stack of papers lying on the coffee table. "I brought home the list of owners who registered porcelain white Jaguars in New York State. Take a look and see if you recognize any names."

I scanned the list. None of the individuals or corporations jumped out at me. I shook my head, frustrated. "I don't know these names."

The phone rang. I crossed my fingers, hoping that Cory was calling to make up with me. Instead, I heard Erica's voice. She sounded a little frightened.

"Sam left five messages on my answering machine. He said I'm going to be sorry for dumping him. He said he'd pay me back. He said when I least expect it, to expect it."

Just what I needed, more trouble. "You did give him quite a shock. He'll settle down. Do you want to come over here and hang out with us? I'm just making dinner."

"No thanks. I'm at work, and Liam is coming to pick me up later."

"Liam?"

"The guy I met last night. He's so-o-o-o great. When I told him what happened, he said he'd be here when my shift ends. He's going to take me to the motel on Route 36 for the night. I always wanted to try out their hot tubs."

Perfect. From the fire to the frying pan. "Do you think it's a good idea to start ... dating so soon? Maybe you should be by yourself for a little while to figure out what it is you really want in a relationship." There, Oprah couldn't have said it better herself.

"I know what I want, Jo. I want Liam." Dial tone filled the line.

I set the phone back on its hook and went back to frying peppers and onions for fajitas. Let Erica be as promiscuous as she liked. It hardly seemed like a matter of life or death after today.

"Ray, can you take the chicken out to the grill?"

He appeared in the kitchen and accepted the dish I held out. His shoulder holster with its shiny firearm was still in place. He caught my glance at it. "Better safe than sorry."

I nodded. As soon as he went out the back door, I ran to check the front. The dead bolt and security chain were firmly in place. Noelle gurgled as she sat on the floor, alternately picking up blocks and throwing them across the room. I scooped her up and carried her into the kitchen, setting her in the highchair.

Dinner made it onto our plates, and we forced ourselves to eat. In between bites of fajita, I spooned rice cereal into Noelle's mouth. The silence in the kitchen didn't bother her, but it weighed on me. I wanted to talk about the threat to Noelle, but I could tell Ray was thinking from the way he shoveled the food into his mouth without chewing. I needed to give him time to work it all out.

I broached the subject after laying Noelle down for the night. Ray's eyes were closed as he rested on the sofa, but I knew he was awake when I sat down on the coffee table next to him. "How do we keep Noelle safe?"

His eyes opened. "I'm taking the next couple days off. The Sheriff owes me the time."

"And we're just going to sit in here like a safe house?"

"Do you have a better idea?"

"No, but if we sit here, who's going to go out and investigate?"

"I'm still convinced that Theo and Heather's associates are the key. Hopefully, Crime Fighters will have something for us within a day or two. The sheriff said he would call as soon as he hears anything."

"What about Social Services?"

"What about them?"

"Are we going to notify them that the child they placed in our care has been shot at?"

"Hell no." Ray sat up and swung his feet off the couch. "They'd want to remove her from our home. Then I wouldn't be able to keep her safe." He took my hand in his. "I am going to keep her safe. I promise."

———

Monday morning Ray played airplane with Noelle while I phoned the shop a few minutes after nine. Cory answered on the third ring.

"I'm sorry, but I can't come in today, Cory. I may not be able to come in for a couple days. Would you be able to cover for me?" I waited for him to ask why, replaying the events of the last few days in my head and still trying to make order of them myself.

His response was clipped and disinterested. "Fine, but I'm only working today until I finish with Barclay."

I could tell from the tone of his voice that I was nowhere near forgiven. "Okay. Thank you for taking care of him."

"That's my job."

He wasn't making this easy. "Cory, I'm really sorry. I never meant to hurt you or let you down."

"Is there anything work-related you needed to speak with me about, boss?" His words were like icicles stabbing my heart.

I tried to sound as detached as him. "I'm going to fax you a list of New York State Jaguar owners who have porcelain white cars. Would you please look it over and see if you recognize any names on the list? If you do, please call me or Ray. We're both home today." I didn't tell him why. If I did, he might relent in his anger, but I didn't want his pity. I wanted his friendship.

I heard the shop's other line ringing in the background. I couldn't let him hang up without one last plea for forgiveness. "Cory, I am really sorry I didn't tell you about Mark right away. Can you come by for dinner tonight so we can talk this through?"

"No. I gotta go, boss. Gotta get the other line. Don't want to keep the customers waiting."

Catherine phoned while Noelle was taking her nap. Ray was outside washing our cars. I was doing laundry, a small pile that had grown into a mountain over the last few days.

"I wanted to suggest to Ray that we tell Heather about yesterday's incident. Maybe if she knows shots were fired, she'll talk."

I carried the phone out to Ray, who tensed the moment I stepped out of the house. His gaze scanned the street until I made it to his side, and I had no doubt he continued to do so as I walked back inside. He had his shoulder holster on, even while he washed the cars. I figured he'd be more comfortable talking to Catherine if I wasn't still in target range. Of course, his male ego prevented him from thinking he might be in danger himself. Or maybe the fact that no one in their right mind ever shot a cop.

Ray came inside five minutes later, leaving wet footprints on our hardwood floor as he crossed the living room to the kitchen where I sat. "We're going to the jail, all of us. Catherine, you, me, and Noelle."

My stomach rolled over. "Why?"

"Catherine wants to load on the guilt. See if we can make Heather talk. I can't leave you home with Noelle alone. I don't want you to go alone. So we're all going."

"When?"

"As soon as Noelle wakes up, I'll call Catherine. She'll make all the arrangements, and we'll meet her there."

———

Noelle cried all the way to the jail. After all, she'd just awakened from her nap. She wanted to play with her toys and her parents, not ride strapped in her car seat for forty-five minutes. I hated to hear her cry. By the time we reached the jail, my nerves were shot. Ray seemed as calm and cool as ever.

Catherine had waited for us in the lobby. She remained seated as we approached her. "I want to talk for a minute before we go in."

We took the chairs to her left. Noelle's eyelashes still glittered with unshed tears, but her gaze darted happily around the room, taking in the other people. A few of them smiled at her. Most ignored us, too engrossed in their own conversations.

Catherine put her hand on Ray's arm. "Let me take the lead today. Let me be the bad guy, because we still want Heather to like you. You're never going to get Noelle if she doesn't like you. So your jobs are to look sad and apprehensive as well as a little helpless and pitiful. Can you handle that?"

Ray frowned. He didn't do helpless and pitiful. Neither did I, until lately. All of a sudden, I had developed a whole new range of heretofore untapped emotions.

Noelle patted my cheek with her sticky palm. Apparently she'd been sucking a few fingers on the way over. I squeezed her tighter. She wiggled in protest.

"Whatever we need to do, Catherine. Just say the word." I didn't bother to look at Ray to see if he agreed. He had to agree.

The guard took Ray's firearm and locked it up. Then we got a cursory pat-down and were admitted to the private consultation room with its bare walls, table, and four chairs. Heather entered minutes later, looking thinner and drawn. She sat in the chair next to me. Ray and Catherine took the chairs across from us.

Catherine leaned forward and touched Heather's hand. "Yesterday afternoon a man shot up the front of Noelle's babysitter's house. No one was injured, but obviously things are escalating. We need you to identify the man who threatened Noelle."

Heather's lips parted and her eyes widened. She pulled her hand from under Catherine's and instinctively reached for Noelle. I let her take her baby onto her lap as one sob escaped from my throat. I fought to get myself under control, but all my fears of losing Noelle had overwhelmed me.

Her gaze met mine over Noelle's head as she planted a kiss in Noelle's hair. She shook her head.

Catherine snapped her fingers. "A name, Heather. We need a name. Now."

"I can't. Just keep her safe with you." This time Heather looked at Ray.

Catherine tapped her pen on the table, clearly losing her patience. "You can't expect Ray to watch this baby 24/7. He has a job. He has responsibilities. If you don't give us some answers today, Social Services will take Noelle and place her in an unidentified home, where no one will be able to find her, including us. It's the only way we can guarantee her safety long term."

Of course, I was once again in the dark, but I kept silent this time. Maybe it would be for the best, although maybe Catherine was just making it up on the fly, too. Ray had said Social Services would not be notified. Would Catherine cross him to win a case?

I studied him. His good-cop, bad-cop, whatever-you-need-me-to-be cop expression was firmly in place. Even a chisel wouldn't crack it now.

Heather examined Noelle's hand, front and back while we waited. Noelle's fingernails could use a trim. One more little task I'd missed.

Catherine tried again. "Heather, we're trying to help you. We're trying to keep Noelle safe. You have to talk to us."

She shook her head, her hair flying back and forth across Noelle's face. "If I talk to you, he'll kill her for sure. That's what he promised. And he'll do it, too."

"Not if we arrest him first." Catherine made it sound as though that would be simple enough.

"What if you can't find him? Theo and I hid for months, and no one found us. If you're careful and have enough cash, no one ever finds you."

"Does this man have a lot of money? Does he have connections with the police department? Are you worried about bribes?"

Catherine's flurry of questions seemed to confuse Heather. She buried her face in Noelle's curls. After a few minutes, she took a deep breath, raised her head, and kissed both Noelle's cheeks before handing her back to me. "He shot at the house to let me know he'll make good on his threat."

She stood. "I'm not going to tell you who he is. I'm going to plead guilty and go to prison. Just announce that to the press and all this will go away"—she laid her hand on my forearm for a second—"I promise."

She crossed the room in three strides and knocked on the door. The guard opened it and stood aside to let her pass. Just before the door closed behind her, she glanced back at me and mouthed "I promise."

I wanted to believe that meant she would sign the adoption papers, too, so that Noelle would be ours forever.

But then, I wanted to believe anything that would make my desire a reality.

TWENTY

RAY CONFERRED WITH CATHERINE in the parking lot while I sat inside the car and gave Noelle a bottle. I didn't catch anything they said, but Catherine looked alternately sad and determined. Ray's expression never changed from impassive. By the time I strapped Noelle in and resurfaced from the backseat, Catherine was sliding into her car on the other side of the lot.

As Ray backed out, I waved to her. "What were you guys talking about?"

A muscle in Ray's cheek twitched, a rare occurrence and not one that comforted me. "Catherine is convinced of Heather's innocence. She says the guilty ones never want to plead guilty. She has no intention of allowing Heather to do so if she can avoid it. She's going to talk to Karen about increasing the reward money we offered. See if more money will entice someone to come forward, and she's going to put the pressure on the cops in this town to knock on more doors. Theo and Heather might have been living somewhere here in the Canandaigua area. In the meantime, she's got other cases pending, and until we find a solid lead for Heather's defense, she's got to focus on the paying customers."

"Is that why Catherine looked sad?"

Surprise flickered across Ray's face. "Did she? I didn't notice, but she's probably worried about losing her first case. She's had a long record of wins until now."

I wondered if he'd told her the bad news. "Did you ever tell her that you're not going to be her sperm donor?"

Now he looked guilty. "I thought it might be in everyone's best interest to wait until this case was over."

"Ray!" I couldn't believe he'd leave her dangling.

He raised one hand off the wheel as if to say "hold on." "If she brings it up again, I'll tell her then, but I don't think it's in our best interest or Heather's to ... ah ... alienate Catherine's affections in any way."

I let it pass for now. Why should I worry about Catherine? She hadn't bothered to consider my feelings before she proposed this ridiculous notion to my husband.

"I know you thought the key to this investigation was Theo and Heather's associates, but maybe we should look at who would want Theo dead instead."

Ray swiped his hand over his face, making his whiskers rasp. "I don't know where to look now. We couldn't find any of their associates. Who knows who wanted Theo dead?"

"I never asked Theo's parents if they knew of any reason why someone would want Theo dead. And I never had Erica ask Sam that question either. I assumed they would have come forward with that information if they had it."

"His parents didn't seem to know anything about his where-abouts for the last seven months. It's not likely they're hiding that information from us, but it never hurts to ask."

"Then let's start with Sam instead. Stop by Erica's apartment when we get back to town. I'll ask her where we might find him."

Ray pulled up in front of Erica's apartment forty minutes later. Amazingly enough, Noelle had remained awake, but silent, the entire drive. I took this as a sign my luck was changing. That was, until I stepped out of the car and got a good look at Erica's front yard.

Chunks of broken pottery and ceramics lay all over the front yard, some entangled in the strings from the chimes which no longer hung from the porch roof. The gnome with the pick axe now had his head buried in the flowerbed and his feet were missing. Erica's newest collections had been trashed.

I wondered if she had done it. In the past, her rage had gotten away from her. She'd destroyed her previous apartment, including her television and furniture. But her latest prescription had kept her demons at bay for so long...

I raced up to the front porch and banged on the door, listening for her footsteps through the door. No sound came from the house.

Ray rolled down his window. "What is this mess?"

I walked to his side of the car. "Erica had a collection of garden gnomes and wind chimes. It looks like someone smashed them to pieces."

Ray scanned the area again, undoubtedly looking for some clue as to the perpetrator. "Do you think Erica did it?"

"She might have." I surveyed the yard again. "Or maybe Sam did it. She said he threatened to get even after she dumped him."

The sound of a throat clearing drifted to my ear from the next-door neighbor's yard. "Did the police notify you about this vicious attack?"

I looked over the car and saw our resident busybody, Mr. Murphy, rushing toward us. "Actually we just stopped by to see Erica."

Mr. Murphy rounded the front end of Ray's car and came to a stop inches from my face. "Erica—" spittle left his lips and spattered onto mine "—that girl is nothing but trouble. Ever since she moved in here, men coming and going. And now one of the hooligans has done this."

Ray's lips started to curve into a smile. "Did you see the perpetrator, Mr. Murphy?"

"I did, Ray. I called the new police chief, but he didn't get here in time."

Ray frowned. He didn't like to hear that the second team was lagging behind. "What kind of a car did he drive?"

"Didn't see any car. Just a hooligan in a baseball hat and shorts, whacking the little guys with an oar. He made such a racket. I came out of my backyard to see what was going on. He ran off when I shouted at him."

"An oar?" I glanced at Ray. "Erica said Sam gives sailing lessons at the yacht club."

Ray nodded. "Okay, now we have two good reasons to find Sam. Darlin', why don't you get in, and we'll see if we can find him at the club?"

Mr. Murphy uttered a "humph" as I rounded the car. "Your sister attracts the wrong kind, Jolene. You need to set her straight."

As if I hadn't been trying for years. I waved to acknowledge his words. Ray thanked Mr. Murphy for the information.

I looked in the backseat as Ray eased the car out of the driveway. Noelle had fallen asleep. What a boring day for her! I felt guilty, but hopefully brighter days lay ahead. I sniffed the air. A diaper change would be good, too.

Ray rolled down the windows. I tried not to hang my head out the window like a dog. Whoever said little girls were all sugar and spice and everything nice?

The yacht club sat on a point at the east edge of Wachobe village, right next door to the arts council. The club was a two-story gray clapboard building with white trim and ships' steering wheels hanging on all four sides. The stucco arts council building seemed plain in comparison. Dozens of people stood sipping cocktails under tents on the grass between the two buildings. It was impossible to tell which building was hosting the gathering and equally impossible to find a parking spot in either one's lot.

Ray parked on a meter three blocks away in the center of town. I jumped in the backseat and changed Noelle while he hauled her stroller out of the trunk. When she was restored to her sweet self, we walked hand-in-hand down the road, Ray pushing her stroller.

We were a little underdressed for the party in our shorts and polo shirts, so we skirted the edge and headed inside the yacht club. On the way in, I spotted Sam's sign offering sailing lessons. At least he'd made good on his promise to get a job. Lucky for our family, Erica didn't honor her promise to marry him. One more oddball in the family and we'd be ready for a reality television show.

I'd never been inside the yacht club before. My family didn't yacht; we drove … and occasionally spent a summer Sunday fishing off a rented pontoon boat before my mother died and my father retreated from life.

The dark paneling and forest-green carpet made the interior cave-like. But a cool cave, compared to the heat outside, with a tantalizing aroma of fried seafood in the air and lots of colorful framed photographs of the club members aboard their assorted vessels with wind in their sails.

As I looked the pictures over, a girl in black pants and a low-cut blouse approached us and addressed Ray. "Can I help you?"

"We're looking for Sam Green. Is he available?"

"Sam isn't here now. He gives sailing lessons in the mornings usually, and sometimes he comes in at night with his parents for dinner." She glanced at the open reservation book on a nearby podium. "But they don't have a reservation for tonight." She smiled, flashing a set of teeth any orthodontist would be proud to claim. "Sorry."

Ray thanked her and we left, strolling along the edge of the crowd. I spotted a tent with framed paintings inside. The party must be sponsored by the arts council, after all. Maybe I would have known about it if I hadn't skipped the last three business association meetings.

I noticed a woman give Ray an admiring glance, and two others cooing over Noelle, who seemed thrilled to get some fresh air and a walk for a change. I smiled back at everyone, proud of my family.

Ray stopped next to our car and knelt to undo Noelle's straps. I checked my watch. "Wait a minute, Ray. It's almost five. What if we walk down to the Lincoln House and have an early dinner? Erica should be working tonight. We can talk to her when she comes in."

"Sounds like a plan."

The Lincoln House sat two blocks outside Wachobe's main shopping district. A log cabin structure, I'd never been certain if it was named for the framed photo of Abraham Lincoln displayed in the foyer or after Lincoln Logs, the architecture the building most resembled. Either way, their food tasted good, their bar poured top-shelf, and their service was renowned, even before Erica started working there.

We sat in a booth overlooking the rose garden. After the waitress took our order, I mixed rice cereal for Noelle while Ray sipped his Corona.

I was happy to be out on the town as a family. Ray's schedule fluctuated so much that we rarely had the opportunity. I hoped for more days like this in the future, and fewer like yesterday. Yesterday, when Noelle was in danger, and Ray and I weren't with her. What if we couldn't keep her safe? What if Social Services did take her away? Or worse yet, what if we managed to prove Heather's innocence and she took her away?

The now familiar sense of fear washed through me, ruining my moment of euphoria. "Ray, we haven't talked about what might happen to Noelle if we prove Heather's innocence and she's released. What if she wants Noelle back?"

"I've been thinking about it. I don't know what recourse we would have."

"But she abandoned her. And she's apparently involved in some kind of criminal activity, even if she didn't murder Theo."

"We don't know that for sure." Ray set his bottle down. "We need to know more. When we know, then we can talk to Greg and go from there. Until then, let's try to live in the moment." He leaned forward and picked up my hand, turning it over to plant a kiss in my palm and send an electric charge up my spine. "For today, just be happy."

Once again, pretty poetic for Ray. It was also the line printed on the shopping list pad I'd attached to our refrigerator with a magnet.

Out of the corner of my eye, I spotted Erica. She had her black pants and white blouse on, her hair done up in a swinging ponytail, but her necktie and her apron were in her hand. I waved, trying to catch her attention. It took her a couple minutes to spot me, since she was busy batting her eyelashes at the hot bartender.

"Hey, what are you guys doing here?" She dropped onto the bench beside me and tickled Noelle's chin.

"We came by to see you and decided to have an early dinner."

"What'd you want to see me for?" Erica picked up Noelle's bottle and made it dance across the table to her obvious delight.

"We stopped by your house. We saw your gnome collection. And your wind chimes. They're destroyed. Do you think Sam did it?"

Erica's laugh echoed in the nearly empty dining room. "First of all, they're not my wind chimes or my gnomes. They belong to the landlord's new girlfriend. Second, what makes you think Sam did it?"

"Mr. Murphy said some guy in a baseball hat used an oar to smash them. Sam's working at the yacht club now, isn't he?"

Erica scrunched up her face and looked at Ray. "Did you help her with this logic or is she making this up all on her own?"

Apparently Ray didn't have a ready answer to that question, because he just forked more salad and shoved it in his mouth, refusing to make eye contact with me.

"Jolene, Sam does not wear baseball hats. Baseball hats give you hat-head, and Sam has a thing about hat-head. He never wears hats. And the oar was from the landlord's new canoe, which he left by the side of the house. He likes to take his new lover out on the lake and paddle her around, serenading her." The sarcasm in Erica's voice let us know exactly what she thought of that idea.

The waitress appeared with our dinners in hand.

When she left, I continued my questions. "So who did smash the gnomes?"

"I don't know, but the landlord expects me to pay for them. He and Mr. Murphy decided it must have been one of those hooligans I hang out with." Erica folded her arms across her chest. "I'm not paying."

I had no doubt. I would pay, just like always. All the bills still came addressed to me. Ray raised an eyebrow to let me know that he realized the same.

"So you have no idea who did smash the gnomes?"

"None." Erica shrugged as though the whole thing was no big deal. "What's the latest with Heather and Noelle?"

I looked at Ray. He nodded to say "go ahead." "We're trying to find people who have had contact with Theo and Heather during the months between the convenience store robberies and Theo's death. We need to find out what they were doing together and why someone would threaten Heather and Noelle and possibly kill Theo. Do you know anyone we should talk to?"

"Just Sam, but I don't think he saw either of them after the convenience store robberies. We were in the psych center for months after that, and no one came to visit except relatives."

Erica looked at her watch and stood. "My shift is starting."

I grabbed her wrist. "Wait. I have a couple more questions. Where can we find Sam?"

Erica shrugged. "At his parents' house or at the bowling alley around eight. It's karaoke night."

"Karaoke night?"

"Yeah, Sam loves karaoke." She pulled her wrist free, slid the necktie over her head and cinched it at her neck, then tied the apron around her waist before bending to plant a kiss on Noelle's head. "See you guys later."

I watched as she made her way across the floor to the bar where she would serve cocktails until two a.m. Then I met Ray's gaze. "Is it me, or does she seem more grown-up?"

He grunted. "She is almost thirty-three. It's about time she started acting it. Now start eating. We have to get to karaoke night."

TWENTY-ONE

WE TOOK NOELLE HOME, played with her for an hour then bathed her, put her in pajamas, gave her one last bottle, and tucked her into her car carrier, where she fell asleep on the drive to karaoke. Trying not to think every moment with her might be my last, I also felt a little guilty taking her into a stinky bowling alley when she should be home, asleep in her crib. I got over it. She would be safest with Ray and me.

Bowl-A-Roll had a sound stage set up in the middle of the lobby with two microphones and a television screen. The disco balls flashed red and green sparkles of light all over the packed room. At a table to the right of the entry, people were in line to sign up for their turn to sing. Tonight the bowling alley offered a one-hundred-dollar prize to the singer who received the most audience votes. Wachobe's answer to *American Idol*.

Ray spotted Sam at the bar minutes after we walked in the door. "Let me approach him alone, okay?"

"You arrested him once, Ray. He might not be so happy to see you."

"Yeah, and your sister dumped him with a phone message, Jolene."

Ray was a little ticked, but I didn't care. "I'm going with you. He'll see the baby. He'll know you're not on duty."

"Fine."

Ray led the way to the bar, carrying Noelle. Sam caught sight of us immediately. His facial expression didn't change, so I couldn't judge our reception. I acted friendly, hoping he would respond in kind.

"Hi, Sam. How are you?"

"Okay, Jolene." He nodded toward Ray. "Deputy Parker."

Ray nodded back. Apparently he wasn't going to follow my lead and be friendly. I ignored him, turning back to Sam and holding up Noelle. "This is Theo's baby, Noelle. Remember her?"

Sam glanced at Noelle without too much interest. "Yep."

"We found out Theo's girlfriend, Abigail Bryce, is really Heather Graus. Did you hear?"

He picked up a few beer nuts and popped them in his mouth. "I saw it on television."

"Did you know she wasn't Abigail Bryce?"

Sam's eyes narrowed as though I had asked him if he was an accessory to a crime. Maybe I had. "No. It was news to me."

"She plans to plead guilty to Theo's murder, but we don't think she did it. Do you know anyone who would have wanted Theo dead?"

"No, Theo was a nice guy."

A nice guy who robbed convenience stores. I guessed Sam's standards weren't that high, then wondered what that said about his relationship with my sister. I pushed those thoughts aside. "Do you know any reason why Heather would want to kill Theo?"

"No."

"When was the last time you saw them?"

Sam gave me a look that said "duh." "When Deputy Parker arrested us and took me back to the psych center."

"You didn't hear from Theo at all after that?"

"No." Sam scanned the room as though looking to escape us.

Another thought occurred to me. "Do you know if Theo and Heather had a good relationship? He didn't hit her or anything, did he?"

"No. He loved her from the first time he saw her, the loser."

"Where was that?"

"At the May Day party."

Wachobe's business association ran a May Day party each year in the town square, where the children danced around the flag pole holding colored streamers and the adults received nosegays of lilies of the valley and coupons to all the shops on Main Street. Ray and I never attended because his birthday is May 1, and we always took a long weekend trip somewhere when we were together. The years we weren't together, I mourned at home, alone, wondering what Ray was doing.

I remembered Heather's beautiful voice when she sang to Noelle in the jail. "Did he know Heather could sing?"

"Yep. I've heard her, too. She's a damn good singer."

"Do you know if she ever worked as a singer?"

"I know she's won karaoke contests before. She told Theo."

I looked at Ray, who smiled. Another clue into Heather's past. I couldn't wait to get home and look up all the karaoke contests advertised in the Finger Lakes area. Maybe someone who had paid out the prize money would remember Heather Graus ... and her associates.

———

While I laid Noelle down in her crib for the night, Ray pressed the button on the answering machine, which had flashed its tell-tale red light when we walked in the living room.

I heard the messages through Noelle's bedroom wall.

"Ray, it's Gumby. We responded to a call at your sister-in-law's house this morning. Someone smashed all the garden gnomes in her front yard. They belonged to her landlord's live-in, but I thought you'd want to know. Later, bro."

The machine announced message two. "Hi, this is Cory Kempe. I'm calling to report to Jolene Asdale that I deposited Mr. Barclay's check and delivered the Datsun to Mr. Barclay's place of business on Martin Road at five o'clock this afternoon. It took me all day because Barclay didn't deliver the check here until after three."

Geez, how long was Cory going to stay mad? For a guy who never got angry, he sure knew how to hold a grudge.

"I should probably mention that Mr. Barclay arrived at his place of business driving a porcelain white Jaguar. I then real-ized the company name on the check I deposited was FLM, Inc., which matches a name on the list from the DMV my boss asked me to review. FLM stands for Finger Lakes Marketing. That's all I have to report to my boss."

Ray stood with his hands on his hips when I entered the living room. "What did you do to Cory?"

"I told him about Mark Wynn."

"And he's mad at you for telling him?"

I sank onto the couch. "He's mad at me for not telling him sooner. He said he expected better from his former best friend."

Ray sat beside me, threw his arm around my shoulders, and hugged me. "He'll get over it."

I hoped so. I would miss his friendship. Not to mention, if he quit, where would I find another Cory who could both make the cars' engines purr and their owners preen with his ego-strokes? "What do you make of this Dave Barclay revelation?"

Ray pulled me back with him as he sank into the couch. "I'm not sure. It sounds like Barclay is the one who gave Theo's parents the bail money."

"Why would he do that?"

"Theo's mom said it was Theo's back wages, right?"

"Right. So Theo worked for Barclay?"

"That's what it sounds like." Ray sighed. "But we checked Theo's employment history after his arrest. He doesn't have any history, with Barclay or anyone else, at least not on the books."

A thought struck me. I grabbed Ray's thigh, digging my fingers in.

"Hey, ow!"

I eased my grip. "Sorry. But Barclay and his wife were at the racetrack the day Theo was killed. In fact, they were standing right behind me when Theo spotted me."

"Is that when he and Heather took off?"

"Yes."

Ray took his arm from my shoulder and turned to face me. "Are you sure he spotted you? Maybe he spotted Barclay and ran."

I closed my eyes and pictured the scene again. "I don't know. I turned and saw Theo. He seemed to recognize me. He pointed me out to Heather and they both started running."

"But it could have been Barclay that they were afraid of?"

"I don't know, Ray. It all happened so fast."

He ran his hand down my cheek. "It's okay. That's why eye-witness reports are so unreliable. It's hard to take it all in objectively when you're in the heat of the moment."

I felt like I'd let him and Noelle down. "So what should we do now?"

Ray glanced at the mantel clock which read nine-fifteen. "It's too late now to visit Barclay. I don't want to leave you alone, and I don't want to send anyone else from the department. Let me call the Sheriff and fill him in. I'll see how he wants to proceed in the morning."

He stood and pulled me to my feet. "Meanwhile, you do an Internet search. See how many karaoke contests you can find. Heather ties into all this somehow. We need to know how."

Halfway across the room, he stopped to face me again. "And while you're at it, see what you can find out about FLM, Inc."

———

An hour later I had compiled a list of ten karaoke contests in the Finger Lakes area within the last year. Six at bars, one ski resort, two churches, and another bowling alley.

I called the six bars immediately. The bartender answered each time. Two remembered the contest but not the winner; three were new to the job; and the sixth seemed like he'd been sampling his wares. All suggested I speak to the management the following day.

In the morning, I would call again and ask if Heather Graus a.k.a. Abigail Bryce might have participated in or even won any of the contests. The managers should know whom they paid the prize money.

Ray sneaked up behind me and rubbed my shoulders.

I leaned into his hands. "I have some karaoke contest sponsors to call in the morning, but I couldn't find FLM, Inc. on the Internet anywhere."

"Don't worry. I'll call Catherine in the morning. Her practice has corporate lawyers, too. They'll know how to ferret out more information about FLM, I'm sure."

I rubbed my eyes. "Okay. What did the Sheriff say?"

"He wants us to ask Heather about Dave Barclay. Even if she won't admit to knowing him, we should be able to tell if she recognizes the name. If she does, he's okay with bringing Barclay in for questioning. He'd like to know what Theo Tibble did for Barclay that was worth all that bail money."

Ray released my shoulders, stretched and wiggled his neck. "I'm going to bed. Are you coming?"

"In a minute." How could he sleep? My mind was racing. I knew the true meaning of sitting on pins and needles. I was full of energy and questions, and it would all have to wait at least another ten hours.

I went into Noelle's room and pulled my rocking chair close to the side of her crib. When she first came home with me, I'd sat here many a night, watching her sleep and worrying about SIDS. Babies were an all-new experience for me, a wonderful, joyous experience fraught with questions and concerns. Thank God Isabelle had been around to advise me.

Isabelle. It had been days since she called. Tomorrow I would have to phone her and bring her up to speed. Otherwise, I might lose another friend.

What to do about Cory? He'd never acted this way before, but then, he'd never had a reason to. Was he still dating Mark or sitting alone at home, pining for his lost love? I didn't dare call him to find out. How could I make it right between us?

Noelle rolled onto her back, smacking her lips and sighing. Such a beautiful baby. I'd been so lucky to have her. But if Heather didn't sign the adoption papers, would Noelle be leaving me soon for good? I didn't think I could bear it. Would my marriage to Ray survive the loss of this child? He'd been very clear that he wanted a child. We'd separated because I'd refused to bear one and didn't like his constant pressure. When the dead man in my showroom Ferrari forced us to face each other, we realized flames still flickered between us. He'd compromised and suggested adoption. Noelle had fallen into our laps. Would she be taken away as abruptly? Where would that leave us?

A shadow in the doorway startled me. "Ray?"

He padded closer, wearing only his boxers. He leaned close to my ear, his warm breath tickling me. "What are you doing?"

"Thinking."

"About what?"

That we might lose our child? That we might not make it to a fiftieth wedding anniversary without her? That I feared all the people I loved were not permanent fixtures in my life? All things I might tell my best friend, if only he wasn't my husband, too. "Just thinking."

He took my hand and tugged. "Come think in bed."

I followed him out of Noelle's room. "I don't want to think anymore."

His thumb stroked the palm of my hand. "Good. I was planning on making you feel instead."

TWENTY-TWO

By NINE A.M. RAY and I were working the phones while Noelle played with her toys on the floor. He called Catherine on his cell while I used our home phone to contact all the karaoke contest sponsors. I struck out with all the bars and the bowling alley. They hadn't kept any records, and they couldn't recall the winner's names. They all thought the winner might have been a girl. The church, however, a more saintly institution, had kept meticulous records about their winner: Abigail Bryce.

"We sent Miss Bryce a 1099 at the end of the year."

"What address did you send it to?"

The church secretary read off the Bryces' home address in Canandaigua.

I wondered what the Bryces had thought when they received that envelope in the mail, six months after their daughter's death. Had they notified the police?

An answering machine was on at the ski resort, but then, it was mid-July. I left a message without much hope of hearing from them anytime soon, especially since their message said they would reopen in October for fall foliage rides on the mountain gondola.

Ray finished his call. "Catherine is going to have one of her associates see what he can dig up on FLM. It will take a few hours. She's going to call ahead to the jail for us so that we can get in to see Heather even if it's not officially visiting hours."

"I found a church that paid Abigail Bryce one hundred dollars *and* sent her a 1099 at year end."

Ray snapped his cell phone open and punched in a number. "Let me call the Canandaigua P.D. I can't believe they didn't follow up on identity theft if the Bryces reported it to them."

I listened to his conversation. It became obvious within minutes that the police were never informed of this 1099. Ray ended his conversation with them and dialed another number.

"Who are you calling now?"

"Mrs. Bryce. I want to see if she remembers this 1099."

She didn't, but she also confessed that, by that time, she'd started to throw out any correspondence addressed to her daughter, assuming it to be junk mail.

Ray clicked his cell phone shut. "Another dead end. Let's head over to the jail and see what Heather can tell us about Barclay."

As I packed a diaper bag for Noelle, Ray brought the car up close to the front door, then stood watch with his hand on his gun while I strapped Noelle into her car seat. Luckily, Noelle was ready for a nap and fell asleep minutes out of the driveway, allowing the ride to the jail to pass in blissful silence.

When Heather entered the jail conference room and saw Ray and me, she hesitated, looking back over her shoulder as though she might prefer to return to her cell. Then her gaze moved to Noelle's face and she seemed to change her mind, moving toward where I sat with Noelle in my lap.

"Can I hold her?" Heather's voice was so quiet I almost didn't make out her words, but her outstretched hands told me all I needed to know.

"Of course." I settled Noelle in Heather's lap. Noelle touched Heather's face and giggled. When Heather kissed her cheeks over and over again, my heart broke.

Ray, on the other hand, managed to keep it together. Sometimes the man was more machine than human. "Heather?" He waited until her gaze met his. "Do you know Dave Barclay?"

Heather's eyes widened and her lips parted. She blinked rapidly. Seconds later she buried her face in Noelle's curls. "No."

Ray sighed. "You're lying."

She didn't raise her head or bother to argue. The wall of silence was back. She started a game of peek-a-boo with Noelle instead.

Ray stood. "Jolene, take Noelle and wait for me outside."

Surprised, I took a second to respond to his request. This time when I took Noelle from her, I thought Heather's eyes widened in fear.

In the lobby, I waited, pacing back and forth with Noelle in my arms. She started to fuss, pulling my hair and crying. I dug her squeaky toy out of the diaper bag and gave it to her, crooning "Hush Little Baby" in her ear. She chewed on the end of the dog's tail as though she was teething.

I wished I had something to chew on myself, other than my fears.

Five minutes later, Ray appeared, strapping his shoulder holster in place.

I darted over to him. "What happened?"

"I pressed her. She gave me nothing. Damn stubborn girl." But Ray sounded almost appreciative. Most of the petty criminals he arrested folded quickly under the lamps. Heather had chutzpa and Ray admired chutzpa, even when it cost him.

On the drive home, Ray tapped his long fingers incessantly on the steering wheel until I snapped. "Ray!"

Startled, he looked over at me. "What?"

I stared pointedly at his fingers.

"Oh, sorry." He curled them tight around the wheel. "I'm thinking about the gambling and the racetrack. The guys at the racetrack identified Theo before anyone else. They said they'd paid him winnings the week before you saw him, then Heather had a winning ticket for that day. What are the odds that they'd win two weeks in a row?"

"I have no idea. I suppose if they won the week before, they'd be more inclined to come back and bet again at the same track."

Ray shifted his weight and pulled his cell phone out of his right pocket. "I don't question that. What I'm questioning is the frequency of the wins." He handed the phone to me. "Scroll though the numbers, would you, darlin'? Find the number for the track. I want to call them."

When I passed the phone back to him, Ray asked the operator at the track to page his contact.

"This is Ray Parker from the sheriff's office again. I need more information on the winnings you paid Theodore Tibble and any paid to an Abigail Bryce. Can you check your records and tell me which races they won, the favorite horse for the race, and the odds on their winning horse?"

He smiled. "He put me on hold. I can hear the race results."

We drove for ten minutes while Ray waited. I started to wonder if he'd been disconnected and just didn't realize it, but then his contact finally picked up again. "Okay, let me grab a pen." Ray looked at me. I pulled a pad and pen from my purse.

"Go ahead … Two winners this month. Okay … Sire Burg and Major Ed were the front runners for those races … Okay … Three months ago, two winners … Sire Burg and Speed Demon."

My pen slid off the page. Speed Demon. I knew that name.

"Okay … and the odds? Big payoffs on all these races?" Ray whistled. "You don't say. All right, thanks for your help."

Ray dropped his cell in his lap. "Theo had a winning ticket once this month, and Abigail had it a second time. Three months ago, Theo had a winning ticket. All combined, they've won over seventy-five thousand dollars at this track in just three races, betting against the odds. How lucky can you get?"

I underlined the front runners' names. "Maybe it's not luck. Maybe it's fixed."

"Yeah, but three different horses, three different owners?"

"No, Ray, not three different owners. One owner. Dave Barclay."

———

Noelle and I spent the afternoon in the conference room at the Sheriff's office, a bare, humid white-walled room that smelled of burnt coffee, shoe polish, Brute, and maybe a hint of stale body odor. Ray hadn't dared leave us home alone, and he wanted to bring Dave Barclay in for questioning himself. I didn't dare let Noelle play on the floor, no matter how clean the vinyl looked, so she spent the afternoon on top of the table I'd wiped down with spray cleaner.

When she tired of patty-cake, peek-a-boo, airplane, pony, and even her squeaky toy, she slept in her car seat carrier, which I rocked back and forth long after she'd dropped off. With my other hand, I dialed Isabelle, hoping she was still a friend who would talk to me, even after I'd ignored her for days.

She was.

All she said when I apologized was "Tell me everything."

So I did. It took me a while, and the story didn't come out chronologically. But Isabelle interrupted so many times to ask questions that I don't think she noticed, and I still managed to cover every last detail of the past few days.

She summed the mess up nicely when I finished. "So everything's up in the air: the adoption and the trial. And you and Noelle are chained to Ray."

"That's about it."

"And Cory's watching the shop?"

I gave myself a mental head slap. "I assume so. I forgot to call him this morning."

"You better call him as soon as we hang up. I'm sure he's on the job, but the least you could do is thank him."

"I will."

Isabelle heaved a huge sigh that reverberated over the phone. "Geez, Jolene, what can I do to help?"

"Nothing, Isabelle. That's what's so frustrating; it's all out of our hands. Heather is the key, and she refuses to talk. But if Dave

Barclay is the one threatening her, maybe Ray can find enough evidence to have him locked up. Once he's locked up and the threat to Noelle is gone, she should be willing to talk." But I didn't sound too confident of that, even to myself.

"Maybe." The doubt in Isabelle's voice mirrored mine.

"What are you thinking?"

When Isabelle spoke, she sounded hesitant to be the bearer of bad news. "It's just that if someone threatened Cassidy, I would be afraid now and forever, especially if he's the vindictive sort. Even prison can have a long arm, you know?"

I did know, and as I hung up, I felt only more discouraged. In the end, would the best place for Noelle be a new home and a new name, far from here? As Catherine had said, Ray couldn't watch her 24/7. Eventually, life would have to go on. And when it did, would Ray and I be the best thing for Noelle?

My hand rocked her seat more rapidly, causing her to stir restlessly. I forced myself to let go of the car seat and reach for my cell phone again to call Cory, fearing another strained conversation with him.

The door to the conference room flew open and Ray blew in like a typhoon. He crossed the floor and poured himself a cup of coffee, stirring in that nasty powdered cream and a spoonful of sugar. He took a sip and turned to face me.

I could tell his interrogation of Dave Barclay hadn't gone well from the twitch in his cheek. I set my cell phone down and waited for him to tell me.

He took the seat across the table from me and held his coffee cup between both hands. "Barclay admits to owning the horses. He admits to giving the bail money to Tibble's parents. He said

Theo worked as a messenger in his office, off the books, before he ducked his arrest. He said he felt sorry for Theo's parents and Theo, so he decided to front the bail money. I'm sure that's a load of crap, but it'll be hard to prove otherwise, especially if any of his other employees can place Theo coming and going from the office. I'm sure Barclay knows that."

Ray took another sip of coffee and continued, "He won't admit to throwing the races, although his wife looked a little nervous when I pushed him on it."

I interrupted, "His wife?"

Ray smirked. "She's his attorney, for the moment at least. She practices general law. She demanded to be present for the whole interrogation."

"How'd that go?"

"I asked him about his relationship with Heather Graus. He said he knew her, because she and Theo were dating. I asked him if he had any other relationship with Heather, and his wife started to fidget in her chair. Her face got real pinched, like she was sucking on a lemon."

That sounded normal to me. "So what do you make of that?"

Ray shrugged. "Maybe Heather and Barclay had something going on before she met Theo. Maybe that's why Heather moved here from wherever she came from. From Kim Barclay's reaction to the question, it wouldn't surprise me if Barclay has a pattern of other women."

Yet another possible explanation for why Kim Barclay looked so strained.

Another thought occurred to me. "But according to her sister, Heather only turned nineteen a few weeks ago. Over a year ago, it would have been an underage relationship."

Ray nodded. "Exactly. For now, he denies any direct relationship with Heather Graus or any threats to her. Without her cooperation, we could never make a case for statutory rape. If we did charge him, the fact that she's given birth to another man's child already will not make for a sympathetic jury. But he's already looking at big trouble with the gaming commission. If we can prove his involvement in Theo's death, he's finished."

"Can we?"

"I don't know, but it makes more sense to me that Barclay would front the bail money to prevent Theo from turning State's evidence. He doesn't want anyone to testify that he's been throwing the horse races. Maybe Theo blackmailed Barclay, and Barclay took the opportunity at the track to kill him. Of course, Barclay and his wife claim they never left each other's sides at the track the day Theo was killed ... and naturally they swear they didn't kill him."

"What about the threat to Heather and Noelle? Did you ask the Barclays where they were the day Marcia's house was shot at?"

"I did. They both claim to have been at work. I'm going to have to make some calls to verify. But with his money, he wouldn't do that kind of dirty work himself. He'd hire it out."

Ray stood. "I'm going to call the racetrack and ask them to look at their security footage again, see if we can spot Barclay elsewhere on the premises when Theo hit the dirt or if he left by a different exit and beat you to Theo in the parking lot."

Another thought occurred to me. "You know, Ray, Kim Barclay is a cold bitch. She doesn't like children. She made that readily apparent when she visited the shop and Noelle was there. I don't think she'd have any trouble threatening Noelle's life."

He leaned on the table. "So what are you saying?"

Kim might have killed to protect Dave. She wouldn't want Heather to expose Dave as a statutory rapist, nor could I imagine her allowing Theo to blackmail him. I pictured Kim Barclay holding the broken beer bottle that took Theo's life. The image came to mind easily, perhaps because the woman's permanently pursed lips oozed malevolence.

"Ask the boys at the track about her whereabouts, too."

TWENTY-THREE

When Ray and I left the sheriff's station with Noelle hours later, the Sheriff had decided to hold Dave Barclay for a few more hours, much to his wife's, or should I say attorney's, outrage. Ray's contacts at the racetrack were combing their security footage as fast as they could, comparing photos of Dave and Kim to the tapes. Ray wanted to drive over and pick up the tapes to do it himself, but the guys at the track assured him they were better equipped for the task. I knew Ray didn't like to rely on anyone else to get such an important job done, but he conceded defeat and drove me home instead.

He flicked on the television and held Noelle while I fixed a bottle for her. She'd been an awfully good sport about her incredibly boring day at the office. I planned to insist to Ray that we take her on a walk around the block before her bedtime. Maybe we'd stumble on one of the cats she loved so much, and Ray could pick it up this time to show her.

"Dammit!"

"Language, Ray. Language."

"Get in here now. You gotta see this."

I carried the bottle with me and handed it to him. The television was playing a cheese commercial. "What?"

Ray gestured to the television set with the remote in hand as he fed Noelle with his other hand. "Just listen."

I sat on the arm of the couch and waited for the commercial to end. Then a perky blond news reporter wearing a turquoise suit looked into the camera, a slight frown creasing her forehead.

"A new twist today in the case involving Heather Graus, the young woman accused of killing her boyfriend, Theodore Tibble, in the parking lot of a Canandaigua racetrack earlier this month. You may remember that Graus was living under the stolen identity of Abigail Bryce, a seventeen-year-old hit-and-run victim from Canandaigua, for months prior to her arrest and subsequent identification by her sister.

"Today, the sheriff's office brought prominent Wachobe businessman Dave Barclay in for questioning. Barclay, a thirty-five-year-old native, owns Finger Lakes Marketing, an umbrella company that includes a home furniture and accessories export business, as well as three racehorses. When Heather Graus was arrested, the sheriff's office discovered a winning ticket in her personal effects for a long-shot horse in the same race Barclay's horse was projected to win the day of Tibble's death. According to our sources, Barclay hired Tibble and Graus to bet against his horse in that race and other races here and across the state in a scheme to defraud the tracks involved. The sheriff's office will contact the Gaming Commission to continue the investigation into whether or not Barclay deliberately threw those horse races.

"Channel Eleven News has also learned that Theodore Tibble fathered a child with Heather Graus, a child currently residing in a Finger Lakes–area foster home. The foster parents are believed to be a local sheriff's deputy and his wife.

"Graus' father and sister requested custody of the child this a.m. after learning of reports of shots fired at the home of the child's daycare provider. The Department of Social Services has declined to comment at this time."

Her eyes wide with amazement, the blond reporter turned to the young Brad Pitt look-alike sitting beside her. "This story just keeps growing."

The man shook his head. "It's the stuff soap operas are made of. We'll continue to follow the story and provide updates as they become available." He smiled at the camera. "And in other news tonight—"

Ray clicked the television off and flung the changer onto the coffee table. "Not good. Not good at all."

I could see the media circus in our front yard already, even though the wire service probably hadn't picked up the story yet. And I'd been worried about local stigma. National headlines never crossed my mind. Noelle could be the next Baby Jessica or Elian Gonzalez, hounded by this story for the rest of her life.

The phone rang.

Noelle stopped sucking on her bottle and looked from Ray to me as we continued to let it ring, avoiding each other's eyes. On the seventh ring, the answering machine picked up.

"Hey Ray. Hey Jolene. It's Greg Doran. I've been trying to reach you. I received a call from Social Services this afternoon. Heather Graus' father and sister have requested custody of Noelle, and based on the six o'clock news, it appears they've released the whole story to the press. Call me."

The living room was silent except for Noelle's steady suck on her bottle. She clasped it tightly in her hands and tried to wrench it from Ray. He let her. The nipple slipped out of her mouth as she dropped the bottle. She wailed. He picked up the bottle and inserted it in her mouth again. This time she let him hold it.

I slid down the arm of the chair onto the seat cushion next to him, resting my head against his shoulder. How did Heather's family find out about the shots fired at Marcia and Jeff's house? Another leak in the sheriff's office like last year? Just some dumb junior deputy who told his mother, who shared the secret tantalizing tidbit with one of her friends, who told one her friends, and on and on? This town never could keep a secret for very long.

Noelle sucked the bottle dry. Ray set it on the coffee table and lifted her to his shoulder, patting her back softly.

The phone rang again. "Ray, this is Jeff. We just got a call from Cindy Barber at Channel Eleven News. She knows you and Jolene are the foster parents for Heather Graus and Theodore Tibble's daughter. She wants to interview you regarding Miss Graus' arrest and the status of your custody. I've got her number if you want to call her back. Marcia and I didn't tell her anything. Talk to ya later, buddy."

And so it begins. Good thing our phone number was unlisted. The press would have to search a little longer for our number and address, but sooner or later, one of the town bigmouths would let it slip.

"Dammit." Ray stood and started pacing the floor with Noelle still on his shoulder.

I watched him with tears brimming in my eyes. We would need a miracle to retain custody of Noelle now. Wordlessly, I held out my arms.

Ray bent and placed Noelle in my lap. She smelled like No More Tears and formula, two of the sweetest smells ever.

Ray sat close by my side and encircled both of us with his arms. The hot tears began to roll down my cheeks, dropping from my chin onto Noelle's chest. Soon her shirt was splotched. She didn't seem to mind. She just looked from Ray's face to mine in wonder.

Ray squeezed us tight, then let go. "I have to go to work. I need to talk to the racetrack and Barclay again. This needs to end now."

He walked out of the living room. I could hear him rustling in the kitchen cabinet high over the refrigerator, the one I never used because I was way too short to reach it.

He reappeared holding a pistol. "Do you remember how to use this?"

I did. Ray made me go to the shooting range with him just once, so I knew how all the guns in our home worked. But I didn't like the guns or shooting, so he'd put this gun away and never mentioned it again.

"It's loaded. It doesn't have a safety." He opened the end table drawer and slid the pistol inside.

Would the true test of my love for Noelle end up being my ability to kill to protect her? I certainly hoped not, but at the moment the gun gave me the feeling of security that I craved, however false that feeling might be.

Ray stared at me until I acknowledged his order with a slight nod. "All right. I'm going to talk to the sheriff about pulling out all the stops, including putting the pressure on the guys in the next county. Someone knows more about Theo and Heather than they're telling. We need to find them fast."

He leaned down to kiss my lips, then Noelle's forehead. "I love you."

More tears spilled down my cheeks. "I love you, too."

He stood for a second, looking at us. I waited for him to say everything was going to be all right.

He turned and walked out the front door.

———

Noelle went down for the night around eight. I sat on the couch and stared at the television, appreciating the noise it made but not deciphering any of its messages. Eventually the strain and heat overcame me, and I felt myself dozing off.

A pounding on the door awakened me with a start. The mantel clock read ten-twenty. The pounding continued, increasing in volume.

I stood, took two steps toward the door, then three steps back toward the drawer holding the gun. I dreaded picking it up. Maybe a quick peek out the window to identify my visitor first?

I headed toward the front door again, but this time the pounding grew frantic. Maybe taking the pistol in hand would be best.

As my fingers pulled the drawer open, I heard Erica. "Jesus, Jolene. I can hear you moving around in there. Are you going to let me in or what?"

Relief washed over me.

I opened the door to find Erica standing on the porch, still dressed in her waitress uniform, necktie askew.

"Can I come in?" She peered over my head into the living room. "What? You gotta guy in here?"

"Of course not." I stood aside and she breezed past me. "What's going on?"

She stopped just inside the door. "You are not going to freakin' believe this. I worked a short shift tonight, and when I got home, my apartment was trashed. Everything is ruined. Someone took a knife to the couch and chair cushions. Stuffing is everywhere. All my dishes are smashed in the kitchen. And all my perfumes and soap bottles were poured over my clothes. It's a mess. I'm too tired to clean it up tonight. Can I sleep here?"

"Sure." I took my seat on the couch again as she flopped into the wingback chair and plopped her feet on the ottoman. "Did you call the police?"

"I called that idiot they appointed police chief. He said he had another call that took precedence and he'd be over in the morning since I wasn't staying there tonight." Erica snorted. "He's totally useless."

The village of Wachobe, as opposed to the township, employed the police chief. The office's main duties consisted of writing parking tickets and emptying parking meters. The village hadn't received a ton of applicants. They had to pick the best of the runt litter. "When Ray gets home, maybe he can go over and take a look around. How did they get in?"

"Broke the window on the back door and turned the lock. The glass is all over the kitchen."

"Did you notice anything missing?"

"No. It looks like they just wanted to trash the place. I'd suspected Sam, but then I heard his parents took him to Bermuda for a few days. They wanted to celebrate the first five hundred dollars he made as a sailing instructor."

I supposed for a boy who rarely worked a day in his life that was a lot of money. "Is there anyone else you've had a spat with lately?" Erica had had a few scratching and clawing fights in the past, mainly with jealous girlfriends who didn't like her hitting on their dates.

Erica made a face. "No, Jolene. I'm acclimated to society again, remember?"

The word "Ha" almost escaped from my lips, but maybe my mother's ghost slapped her hand over it. It was about time she helped me with something. "What about your new boyfriend, Liam? He's not married, is he? Does he have a wife who might not be happy with you?" It wouldn't be the first time.

"He says not. He doesn't wear a ring, and he never worries about getting home at night. Besides, he doesn't know where I live. I always meet him at work."

"He could look you up in the phone book, couldn't he?"

Erica rolled her eyes. "No, Jo. You're still listed in the phone book at my address. You still get all the bills, remember?"

I should have, shouldn't I? But one check on bill-paying day blurred right into the next. My stomach sank as a new suspicion crossed my mind. "Did you put a new sticker on the mailbox?"

"No, it still says Asdale/Parker."

I mulled over that fact. Ray and I kept this address and phone number private, because he worked for the sheriff's office. Only a few friends and relatives and, of course, the sheriff's office, knew our number here. Anyone who looked in the phone book or on the Internet would think we lived at Erica's address. Had all the vandalism at her apartment really been targeted for us? Was it just another scare tactic like the shots fired at Marcia and Jeff's house? I should call Ray and find out if Dave Barclay was still in custody. Of course, he could have hired someone to do his dirty work for him, even before he was taken in for questioning today.

Erica's roaming gaze fell on the open drawer and the pistol. "What is that?"

I jumped to my feet and shoved the drawer closed. "Ray left it for me. He had to go into work and didn't want Noelle and me home alone and unprotected."

"Do you know how to use it?"

"It's a point and squeeze, Erica, but I won't need it."

She rose and followed me into the kitchen, sitting at the breakfast bar while I heated some water for tea. "So what's the latest on Heather and Noelle?"

"Did you see the news tonight?"

"No. The bar had the sports channel on."

"The press knows Noelle is Heather and Theo's child, and that we're the foster parents. They know Noelle was in danger. They announced that Heather's father and sister spoke to the Department of Social Services today about getting custody of Noelle."

Erica slammed her hand on the kitchen counter. "Well, they won't get it. You and Ray are model citizens and parents."

"I wish." I filled her in on the shots fired at Marcia's home and our failure to report them to Social Services. "They may not be too happy with us right now."

I fixed two cups of orange spice tea and placed one in front of Erica, then climbed onto the stool next to her. "And now I'm thinking maybe all the action at your apartment was targeted at us, too, since my name is still listed in the phone book and on the mailbox. Social Services will say that we're no longer able to provide a safe, stable environment for Noelle, and I'm afraid they may be right. We won't have much of an argument if Social Services decides it's in Noelle's best interests to place her with her aunt and grandfather."

"Didn't you find anything about Theo and Heather?"

I sipped my tea. "We did. We found out Heather won a few karaoke contests. Did you know that?"

Erica shook her head. "Nope. Didn't know she could sing."

"And we found out they were placing bets against the odds at the racetrack and winning. It looks like Dave Barclay was throwing horse races and probably sharing the profits with Theo and Heather."

"Uh huh." Erica avoided my gaze.

"You knew about that."

She chewed on a fingernail. "I knew something was up with Barclay. He called Theo's cell phone once while we were at the casino last year. I was surprised they knew each other."

"Surprised Theo knew him, or surprised Heather did?"

"Heather? I don't think she really knew him, just through Theo; that's all."

"Are you sure? Ray and I thought they might have had a prior sexual relationship."

Erica's blond curls flew as she shook her head. "No way. Theo and Heather really loved each other. I don't think he would have been so into her if Barclay had been in the picture that way."

"I don't know. Maybe Heather was part of the plan. Maybe she was supposed to keep Theo happy and tied to Barclay."

Erica shook her head more adamantly. "NO WAY. I know true love when I see it."

With her dating history, I couldn't help but laugh. "When have you seen it?"

Erica smiled with smug satisfaction. "Whenever Ray looks at you."

TWENTY-FOUR

I CALLED RAY TO tell him about the break-in at Erica's apartment. His cell phone went directly to voicemail. I called the operator at the sheriff's office. Ray was in conference and couldn't be disturbed. I didn't recognize the voice on the other end of the line who told me this, so I didn't press. I just called his cell again and left a voicemail asking for him to call me when he got a chance.

Erica's cell phone rang as I hung up from my call. I could tell from her excited expression that Liam was her caller.

"You did? I worked the short shift tonight since the bar was slow. I'm over at Jolene's, hanging out, because someone broke into my apartment and trashed it while I was at work. It's a mess. I can't stay there tonight."

She listened for a moment. "I live on Wells Street. In a first-floor apartment."

Listening again, she looked at me with concern. "I'm not sure. Hold on." She pressed the phone to her chest. "Liam wants to go bar-hopping. I probably won't be able to sleep anyway, but I don't want to leave you alone, if you and Noelle need me."

I waved her off. "Go ahead. Have fun."

She frowned. "Are you sure?"

"Yeah, I'm sure. Why don't you have him pick you up here so I can get a look at him?" I smiled and wiggled my eyebrows.

She grinned as though my interest made him all the more appealing—a tactical error on my part. "Liam? Would you mind picking me up at Jolene's? She'd like to meet you."

Erica rolled her eyes. "No, Ray isn't home. He's at work. He doesn't really act like my dad anyway. I just say that."

Liam must have agreed to pick her up, because Erica proceeded to give him directions to our street. Then she disconnected and headed into my closet again to see what she could find to wear.

She appeared five minutes later in an old but still very hot pink T-shirt dress. She'd wrapped a black silk scarf around her waist as a belt and tied her hair in a ponytail using a black velvet ribbon belt from another one of my old dresses. First, I had to applaud her ability to mix-and-match. Second, I had to admit, in the same outfit, I would have looked ridiculous. Erica looked fabulous. Her feet, however, were bare.

"You look great, but no shoes, no service, you know."

"I have a pair of flip-flops in the car. I'll get them when we leave." She peered out the front window, impatient for Liam to arrive.

I watched her, pleased to see her excitement. A twinge of jealousy coursed through me, too. The excitement of a new love was intoxicating, and I'd only felt it with Ray. True, I'd gotten a prince, but it might have been nice to experience the thrill of a new love more than once.

Shame on me for thinking that way! Ray was like an Academy Award, timeless, respected, and coveted. Liam was probably more like the kind of cheap plastic prize the carnival sharks pull out from under the counter, just like all the rest of Erica's choices. I tried to remember what she'd told me about him. Not much, but then I hadn't really had time to ask her either. "So what does this Liam do?"

She didn't take her gaze off the street. "He's in sales."

"What does he sell?"

"Frozen food like hamburgers, chicken patties, french fries."

"Who does he sell to?"

Erica let out an exasperated sigh. "I don't know. Places like water parks, ski resorts, and carnivals. You know, places that sell crappy food."

The carnival connection. I knew it. I'd become psychic.

Since my questions were clearly irritating my sister, I went into the kitchen to put our teacups into the dishwasher and wipe down the counter. Plus, I thought it would be nice to give her a minute alone to greet him at the door. I wasn't really interested in watching them suck face, as Erica was known literally to do.

Funny, water parks and ski resorts. Wachobe had neither. So what brought Liam to our town to do his drinking?

I called out to Erica "Does Liam live in Wachobe?"

"No."

"So where does he live?"

Silence. Dear God, had she not even thought to ask him? Why did I think this relationship was doomed?

Would Liam know Abigail Bryce's stepfather? He worked in food services, and Mrs. Bryce said her husband worked at the water park in the summer and the ski resort in the winter. He had to work at the ski resort south of Canandaigua. It was the only one within a reasonable commuting distance.

It was also the ski resort where Heather won the karaoke contest over a year ago. Liam might know her, too. Such a coincidence.

I stopped in the middle of the kitchen floor. Too much of a coincidence. What did Ray always say? It's always best to stick as close to the truth as possible when making up a lie.

The sponge slipped out of my hand, dropping to the floor. I bent to retrieve it, trying to quell my growing nausea.

A discreet knock sounded at the front door. I heard Erica open the door and the sounds of passionate kissing. My hand reached for the phone and hovered over it. Was I jumping to all the wrong conclusions? Dave Barclay or his wife had been responsible for Theo's death, hadn't they?

I heard footsteps on the floor and a familiar jingling sound, like the sound of keys.

Theo Tibble's bloody neck and glazed eyes flashed before me. Heather's fearful and frozen gaze. I'd heard it that day at the racetrack. I'd heard it move away before I screamed for help. And I'd heard it once before, at the—

"Hello, Jolene."

My hand seized the phone. I tried to lift it, but my fingers were still wet from the sponge. The phone slipped out of my hand and crashed to the floor. The battery fell out and skittered across the floor.

Dressed in a long-sleeve white dress shirt and jeans, key chain hanging silent now at his side, Abigail Bryce's stepfather stood two paces behind Erica, who frowned at the phone on the floor, completely unaware of who she'd brought into my home. "Jo, this is Liam. Liam Bennett." She grabbed his forearm.

He winced and jerked it away.

"Actually, Erica, it's William. William Bryce," I said.

Confusion flashed across Erica's face before she turned to face him. "What?"

I took a few steps and grabbed her dress, pulling her back against me and positioning the breakfast bar between us and Bryce. "William Bryce, Erica. Abigail Bryce's stepfather. And the man who killed Theo Tibble."

He flashed his teeth again. His canines were particularly long, suitable for the wolf he was. "I didn't kill Theo. Heather did. She even admits it."

I felt sweat dampen my shirt even though I'd started to tremble. "Only because you threatened her."

He feigned shock. "No one threatened her, although I understand her baby ... or is it your baby? ... was threatened." He shook his head in mock dismay. "Shocking." He glanced around the room. "Where is the little princess, now? Sleeping?"

Sweat rolled off my brow and burned my eyes. I edged toward the knife rack on my kitchen counter.

"No, no, Jolene." Bryce pulled a pistol from his pocket, not as big as Ray's spare but just as intimidating. "Let's go sit in the living room, shall we?"

My heart felt like it would explode out of my chest. Teeth clenched, I held Erica's hand and led her to the couch. Her hand felt cold to my touch. She'd begun to shake uncontrollably. Big tears rolled down her face.

She hiccupped. "This is all my fault."

I squeezed her hand. "It's his fault. He lied to you about everything. He's an evil man."

Bryce positively preened as he perched on the edge of the ottoman next to me and the drawer holding Ray's gun. Apparently, he was rather proud of his criminal mind.

My fingers itched to reach for the gun, but he'd be on me too fast. I couldn't risk it. I decided to keep Bryce talking in the hopes Ray was on his way home. He'd notice the strange car in the driveway and enter with cautious suspicion.

I thought back over the last few weeks and tried to piece the rest of the story together, all the little details falling slowly into place. "You met Heather at the ski resort where you worked."

Bryce nodded. "I'm surprised none of the other resort employees have stepped forward yet to claim the reward you've been advertising, although Heather does look different now. She won a karaoke contest in December the year before last. I hired her to work in the café after that."

Candace Morton told me Bryce had a thing for the young girls where he worked. "You had an affair with her, but you didn't know she was under eighteen."

"She had a fake ID. She used it to fill out her paperwork. How could I have known?"

"But you dropped her when you found out."

He shook his head, looking almost gleeful that I didn't know it all. "The ski season ended and the relationship had run its course. I didn't know she was under eighteen until later."

"How did you find out?"

"If I tell you that, then I'll have to kill you." He examined the gun in his hand, turning it to the right, then the left. "But then I planned to do that anyway."

I wasn't surprised, but my heart started beating even faster than before. The pressure from the Crime Fighters announcement had forced Bryce into action. But he must realize Ray would go on looking forever if he killed us. Was he insane?

Erica began to sob loudly. Bryce pointed the gun at her. "Stop it, Erica." She continued to wail, the volume increasing with each heave of her chest.

He waved the gun in my direction. "Make her stop."

I gathered Erica to my chest and attempted to soothe her. I was sure the trembling of my own arms didn't support my whispers of assurance in her ear that Ray was surely on his way. She did manage to stifle her sobs.

I looked at Bryce over her head. "So how *did* you learn Heather's age?"

"She met my stepdaughter, Abigail, at the ski resort and struck up a friendship with her."

Erica wiggled in my arms. I released her, thinking I'd been squeezing her too tight. She leaned back against the couch and glared at Bryce.

I continued with my questions. "And Heather told Abigail about your relationship?"

Bryce's lip curled. "Months later. They kept in touch after ski season ended." He looked off into the distance and sighed. "Abigail told Heather it wasn't the first time I'd had a relationship with a young woman. Heather thought she was special. She thought I loved her and wanted to marry her, but couldn't bring myself to break my wife's heart."

He brought his gaze to meet mine, then shifted it to Erica. "You know, those stupid romantic notions of childhood."

Erica stiffened. I held onto her hand a little tighter.

"The girls planned to tell my wife and the police. As I said, we left Lockport because of a similar little incident." He pulled himself taller and grimaced. "It's really not my fault. All these little tramps lie about their age. They all have fake IDs and MySpace accounts. They're asking for it. And they've had it before. It's not like I was their first."

Erica started to shake uncontrollably.

"But then your stepdaughter was killed and somehow Heather got her ID." That part had me stumped and I wanted to hear his explanation.

Bryce smirked. "I tried to hit them both that night, but I missed Heather."

I heard a gasp. It was me. I couldn't believe this man had just confessed to killing his own stepdaughter. He was insane. He wouldn't hesitate to kill us. *Ray, where are you?*

I closed my mouth and thought for a moment. "How did you come to be at the racetrack the day Theo died?"

Bryce smiled a sadistic smile. "To tell the truth, I'd stopped worrying about Heather. She never came forward, never contacted me again. I thought she was gone from my life. Then I saw her one night at a motel outside of Canandaigua. You know, a no-tell motel where you pay cash and the desk clerk has more to hide than you. She and Theo were staying there."

He brushed his hand over the gun's barrel. "I started to keep an eye on them, tracking them from motel to motel. When you came to see my wife and me, I knew you'd find Heather eventually, too. I needed to prevent that. I just had to wait for the right time. That day at the track was manna from heaven."

Erica began to wail again, drowning out all conversation and my thoughts. I'd never seen her like this before, even at her worst moments. But then, in the past, she'd been the one in control of her impending death.

Bryce stood and walked around to the other side of the coffee table, coming to a stop a few feet from Erica, who wailed louder. He waved the gun in my direction. "Make her stop!"

I reached for Erica, but she sprang from her seat, slamming her arms into Bryce's chest and knocking him backwards onto the floor. She landed on his chest and pummeled it with her fists, screaming "YOU BASTARD!"

Bryce reached for his gun that had fallen out of his hand. I scrambled over the coffee table and dived for it. He got there first, swinging the butt of the pistol into Erica's head. She slumped alongside of him, dazed.

I grabbed for his wrist and missed. He scooted backward against the fireplace and held the gun on me. I froze, my heart still beating wildly.

Noelle began to cry, softly at first then with increasing intensity. All the banging and crashing must have awakened her. My hands started to shake. I couldn't stop darting looks at the doorway to her room only steps away.

Bryce pulled himself to his feet. His white dress shirt had a spot of blood the size of a quarter on it where Erica had touched his forearm earlier. Marcia had winged him after all.

He took a step toward me, waving the gun toward Noelle's room. "Go get her, Jolene. I'd like to meet her."

No way in hell. I looked up at him, face burning and throat swollen shut with fear.

He came closer and waved toward her room again. "GO GET HER, JOLENE!"

I continued to meet his gaze, refusing to move. *Ray, where are you? We need you!*

Bryce took a few steps in the direction of her door. I slid across the floor to block his path.

He kicked me in the leg, hard enough to get my attention but not enough to disable me. "Get her, or I'll get her myself."

I stood. Now I was directly in his path to Noelle's door. I'd die before I'd let him near my child. I folded my arms across my chest, trying to hide my shaking. Sweat rolled down my forehead and burned my eyes. "No."

He pointed the gun at my forehead. In reflex, my eyelids closed.

I heard a shot.

My eyes popped open. At first, Bryce's brow furrowed as though he was confused. Then he twisted and tried to see his backside. He reached around with his left hand, turning to look at Erica and moving a few feet away from me. As he turned, the gun in his right hand swung around toward her.

She held Ray's gun in both hands, legs shoulder-width apart. Without hesitation, she shot again. This time the bullet hit him in the left shoulder. She emptied the rest into his chest, blood spraying everywhere and flames flicking out the gun's tip.

I felt warm, wet spots on my face. My hand moved of its own accord to wipe my cheek. I jumped backwards to escape the gore. My stomach rolled.

Bryce slumped to the floor. His gun fell useless by his side. He looked confused for a moment as though he couldn't believe things hadn't gone as he planned. Then he began to twitch. The blood gushed from his wounds faster. His eyes widened as if a shock had run through his body. He let out a gasp. Then he was gone, the now all-too-familiar glaze filling his eyes.

For a moment, the roaring in my ears drowned out all sound and thought. I swayed and feared I might faint. I bit down hard on my lower lip. The pain felt refreshing. I returned to reality and my living room.

Noelle continued to cry. I rejoiced in the sound. It meant she was still alive.

I swallowed my nausea and stepped toward Erica, who had dropped Ray's gun to the floor. She stood frozen, looking catatonic, gazing down at Bryce's body.

My first thought was "All those years of therapy down the drain." Even Ray had taken months to recover from shooting a man. Erica might never recover.

I reached for her arm and rubbed it gently. "Erica?"

Her gaze shifted to me.

"I'm so sorry, honey. I'm so sorry you had to shoot him. It'll be all right. Don't worry."

She blinked. "What do you mean 'sorry'?"

I swallowed the bile burning my throat and tried again to reach her. "I know it's a horrible thing to have to take a life. But he was an evil man. It's not your fault."

A hint of a smile touched her lips. "You think I'm freakin' out because I killed him?"

I blinked. "Aren't you?"

"Hell no. He was going to kill you." She stood a little taller. "I *love* you."

She shot a contemptuous gaze at Bryce's body.

"I should have shot him in the balls and made him suffer longer."

TWENTY-FIVE

RAY, JEFF, GUMBY, AND the sheriff himself arrived at the house within minutes of my 911 call. By then I had washed Bryce's blood off my face and changed my shirt so that I could pick up Noelle, who greeted their arrival with much interest.

Ray threw his arms around both of us and held on tight. Gumby hugged Erica.

Erica seemed to welcome the support. She'd started to sway a little bit while I called the police, as though the full magnitude of what she had done had finally hit her. An emergency appointment with Dr. Albert, her psychiatrist, was definitely in order. I might even make one for myself.

Ray left his friends to bag the evidence and sat next to me at the breakfast bar as Erica and I told our story to the sheriff, who bore some resemblance to Santa Claus, except he wasn't a right jolly old elf. He had on red suspenders, a plaid flannel shirt with a cigar burn in the sleeve, and khakis that folded over beneath his big belly to reveal the white lining on the waistband. One of his stogies stayed clamped firmly in his teeth as he asked questions and noted the answers. He grumbled a little bit under his breath when he heard Ray had left his extra revolver at home with an untrained, unlicensed woman, but he never argued with the end result. Instead, he ambled off to call and update the prosecutor.

It took a couple hours for Bryce's body to be removed from our living room. By then, Erica, Noelle, and I were fast asleep in my bed. When Noelle awakened around seven a.m., we rendez-voused with Ray at the breakfast bar, where he served us his spe-cial Sunday Belgian waffles, even though it was only the middle of the week.

The doorbell rang at nine as we finished the dishes.

I walked through the living room and couldn't see any signs of the carnage from the night before, although I could smell carpet and upholstery cleaner. Ray must have cleaned all night. I looked through the peephole and swung the door open wide. "Isabelle!"

Isabelle did not look herself. Usually she dressed in a form-fitting suit with fashionable shoes and elegant jewelry from her husband's store. This morning she wore faded jeans, a T-shirt, and flip-flops, her mousy brown hair hanging in straggles around her face.

She hugged me, and hugged me, and hugged me until I started to feel uncomfortable. I pried myself loose. "You saw the news this morning, didn't you?"

Tears sprang to her eyes. "You were the lead story. It lasted a full five minutes. I had to come."

I hugged her quickly again. "I'm glad you did. Come sit down."

She hugged Erica and Ray, and kissed Noelle's cheeks, lingering over her as though taking in every feature of her face. My feeling of unease returned.

We all sat in the living room, Isabelle bouncing up and down nervously on the couch. She turned to me. "I was thinking about what you told me the other day, about how Heather and Theo met at the May Day celebration last year."

I nodded and looked at Ray, who shrugged.

She glanced at Noelle, who sat in my lap holding her favorite doggie squeeze toy. "Noelle was born in December, a week before Christmas, right? That's what her birth certificate says, right?"

My feeling of unease increased. "Right."

"Are you sure that information is correct? I mean, I know her birthmother's name was incorrect. Do you think the birth date is correct?"

Ray spoke up. "The hospital confirmed that date."

Isabelle squinted as though pained. "Well, you know babies usually stay in the womb for nine months, and Noelle was full size, eight pounds, when she was born. It seems to me that Theo and Heather had to have met sooner or …" She trailed off then seemed to find her courage. "I don't think Theo is Noelle's real father."

I pulled Noelle closer to my chest. "Could she have been a preemie?"

Isabelle sighed. "Babies gain most of their weight in the last few weeks of the pregnancy, approximately a half pound a week. It's highly unlikely that Noelle would weigh eight pounds if she was born after less than seven months of gestation."

I wanted to believe that Isabelle was mistaken, but I caught a guilty and knowing look in Erica's eye. "Erica, was Theo Noelle's father?"

Erica squirmed and then her shoulders dropped. "No. He knew that, but he fell in love with Heather. He didn't want her baby to end up unloved like him. His mother was already knocked up when she married his dad. He never knew who his real daddy was and the one he grew up with treated him like a dog. He wanted Noelle to have a father who loved her."

Ray asked the question we all wanted answered. "So who is her real father?"

Erica shrugged. "I don't know. You'd have to ask Heather."

Our doorbell rang. Four heads swiveled in that direction. No one got up.

The doorbell rang again. This time even Noelle raised her head from her toy as though she recognized something needed attention.

With a sigh, Ray answered the door.

I hoped Cory would be behind the door. I needed all my friends at a time like this.

Instead, Greg Doran, the sheriff, and a man and a woman in business suits stood on our porch. Greg introduced the man as Mr. Simpson and the woman as Mrs. Bindle, both from the Department of Social Services.

I ran into the kitchen with Noelle. Isabelle followed me.

I backed into the corner against the stove. "Why are they here, Isabelle?"

She didn't want to tell me, but she was my friend. "The news interviewed Karen and her father about the petition they filed for

Noelle's custody earlier this week. Karen and her father knew all about what happened here last night." She glanced at her watch. "They said they planned to call Social Services first thing this morning."

My chest felt like it might burst.

Ray appeared in the archway. He looked at Isabelle. She touched my arm and walked around him, back into the living room.

He approached me, resting his hands on my shoulders. "Mrs. Bindle is here to take Noelle into temporary custody. They scheduled an emergency hearing with family court this afternoon. It's possible they'll award custody to Heather's sister."

I clutched Noelle tighter. My temple throbbed. "No-o-o-o-o."

Ray's cheek twitched. His eyes closed for a second as though he were gathering his strength. "Darlin', we have to give Noelle to Mrs. Bindle. We don't have any choice. Greg will do everything he can."

"No-o-o-o-o-o!"

Undoubtedly sensing our distress, Noelle began to cry.

Ray crouched next to me. "Please, darlin', give her a hug and kiss for now. We'll see her again."

"No-o-o-o-o!" I buried my face in Noelle's curls. She wailed.

"Jolene, you're scaring the baby. You're holding her too tight. Let me take her, please."

I loosened my hold on Noelle and looked down at her adorable little face, recalling the first time I'd seen her. She'd cried then, too. A little red face, cheeks like roses and lips like cherries, all snuggled up in a pink fleece snowsuit—the perfect baby.

My tears fell on those cheeks now. She continued to cry, sounding fearful. My fears had filled her, too.

My throat had swollen shut. I brushed her right cheek with my lips, then her left. I hugged her close and breathed in her familiar and wonderful No More Tears and formula scent. Then I let Ray take her from my arms. I dissolved onto the floor.

———

At three o'clock Ray and I appeared at the courthouse, dressed in business suits. Greg met us just inside the door of the historic stone building with its polished wood banisters, shiny marble floors, and gleaming brass elevators. But all that paled in comparison to the despair that lingered in the air.

"Heather asked to meet with you privately before the case is called. She's in a conference room on the third floor. Do you want to see her?" Greg looked from Ray to me.

"Of course." Ray took me by the arm and steered me toward the elevator. The three of us rode in silence to the third floor.

Greg escorted us to the conference room door. At the far end of the hall, I saw Heather's sister Karen, standing beside a handsome younger man and a distinguished-looking older man, all in their Sunday best. Greg opened the door and stepped aside. "I'll wait for you out here."

I followed Ray inside to find Heather dressed in a navy suit with matching pumps, her hair pulled back into a ponytail that covered the back of her neck and her flying eagle tattoo. She stood when we entered, but didn't move from her place on the other side of the conference table.

The lines were clearly drawn.

Ray and I took the seats opposite her. She waited until we were seated to resume her chair. She met my gaze. "I'm sorry."

My throat swelled shut.

Ray clasped my hand where it rested on the table. "I know you spoke to the sheriff at length this morning, but we haven't heard your whole story yet. Can you share it with us?"

She nodded. "I met William at the ski resort. He came onto me. I didn't have anywhere to go, so when he offered me a job, I took it. We dated." She shrugged. "He was nice to me. Then I met Abigail and realized he was married."

She blushed. "I kept on dating him anyway, but I made friends with her, too. I just didn't tell her about him and me. Then ski season ended. I had to move on and get another job. I figured it was all over anyway.

"I worked at a motel for a few months, cleaning rooms, but then I started getting sick from the smell of the cleaning stuff. At least, I thought so." She stared at the table for a moment then went on. "It took me about a month to realize I was pregnant. Then I panicked. I didn't know what to do. I thought William should at least support the baby. So I hitched a ride and went to see him at his house. He wasn't home, but Abigail was. I told her about the baby." Heather swallowed and made a face as though she'd eaten something spoiled. "Abigail told me about the other girls.

"I went over to the water park to talk to William. He said everything would be fine. He said he'd take care of me. He said he'd leave his wife. He said to wait for him at the bar on the corner near his house."

She sighed. "I waited for hours. The place closed. Finally I called his house. Abigail answered. She said her mother was

265

asleep and William wasn't home yet. She offered to come meet me.

"I met her in the parking lot. She invited me back to her house. She said we should tell her mother everything. We started walking toward her house. Then a car started up by the parking lot. It came fast. Abigail looked back, saw him coming and pushed me aside. He hit her dead on."

Heather cupped her face in her hands. We waited in silence until she gathered herself to finish the story.

It took a few minutes before she raised her face from her hands and continued. "I didn't know what to do. I started toward her and he got out of the car. When I saw him, I panicked and ran. He said, 'You better run or I'll kill you, too, and the little bastard.'

"I ran. I ran all the way to the grocery store clear on the other side of town. When I got there, I realized I'd picked up Abigail's purse with mine from the road. My stomach was cramping. I thought I was going to lose the baby. So I asked a trucker parked outside the store if he'd take me as far as he was going. He was only going to Wachobe, but I figured that might be far enough."

Heather stared at the table, appearing to gather her thoughts. She took a deep breath and continued.

"I got a cheap motel room with the money from Abigail's purse. I watched the news and read the newspapers for a week. After two days, they didn't talk about it anymore. The police never figured out it was William. Nobody ever mentioned Abigail's purse was missing. I was too scared to go back and tell the police the truth.

"When I entered the karaoke contest in Wachobe, I shaved my head and used Abigail's name, like a tribute to her or something. Then I met Theo. I didn't want to explain why I had used a dead girl's name. I just sort of became Abigail Bryce."

Heather glanced at Ray. "Maybe I wanted to get caught. I don't know. I was afraid to go to the police. I thought they might arrest me for leaving the scene and withholding evidence, not to mention stealing Abigail's purse and identity. But I felt guilty that I didn't tell them the truth about Abigail's death. I was really confused, about the baby, about William, about what to do. It was just easier to do nothing."

She shifted her eyes to me. "But the day you chased us out of the racetrack, I got separated from Theo in the parking lot. He fell and he told me to keep running, to meet him at the car. I couldn't remember where we parked. I kept running up and down the aisles, and I couldn't find it." She spread her hands wide and a little of the panic she must have felt that day returned to her eyes.

"Then I smacked into William. He recognized me. He grabbed my arm and started dragging me. Theo came. They fought. William grabbed a beer bottle from the ground and the next thing I knew, Theo was bleeding. I heard running. William pushed the bottle into my hand and said, 'I know where your baby lives. If you talk, your baby's dead.'"

I felt sorry for her, I really did. She'd made a lot of bad choices and lost people she cared about, who had cared for her in return. Abigail Bryce was dead. Theodore Tibble was dead. I'm sure Heather had suffered, too, but she was still here. I held onto the tiniest glimmer of hope that she might leave Noelle with us.

Ray squeezed my hand. "So what happens now?"

She brushed her hand over the lapels of her suit. "I'm going to be charged with something, Catherine's sure of that. I may get out on bail, but I'm a flight risk." Her lips turned up ever so slightly as though she realized the irony of that. "Today the judge is going to ask me about Noelle."

I tensed.

Ray seemed impervious. "What are you going to tell him?"

"I'm going to say I made mistakes. That I was afraid, but I tried to act in the best interest of my baby. That's why I gave Noelle to you."

I dared to hope.

Heather leaned back in her chair as though to put some distance between us. "But now I want a fresh start. I want my sister Karen to get custody of Noelle, so maybe I can be with her too, eventually. My sister's husband is a minister. He said God believes in giving people second chances. I want my second chance."

Noelle had been Ray's and my second chance. If she was taken from us now, where would we be without her? Why did we have to lose the baby we'd come to think of as our own? This girl wasn't equipped to handle a baby alone. And her sister and father hadn't taken the right care of her. Why else would she have run away from home in the first place? These people were not the best thing for Noelle. Noelle belonged with us.

Without a word, I stood and walked out of the room. After a second, Ray followed.

———

I shared all my earlier thoughts and more when the judge gave me a chance to speak. A lot of tears were shed, and not just by me. Heather and her sister cried for themselves, and for me. I could tell. It didn't make me like them any better. They were trying to take my baby away.

When the state's attorney asked me about my sister, I knew it was over. Being her surrogate mother all these years didn't make me look like June Cleaver, nor did the final image of my sister shooting "her boyfriend" to death in my living room make her look like good aunt material.

Ray did us proud when he took his turn on the stand. He appeared calm, competent, and totally in charge of the situation. But I saw his cheek twitch once or twice, especially when the state's attorney asked him about the man he'd shot to death last year in order to save my life.

The judge said many words at the close of the hearing. I don't remember them. I do remember the gist.

Karen won.

TWENTY-SIX

By ten o'clock that night, I had run out of tears. Ray undressed me for bed like a baby, slid a nightshirt over my head, and climbed in next to me, spooning.

We'd spent hours at home with Greg Doran and Catherine, brainstorming ways to get Noelle back. Neither one of them held out much hope, but they let us talk until we ran out of words, more friends than lawyers.

Catherine hugged us both before she left. "You guys deserve better than this."

Greg apologized. "I never should have let Heather leave the baby with you in the first place. It was very slipshod lawyering."

Ray had shaken his head. "We were lucky to have Noelle, even for such a short time. It's not your fault."

Now he murmured in my ear, "It'll be all right, darlin.'"

I didn't answer him. It would never be all right. Noelle was gone. My chest ached. My head throbbed. I couldn't stop crying. I felt as though she'd died. We were alone and childless. Another child could never replace her. And now the one thing my husband had most wanted to have, a child, was the one thing I never wanted to risk my heart on again.

I must have slept, because when I opened my eyes, it was morning. Sunlight streamed in through the bedroom blinds we'd forgotten to close the night before.

The clock read eight a.m. When I turned over, Ray was no longer beside me. Erica was there instead.

"Ray went to work. I think he's hoping he'll find someone to beat into submission today."

I knew him better than that, although he would find solace in just doing his job. I rolled over to face her. "How did you get here?"

"He called and asked me to come. He said you didn't hate me."

I studied her blue eyes, which had filled with tears. "I don't hate you. It's not your fault."

"I never should have tried to arrange the adoption. I should have known Heather was hiding something more than the father's name. I messed everything up."

I repeated Ray's words. "We were lucky to have Noelle for as long as we did."

Erica lifted her head off the pillow and rested on her elbow. "How can you say that? This whole thing sucks."

What else could I say? My baby was gone. My tears began to flow again.

"Oh, Jo." Erica gathered me into her arms and held me. "I'm so sorry. I'm so sorry."

She stayed with me all day.

Early in the day, she tried to convince me to get out of bed and take a shower. I pulled the sheet over my head. She tried to feed me lunch. I wasn't hungry. She tried to talk with me. I was too tired. She offered to share her anti-depression medication with me. I declined, for the time being. She ended up lying beside me and taking a nap.

Ray came home at five. He climbed in next to me and spooned, stroking my thighs. "What do you want me to make you for dinner?"

"Nothing."

"You want takeout?"

"I'm not hungry." I wiggled out of his arms. "I just want to sleep. I'm so tired."

He flopped over onto his back and lay still for a few minutes. "I'm here when you're ready." He rolled off the bed. I heard his feet pad down the hall, then the television in the living room.

I wondered what Noelle was doing now. Was she eating? Was she wondering where we were? Was she afraid of these strangers who were her aunt and uncle and her grandfather?

Or worse, had she forgotten us already? How attached could a child be at seven months? As long as she was fed, changed, and cuddled, she'd be happy. In a few weeks, she'd forget about us entirely. When she learned to say 'Mama' for the first time, she would be calling someone other than me.

I closed my eyes and let the warm tears soak my pillow.

The next morning I found Isabelle in bed next to me. She was sitting up with her back against the headboard.

"How long have you been here?"

"Since eight o'clock."

I looked at the clock. It read ten-fifteen.

Isabelle yanked on the covers, trying to pull them off me. "Come on, you have to get up, at least to pee."

I'd peed in the middle of the night. Some things in life must go on, no matter what. I'd stumbled into the bathroom and cried into a towel for a while last night, trying not to wake Ray. Then I'd taken care of business. "In awhile, I'm fine for now."

Isabelle frowned. "I don't like seeing you like this."

"Then leave." But I smiled to try to lessen the blow.

She folded her arms. "You're not going to get rid of me that easily."

"I hope not." I rolled away from her. "I need to sleep."

"Don't you want to call the shop? Don't you want to talk to Cory?"

Cory. He must still hate me. He hadn't called. He hadn't shown up. Maybe he didn't even work for me anymore. Maybe he'd left me, too.

I couldn't bring myself to share another of my failures with Isabelle. Maybe she'd leave me.

Instead, she stayed with me all day, alternately cajoling and threatening. I felt loved, but not the least bit inclined to eat or get out of bed. Why bother? And I was just too sleepy.

When the mantel clock chimed six o'clock, I opened my eyes to find Ray in a chair next to my side of the bed. "Do you want to hear the rest of the story about Dave Barclay?"

I flopped on my back, which had begun to ache from too much time in bed. "Sure."

"Turns out Kim's grandfather was the one who took everything in the divorce, except for the Datsun. The racehorses belonged to the ex-wife's family, and he stole them from her in the divorce settlement. He forgot about the Datsun until it was too late."

"But now he has everything."

"He's dead. He died yesterday."

"And they plan to bury him in the Datsun?"

"No."

This was a surprise. All our scheming and now the man wasn't even going to be buried in the car. "Why not?"

"Cory was really ticked at you Monday. Barclay showed up to pay for the Datsun with a personal check, and Cory accepted it, even though he knew your policy was bank checks only. Anyway, Barclay's check bounced. Cory freaked, called Gumby, and they went to visit him. It was right after we brought him in for questioning. He gave the car back."

The good news was Cory apparently still worked for me. The bad, he still hated me. And it only got worse. "So now I own a Datsun racecar?"

Ray held up his hands as if to say "wait." "No. Cory went to Chautauqua to see Sylvia Wilder a day later and told her the truth, apologized, and offered to sell the car back to her. She didn't want it, but she gave him the name of another guy who did."

Relief coursed through me. At least my business wasn't a total failure like my personal life. "Why would she do that? I would think she'd be furious with us for the charade."

"She was too excited. She has her three race horses back."

Another surprise. "How'd she get those?"

Ray smiled. "Barclay is looking at a lot of legal fees. Apparently, he's been playing fast and loose with not only the gaming commission but also the IRS, which served him a couple months ago for tax evasion. He needed to sell the horses, and Sylvia Wilder had the money to buy them."

No wonder Kim Barclay had the permanent pinch to her lips. She and her husband were cooked. "Sylvia used the money we gave her for the car?"

"That helped. The horses are worth a little more than that."

At least I didn't have to wonder anymore if losing Noelle was punishment for tricking Mrs. Wilder into selling us the Datsun. Things had turned out all right for her. She must have good karma, unlike me.

Ray stood. "Get up. I brought Chinese home for dinner."

I managed to roll out of bed, freshen up, and follow him to the kitchen table. But when I saw Noelle's empty highchair, I burst into tears. Ray pulled me into his arms. "I put everything of Noelle's in her room for now. I guess I missed that."

I sobbed into his shoulder. "It's all my fault."

He pulled back and looked at me. "How do you figure that?"

"I refused to have a baby with you. I let my sister run around trying to arrange an adoption for us instead of making sure she was in the psych center the way she should have been. I let her believe Mom still talks to her from the beyond. That's who told her to get Noelle for us, you know."

He sat me in a chair. "Jolene, you've got to snap out of this. It's nobody's fault. It just happened. Noelle wasn't meant to be with us any longer; that's all."

"Didn't you love her?"

His cheek twitched. "I loved her. I still love her. I miss her. But I miss you, too. We have to go on."

I opened my mouth to ask why he still wanted to go on with me when he no longer had the child that brought us back together. I didn't have the strength to ask him. I just sat at the table and ate a little of the food he placed in front of me. Then I climbed back into bed.

I stayed there all the next day. Erica sat with me most of the day, watching game shows on the television in the bedroom. The drone of the shows almost drowned out my thoughts, all of which swirled around Noelle. Sweet, adorable, kissable, lovable Noelle.

Later that day, long after Erica had gone into work, someone climbed onto Ray's side of the bed. I figured it had to be Ray.

"Hi, Jo."

Tears filled my eyes. This time they were tears of joy. I rolled over. "Cory!"

He grabbed my hand. "I'm so sorry about Noelle."

I nodded, my throat swollen once again. I managed to whisper "I'm sorry about Mark, too."

He made a face that said "That's life." "You know the worst part about losing someone you love?"

The heartbreak? The loneliness? The guilt? The never-ending what-ifs and if-only? The knowledge that your heart's desire remained forever out of reach? "What?"

"It's not having your best friend to comfort you."

I squeezed his hand. "Do you want to talk about Mark?"

"Not really. Do you want to talk about Noelle?"

I shook my head.

We must have fallen asleep holding hands, because the next time I woke, the clock read ten and Ray was standing over us. "I see Cory's here."

"Yes." Even I heard the hint of happiness in my voice.

He sighed, a resigned sort of sigh. "I'll sleep on the couch to-night, but don't ever tell the guys at work that Cory slept in my bed, okay?"

"Deal. Thank you."

Ray tiptoed across the room.

"Ray?"

He stopped and turned back. "Yes?"

"I love you."

"I love you, too, Jolene."

THE END

BOOK CLUB QUESTIONS

For Richer, For Danger opens with a case of stolen identity. Throughout the story, identity remains a theme, including Jolene's need to feel like "Noelle's mother" and "Ray's wife" as well as her concerns regarding any stigma that might attach itself to Noelle if the facts about her parentage became public knowledge. Discuss what key elements constitute a person's identity. How do differences arise between self-identity and public personae? Can someone truly steal your identity?

As with most mysteries, a whole lot of lying goes on in *For Richer, For Danger*: the villain(s) trying to cover up the evidence, the secondary characters trying to hide their secrets, and the "good guys" trying to ferret out the truth any way they can. And Jolene and Ray tend to omit the facts whenever it's more expedient in dealing with one another. Identify some of these lies, both white and otherwise. When, if ever, is it acceptable to lie? Is it even possible to get through life without lying?

In the course of the story, Jolene learns new information about Cory's love, Mark Wynn, and Cory stumbles on an interesting fact about Ray and Catherine. Neither one is sure if they should share their discoveries with the other. When is it the right thing to share? When is it best to keep quiet? Can you ever be certain which is the right choice?

How realistically do you think Jolene and Ray's marriage is portrayed? Jolene and Erica's relationship as sisters? Jolene's friendships with Cory and Isabelle?

What did you think of Ray's relationship with Catherine and how he handled that relationship?

Often mysteries build to the moment where the villain receives his just desserts. How did you feel about what happened to the villain(s) in this story?

A dying ex-racer wanted to be buried in his Datsun 240Z. Is this an example of trying to take your possessions with you or of being with the thing you loved most throughout eternity? What's the most unusual burial or funeral request you've ever heard?

So where does *For Richer, For Danger* leave Jolene and Ray's relationship? Is it where you hoped? What do you expect or hope will happen with their life and relationship in the third book in the series, In Sickness and In Death?

ABOUT THE AUTHOR

Lisa Bork lives in western New York and loves to spend time in the Finger Lakes region. Married and the mother of two children, she worked in human resources and marketing before becoming a writer. The first book in the Broken Vows mystery series, *For Better, For Murder*, was released in 2009. Please visit her website at www.LisaBork.com.